CW01066974

Drug
Trial

Drug Trial

Rosemary Richards

PIATKUS

Copyright © 1987 by Rosemary Richards

First published in Great Britain in 1987 by
Judy Piatkus (Publishers) Ltd of
5 Windmill Street, London W1

British Library Cataloguing in Publication Data

Richards, Rosemary
  Drug trial.
  I. Title
  813′.54[F]   PS3568.I316/

  ISBN 0–86188–660–7

Phototypeset in 11/12pt Linotron Times by
Phoenix Photosetting, Chatham
Printed and bound in Great Britain by
Biddles Ltd, Guildford & King's Lynn

To Mark,
Who makes anything possible and everything worthwhile,
with all my love.

Chapter One

The sound was penetrating and instantly alarming. The shriek and rasp of crumpling metal caused attendant Jack Peterson to slop his coffee over the crossword he was pondering and curse softly, his enjoyable early morning apathy rudely destroyed. Hearing an engine rev wildly, then stall, he moved swiftly to the door of the booth to see just what the hell was going on in his domain – the carpark of Newcastle's Royal Northern Infirmary.

The offending vehicle was easily identified, angled against the neat row of parked cars like a badly broken limb. Clearly, it had been aimed towards one of the few remaining empty slots but in turning too soon the passenger door had caught the bumper of the car alongside. The driver was the sole occupant.

'Women drivers,' muttered Jack, shaking his head sorrowfully. He turned his collar up to combat the chill of the early December morning and sucked in air noisily through his teeth, watching to see how she would deal with the problem.

Mike Jennings, a junior housesurgeon at the Northern, was also watching. Leaving the hospital late after a night shift on Accident and Emergency, he walked briskly towards his own car, white coat hanging over one shoulder and a pile of books cradled under his other arm. Mike's frown deepened as he neared the car in difficulty. Suddenly he dumped the books on to the bonnet of the nearest car and his coat slipped unnoticed to the ground as he began to run.

Jack left the booth. He also broke into a run.

The driver was hunched over the steering wheel, her

1

knuckles protruding whitely where she gripped it. She looked up as Mike wrenched the door open. The housesurgeon's glance took in a small plastic canister on her lap, noting in almost the same instant her dilated pupils and the droplets of perspiration beading her face. She was struggling to breathe and her plea for help was almost inaudible due to the agonised wheezing sounds she emitted.

'Asthmatic?' Mike queried tersely, pocketing the canister.

The young woman nodded.

'Put both your hands around my neck and hold tight,' he directed.

He eased her out of the car, balancing himself to cope with her weight.

'Bring her handbag, will you please, Jack?' he called, moving swiftly in an awkward loping stride towards the ambulance entrance of the Northern's Accident and Emergency department.

People scattered as Mike barged through the casualty waiting area. A woman picked up a child and pressed herself against the wall. A nurse hastily dragged a wheelchair out of his path, the locked wheels leaving rubber marks on the tiled floor. All conversation ceased as they gaped at the drama. Mike didn't pause until he entered the resuscitation room, equipped for all major medical emergencies and luckily unoccupied at present. He was closely followed by several staff members, including the senior registrar on duty, Bob Matthews, who had abandoned his examination of a sprained ankle on hearing the commotion.

'Status asthmaticus,' said Mike, now out of breath himself, as he gently deposited his charge on to the gurney. She sat, shaking, hugging her knees. The registrar reached for his stethoscope as he spoke to the young nurse beside him.

'Load the nebuliser trolley with 2 millilitres of salbutamol solution in 5 millilitres of water and start a low flow of oxygen.'

Bob helped Mike remove the cardigan their patient was wearing and loosen her blouse.

'What's your name, love?' he asked.

Her breathing was quieter now though still obviously difficult. Both doctors recognised that the decrease in sound

2

indicated a worsening of her condition. She strained to speak, her voice emerging as a hoarse whisper.

'Shar . . . Sharon Andrews.'

'OK, Sharon. Have you taken any medication recently?'

She nodded.

'What was it?'

'I . . . don't know.'

'What?' Bob's harsh tone reflected disbelief. Sharon became agitated. Tears rolled down her cheeks and sobs further convulsed her breathing efforts. Her words were nearly incomprehensible but Mike thought he caught the gist.

'Take it easy, Sharon,' he said. Digging in his pocket he handed the inhaler in its plastic case to Bob, then turned and ducked past the curtain to rescue her handbag from Jack, who was explaining his presence to the receptionist. When he returned to the resuscitation room, having found the bottle of capsules, Bob was removing his stethoscope from Sharon's back and the nurse was fitting the primed nebuliser mask to her face. The sister looked up from a sphygmomanometer, the cuff of which was secured around Sharon's upper arm.

'Pulsus paradoxus 25 millimetres mercury. Heart rate 70,' she reported.

Mike glanced at the registrar.

'That's a low rate, Bob.'

'Mmm.' He was busy inserting a small plastic cannula into a forearm vein. The task was being made difficult by Sharon's agitated movements.

'Find a splint,' he ordered the staff nurse, 'and draw up 200 milligrams of hydrocortisone.'

He turned to the sister.

'Draw up 250 milligrams of aminophylline in 10 millilitres, Carol, and then another 250 for the intravenous line please.'

He looked up at Mike, standing at the foot of the gurney.

'What was it?'

'Week five of a double-blind, crossover drug trial being run by Tony Lawrence. They're contacting him but it's either salbutamol or placebo.'

Bob gave a curt nod. It would not interfere with the standard regime.

Sharon gave up any attempts to communicate within the next few minutes, and concentrated her struggle on her breathing. Her efforts at respiration were rapid and chaotic. Mike had difficulty trying to keep her lying down as Bob injected the dose of hydrocortisone and then made an arterial puncture near her elbow for a sample to test blood gases. He spoke reassuringly to Sharon as he worked, quietly explaining the procedures.

The blood was dispatched and Bob had time to observe the condition of his patient closely as he slowly injected the priming dose of aminophylline. Sharon was staring at him, looking terrified. Her face was a dreadful shade of grey and she was sweating profusely. Beads of perspiration were collecting on her forehead to form rivulets which matted her hair into a dark tangle and drenched the pillow and sheet beneath her. Small conjunctival haemorrhages were noticeable, a red spiderweb around the green of her irises. Through the clear plastic of the Venturi mask Bob could see that her lips were blue. What worried him more than anything, however, was that the sounds of her breathing were still decreasing despite her desperate efforts to shift air. He completed the injection and connected the saline solution containing the second dose of aminophylline to the IV cannula.

Bob shifted his gaze to Mike, who was reinflating the cuff of the sphygmomanometer, his eyes fixed to the mercury column. Mike frowned as he finished checking Sharon's blood pressure.

'Pulsus paradoxus way over 50 millimetres,' he reported grimly, removing the stethoscope.

The blood gas results arrived but as Bob glanced at them he was aware of an abrupt change in the room's atmosphere. He turned sharply to see that Sharon had lost consciousness. Her panicked movements had ceased and her face was a dusky blue, the eyes half-open, staring ahead sightlessly.

'God,' muttered Bob. He rapidly organised his thoughts as he snapped directions.

'Get the anaesthetics officer down here, stat.'

'Start 100% oxygen.'

'Endotracheal tube, size 8.'

'Draw up 50 mg suxamethonium.'

'Bring that anaesthetic trolley over here.'

The staff reacted to the situation with practised skill. Sharon's clothing was swiftly cut and removed. Electrocardiograph electrodes were positioned on her shoulders and chest to monitor her heartbeat and a black ambu bag pressed to her face in place of the nebuliser. The initial attempt to get the endotracheal tube down Sharon's throat failed due to the convulsive gagging response it provoked. Bob suppressed the old horror that often surfaced at times like this – that the patient was really conscious enough to be aware of what was happening. He pressed the arrest button on the wall to summon extra assistance before reaching for the short-acting paralyzing agent Carol had drawn up for him.

The electrocardigraph showed the pulse rate to be decreasing into a bradycardia and the spikes of the QRS complexes indicating cardiac electrical activity, showed abnormal widening. Mike closed off the IV line to prevent the aminophylline being given possibly contributing to the arrhythmia. He continued compressing the ambu bag as they waited thirty seconds for the characteristic muscle tremors, which looked like a mild electric shock, to indicate that the paralyzing agent had taken effect. Then he placed his thumbs under Sharon's jaw and lifted it forward to aid the repeat attempt at intubation. With the ET tube successfully placed this time and the ambu bag reattached, Bob began to try and respire Sharon. Even with the paralyzed muscles offering no resistance he needed both hands to try and pump air into her lungs. He watched her chest for signs of movement but Sharon still looked overinflated, as if she were holding her breath, and there were no signs of a significant air volume being shifted.

Bob ordered another blood gas sample and cast an anxious glance at the ECG screen where the tracing was becoming more erratic. Mike was moving his stethoscope from one side of Sharon's chest to the other, listening carefully. He shook his head in response to Bob's raised eyebrows, his expression grim.

'Could be a pneumothorax.'

The blood gas analysis was returned and Mike read out the information which revealed Sharon's deteriorating condition. A sharp increase in carbondioxide had reached a dangerous level, causing a severe buildup of acid in her blood.

The crash team arrived and filled the remainder of the resuscitation room, poised for action. Bob turned over the ambu bagging to one of its members and selected a large bore angiocath needle from the trolley of sterilised equipment beside him. Feeling for a rib space at the side of Sharon's chest Bob plunged the needle in confidently, feeling the pop of separating muscle and the needle grazing a rib. The needle was removed leaving the plastic casing protruding. He repeated the procedure on Sharon's other side, hoping for the gush of air that would indicate release of a tension pneumo-thorax, where air trapped outside the lung prevented it functioning. None came.

Someone barked a warning as the ECG screen displayed the wild pattern of fibrillation. An alarm went off stridently as it changed to the straight line of asystole. Sharon had arrested.

Bob stepped back to gain an overview of the crisis. His mind seemed automatically to supply the necessary directions to co-ordinate the increasingly determined efforts of the small army of trained personnel. The anaesthetics officer arrived but could only become a spectator. The young nurse standing beside him was pale and her quiet comment might have been his own.

'She's only twenty-eight.'

By the time Dr. Tony Lawrence arrived at the scene it was all over. With an almost painful sense of shock he realised Sharon was dead. Her eyes were open and surprised-looking with widely dilated pupils. She was almost navy blue in colour and her face had a puffed and bloated appearance. A nurse was wiping saliva from her chin, another removing electrodes and needles. The arrest team were silently gathering up their equipment, preparing to leave.

Bob looked exhausted, He wiped his hands on a towel and then extended one to the newcomer.

'Dr. Lawrence? I'm Bob Matthews.'

The older man's handshake was firm and the eye contact managed to convey sympathy without a patronising overtone.

'I'm sorry I couldn't get here sooner, Bob. We had an arrest on the ward just after I got your message.'

By unspoken agreement they left the resuscitation room. The waiting area was crowded and the owner of the abandoned sprained ankle was complaining loudly to the receptionist about the delay. Tony Lawrence smiled wryly.

'Your public awaits. I'll have to catch you later. Has her husband been notified?'

'They're still trying to contact him.'

'Give me a yell when he arrives.'

Bob nodded. 'I expect there'll be an inquest.'

'Yes. Could you also ask pathology to let me know when they schedule the autopsy? I'd like to be present.'

'Sure.'

'Thanks, Bob.' Dr. Lawrence turned to leave, then paused briefly.

'We broke the code, by the way – she was on placebo.'

Chapter Two

Dr. Anthony James Lawrence was angry.

Unreasonably, part of his anger was directed at the unfortunate Sharon Andrews for dying. Without recognising this primal reaction, Tony Lawrence fed the anger directed at himself, for not having prevented her death. In the face of such a disturbing event, his years of training, hard-won knowledge and even the ideals of his chosen profession seemed a waste of time.

Tony had decided to become a doctor at the age of ten, the desire being a direct result of his father's redundancy. A joiner in a quiet Yorkshire village, Jack Lawrence had lost his job at the age of forty-eight and in his son's opinion, had never made any effort to find himself other employment. Tony had watched his father's degeneration into bad temper and apathy, blaming the world's ills on the government and complaining about the meagreness of the benefit he collected weekly. The boy had unconsciously chosen a new father figure, the village doctor, and modelled himself on this man he respected and admired.

Possessing a keen intelligence, Anthony Lawrence had excelled in his early education and won a scholarship which enabled him to attend medical school. He helped support himself by taking a series of part-time and holiday jobs, working as a porter, laboratory technician and later an ambulance driver, but still managing to fit in a fairly active social life. Breaking out somewhat after his quiet village upbringing, Tony enjoyed these years thoroughly and his academic record did not reflect his full capabilities, a fact commented on by more than one of his professors. In spite of this he managed to pass with flying colours, and while disappointed that his father was not alive to witness his achievement he recognised that it had been more appropriate in many ways that the village practitioner had accompanied his mother and sister to the graduation ceremony.

Since then Tony had made up for his lack of application at medical school many times over. He had become a perfectionist, demanding the highest standards from himself and expecting the same from the people he worked with. When these standards were not met his normally even temper was liable to fray, but the strength of his personality was such that his colleagues and even patients were generally eager to give the best they had to offer.

What people remembered most after meeting Dr. Lawrence was his enthusiasm. He had a genuine and avid interest in everything medicine had to offer and how it could be harnessed to maximum effect. Tony had done his housesurgeon years at Leeds General Infirmary before taking up a junior registrar post at the Northern in Newcastle and rotating through several medical runs. He had delighted in each speciality he had encountered, with the exception of geriatrics. Addicted to the excitement and challenge of treating acute and serious conditions he quickly realised that general practice was not for him, but deciding which area to specialise in had been very difficult.

He almost decided to stay in general medicine so he could have a taste of everything but the job opportunities for general physicians were becoming increasingly rare and reluctantly he had narrowed his interests. The decision to specialise in respiratory medicine had come about mainly because it was on this run that he was first introduced to medical research, an area considered inferior and entirely ignored during medical school training. Research provided a scope for Tony Lawrence's creativity and interests that purely clinical work could not.

Tony Lawrence had a charm he was refreshingly unaware of. From a distance he was an unprepossessing figure, of slightly above average height and lean build, favouring comfortable clothing more appropriate for a housesurgeon than someone approaching consultant status. The soft-soled

9

shoes, tidy but definitely casual wool or corduroy trousers, worn-in shirts and in particular a favourite, and now stringy, brown leather tie were Tony's uniform and the despair of his fashion conscious wife.

Closer to, the first impression was forgotten. Tony's intensely blue eyes, which tended to turn a deep shade of grey when he was angry, were arresting. They were framed by unusually long eyelashes, a darker shade of brown than the wavy hair which reflected golden tones under artificial light and changed to a streaky blond with a good dose of sunshine. The sincerity and gentleness these eyes advertised might have been disconcertingly intense, but the effect was charming in conjunction with Tony's engaging, almost cheeky grin that appeared with spontaneous frequency.

Right now, his eyes were a steely shade of grey and the anger he was struggling to turn to a constructive purpose made Tony Lawrence oblivious to his surroundings as he started the long trek from casualty to the respiratory department of the Royal Northern Infirmary. Rationally, he knew that he was not responsible for Sharon's death. The drug trial the young woman had been involved with could not have contributed to the tragedy. In fact, the exhaustive lung function tests and monitoring over the weeks of the trial should have been the best possible protection.

With highly developed, scientific thought processes, Tony gradually sorted the accusations he was levelling at himself into a list of questions, graded according to priority. With no benefit to be gained from immediate attention to them, he mentally added the questions to the long list of important issues to be attended to as soon as possible. As his anger faded, Tony focused on another high priority.

His twelve years of working at the Northern enabled him to negotiate the labyrinth of corridors and walkways automatically. The central part of the hospital, where Accident and Emergency was situated, had been built around the turn of the century. It was by now rather dilapidated and had many architectural shortcomings. The over-high ceilings caused enormous heating bills, there were frequent complaints about the presence of silverfish and cockroaches, and the narrow corridors, which didn't allow two beds to pass with ease, led to congestion and bad-tempered porters. Layer after layer of paint had been applied over the years and dampness caused large chunks to fall off which gave the walls the appearance of an unfinished jigsaw puzzle.

Over the last eighty years additional buildings had sprouted in all directions. The respiratory department was on the outskirts of the complex. Before he reached it Tony made a detour into what was the latest addition to the Northern. This wing, completed only last year, housed some sophisticated operating theatres, the Intensive Care and Coronary Care Units. It was CCU that Tony entered. The patient who had arrested earlier in the ward had been transferred there immediately after the successful resuscitation attempt.

Tony picked up his patient's wrist, his mind correlating the pulse he felt with the tracing he watched on the bedside ECG monitor. The patient's eye lids immediately flickered open, the appearance of a pair of beady brown eyes bringing life to the florid face. Tony said gently, 'Hullo, Harry'.

'Hi, Doc.' The voice was much weaker than usual but still cheerful. 'I nearly kicked the bucket that time, didn't I?'

'You certainly gave us a fright, Harry, but you're looking pretty good again now.'

'Aye. Think I'll stick around a while yet, right enough.'

'We'll have to cancel your biopsy for the moment, old chap – just to make sure we've got you under control.'

Harry grimaced under his oxygen mask and gestured towards the spaghetti-like jumble of wires and tubes surrounding him.

'Can't go far, that's for sure.'

'Make the most of it and have a good rest. I'll be up to see you again later.'

Tony chatted to the registrar on duty briefly before he left CCU. He checked his watch. It was now a choice between catching up on the patients he had missed on the interrupted ward round, or having lunch. He walked decisively towards the ward.

By the time he felt happy that he was aware of all new developments there, Tony was running late for his outpatient clinic. He sighed, knowing he wasn't so popular with the staff down there. Tuesday afternoon was basically a review clinic

11

for patients who had been coming for some time. A ten-minute slot was allocated to each one after they had had their lung function tests, x-rays and so on. Tony's unpopularity stemmed from the fact that he insisted on taking as much time with each patient as it took for both himself and the patient to feel satisfied. This meant that he invariably ran well behind time and even with his junior registrar working flat out, patient delays became extended and the outpatient support staff never got home on time. The receptionists were the ones to suffer most, as they dealt with a crowded waiting room and the complaints about delays. Even so, they suffered with a grudging good humour. Tony's slightly disreputable appearance tended to foster an affectionate maternal instinct in the females he encountered, an affection which quite a number admitted to each other had become something of a crush. Not that Dr. Lawrence had ever shown more than a friendly interest in any of them, but they were also all aware that should they ever become sick themselves, he was exactly the type of doctor they would want.

The first case of the afternoon was straightforward enough, a seventeen-year-old girl who had suffered from asthma since early childhood and had had three admissions for severe attacks, the last one twelve months ago. Her lung function tests were now all within the lower limit of normal and Tony was considering discharging her to the care of her general practitioner. During his routine examination and questioning he changed his mind, however, concerned to hear that episodes of wheeziness over the last three months occurred more often in the morning. Asthmatics who woke with breathing problems were at greater risk of severe or even fatal asthmatic attacks. Tony did not want to see a repeat of the morning's disaster. He rummaged through a desk drawer and produced two small plastic cylinders.

'Have you ever used one of these before, Lesley?'

The girl shook her head and smiled shyly. She wished her current boyfriend had blue eyes like Dr. Lawrence's. They were as gorgeous as Steve McQueen's. The thought made her squirm slightly and transfer her gaze to the buttons on her blouse.

'It's a Wright's peak flow meter,' explained Tony. 'It

12

measures how much air you can get out of your lungs, just like the spirometry test you did today. I'll show you how to use it.' He skirted the desk and bent down beside Lesley. She bit her lip and tried to concentrate on what he was telling her.

'You slide this button down so that it sits at the bottom.'

What amazingly long fingers he has, the teenager thought, then blushed crimson as she remembered what the girls at school said that was supposed to mean. Guiltily she glanced at Tony's nose. That was said to be another good indication but Dr. Lawrence's nose was of very average proportions.

'Right.' Tony handed the other meter to Lesley. 'Now you try it.'

The girl put the mouthpiece to her lips obediently.

'Check that the slide is down,' Tony reminded her.

She checked and raised the mouthpiece again. He sighed imperceptibly.

'Let me show you again, Lesley. Let your breath out and then take a really big breath in. Hold it for a moment, keeping your mouth open, *then* put it in your mouth and blow as hard as you can. Like this.'

She watched in some embarrassment as Tony repeated the performance then copied him correctly.

'Good girl, that's fine. I want you to take that meter home and use it every morning and evening. Record the number that the white mark gets to each time and make a note if you felt particularly wheezy that day. Bring the chart back with you the next time you come.' Tony moved back to the desk and made a quick note in her records. 'I'll see you again in two months. We just need to sort out your prescription and that's all for now.' He smiled cheerfully at his patient, totally unaware of the adulation he received in return.

The hold-ups began with the second case. The receptionist's heart sank when she called for the patient.

'Mr. Thornton? You can go through now, please.'

As he passed the desk she muttered to her companion: 'I'll put fifty pence on him taking longer than half an hour.'

'You're on,' replied the other receptionist. 'He was only in two weeks ago.'

Tony's own heart sank as he watched John Thornton enter the examination room. The forty-seven-year-old man had developed asthma late in life and it was steadily becoming more severe. Nothing they had tried so far had helped, and judging by the way his patient shuffled into the room and then sat, with his shoulders hunched up almost to the level of his ears, the most recent combination of drugs was also a failure.

'Things still not too good, Mr. Thornton?'

'No, Doctor.' John Thornton spoke in short sentences, all that he could manage on a single breath. Tony looked at him carefully and felt more depressed. He was on maximum therapy. Atrovent and salbutamol inhalers, four puffs six times a day, theophylline and 30 milligrams of prednisone a day. The steroids were causing central body weight gain, the hump of fat on his shoulders contributing to the hunched appearance, while his arms and legs were becoming thin and wasted. The skin on his hands was mottled with bruises where blood vessels were becoming fragile. Tony sighed as he read the abysmal results from the lung function tests and the most recent chest x-ray. He pressed the intercom button on his desk to summon the clinic sister.

'Could you bring in a trolley for an arterial blood gas please, Sister? I'm sorry about this, Mr. Thornton,' he said apologetically, 'but we'd better see just how much oxygen you've got circulating right now.'

Puncturing an artery for a blood sample could be a time-consuming procedure. Tony scrubbed up at the sink in the room and then donned surgical gown, mask and gloves. Luckily the needle slid easily into the artery on this occasion, in spite of the local anaesthetic injected into the area first. Tony let the blood gas syringe fill itself from the pressure of the blood pumping from the artery then handed it to the sister. She carefully checked for any air bubbles that would ruin the analysis before leaving with the syringe nestled in a bowl of ice. Tony pressed firmly on the puncture site at John Thornton's elbow. He glanced at the wall clock. The ten minutes of applying pressure to seal up the puncture in the artery could seem a long time but he was going to need even longer to discuss the options of treatment left with this patient. They could experiment with a different combination of drugs but judging from John's obvious depression, something more effective was needed immediately. Perhaps admitting him to hospital for intensive physiotherapy and high doses of intramuscular steroids, or even pulmonary lavage where one lung was kept open while the other was washed to flush out the accumulation of mucus.

Ginette, at the reception desk, collected her fifty pence after forty minutes and sighed theatrically as she surveyed the packed waiting area. Tony's junior registrar, Hugh McGinty, was working flat out and managing to keep interview times to between ten and fifteen minutes. Ginette relaxed slightly after Mr. Thornton emerged and Tony had seen two more cases within thirty minutes, then was dismayed to receive an internal telephone call demanding a connection to Dr. Lawrence. Tony was equally annoyed at the summons from the chief respiratory physician's secretary.

'Can't it wait, Mrs. Dogerty?' He held the phone to his ear with a hunched shoulder, his hands occupied with the pile of results that preceded the arrival of his next patient. 'I'm up to my eyeballs in an OP clinic.'

'I'm afraid not, Dr. Lawrence,' intoned Mrs. Dogerty crisply. 'Dr. Davies requires your presence immediately.'

Tony's rueful grin mollified the receptionists only slightly as he left.

'I'll be as quick as I can,' he promised.

The office of Dr. Gordon Owen Davies – dubbed God by his less reverent subordinates – was on the fifth floor. The long pointed nose of his secretary, which looked to have been designed for haughty sniffing, performed exactly that function as she let Tony in to the inner sanctum.

Dr. Davies was a large man with strands of steel grey hair arranged carefully to conceal his baldness. He had a permanently patronising awareness of his own importance and always wore his white physician's coat firmly buttoned, the handles of a stethoscope protruding from his top pocket with military precision. Today his customary aloofness was obviously disturbed and the look that Tony was bombarded with had distinctly hostile undertones. He was not alone in his office. A younger man sat in front of the ornate desk, his head buried in his hands.

'Ah, Lawrence.' Gordon Davies' tone held a measure of

15

satisfaction. He gestured towards the man by his desk. 'This is Mr. Andrews.'

The young man's head snapped up at the mention of Tony's name. He leapt to his feet.

'You're the one who killed my wife!'

'Mr. Andrews, please – ' Tony stepped towards the young man.

Shane Andrews was distraught, unaware of the tears on his face. His voice rose to a hoarse shout. 'She only had asthma, for God's sake.' His movements were jerky as he blundered to the window, then turned sharply to face Tony. 'Then she becomes your bloody guinea pig, and now she's dead. Christ, she was only twenty-eight!' Shane's eyes were wild and he clenched his fists with enough force to make his whole body shake. 'I'll sue, damn you – sue you, sue this bloody hospital.'

His voice broke and he sank into the consultant's leather chair, his body racked with painful sobs. Gordon Davies folded his arms and adopted his preferred observer's rôle. Tony swiftly rounded the desk and gripped both of Shane's shoulders. He spoke with a calm which belied his own distress.

'Mr. Andrews, I'm terribly sorry about your wife's death. I wasn't present when she came into hospital but I know everything possible was done for her. Asthma is so common a disease, its potential as a killer is sadly underestimated at times. There are more than two million people in Britain who suffer from asthma, and nearly two thousand die from asthmatic attacks every year.' He felt his words were totally inadequate. He should be offering some comfort to the man, not a statistical lecture, but Shane was quieter now and might be listening.

'The trial Sharon was involved in couldn't possibly have caused her death, Mr. Andrews,' he continued. 'She was receiving the best of care and almost continuous monitoring – much more than she usually had. It's a tragedy that she died, and we're all very unhappy about it, but you can't hold the trial responsible.'

Shane rubbed his eyes. 'I'm going to see my lawyer,' he mumbled, but his voice lacked conviction. He looked exhausted and his anger was giving way to shocked disbelief.

Dr. Davies seemed willing to take part again, now that things were more under control. Shane Andrews was looking merely bewildered, ready for the reassurance that Gordon Davies' years of experience had made him an expert in imparting. He ushered Tony out of the office, pausing at the door, his gaze level and tone of voice chilly.

'I want a copy of the protocol, patient records, the informed consent and the post mortem report on my desk. Tomorrow.'

Chapter Three

The outpatient waiting area was overflowing as Tony hurried through on his return. Hugh McGinty, the nursing staff and receptionists were all looking harrassed. He paused by the desk to check the list of patients remaining to be seen.

An attractive peal of laughter made him glance up. A toddler was standing with his chubby legs splayed, making faces through them at a woman whose long black hair rippled as she shook her head at the infant and laughed again. The toddler overbalanced and hit his head on a wooden train. His crescendo of wails sent people diving for the cover of their magazines. Dr. Lawrence retreated to the relative calm of patient interviews.

An hour later the waiting room was getting emptier but it was a very annoyed-looking receptionist who poked her head around the door of Tony's examination room as a patient left.

'Dr. Lawrence?'

'How's it going, Ginette?'

'Not very well. Mrs. McTavish is insisting on seeing you.'

'She's not on the list for this afternoon, is she?'

'No, she isn't. I've explained that we're busy and running late but she says it's important and she'll wait.'

Tony drew in a long breath. Irene McTavish was another of his trial patients.

'Let her wait, Ginette. I'll see her when I can. Sorry.'

She shrugged. 'My stars forecasted a bad day. I guess it can't last forever.'

It was half-past five when Irene McTavish bustled in and settled her bulk in the chair opposite Tony. He was dismayed

18

to see that her rather obnoxious eight-year-old son was in tow. The boy sidled around the desk, fingering objects within his reach, and Tony quickly put his stethoscope into his pocket. Mrs. McTavish beamed at him. He was astonished. Good humour was not a virtue he had previously associated with her.

'How are you, Irene?'

'Wonderful, Doctor – and I have some wonderful news.'

'Oh?'

'I have to withdraw from your trial.'

Tony was rendered momentarily speechless. He caught a movement out of the corner of his eye and automatically said, 'Put that back, please, Brent.'

The child's lip curled slightly as he took a pen out of his pocket and flicked it back onto the desk. His mother hadn't noticed. She leaned forward conspiratorially.

'You see, Doctor, it happened last night.'

'Yes?' Tony was aware of a sinking sensation. Today was going from bad to unbelievable. Mrs. McTavish merely nodded and smiled, so he tried again. 'I don't quite follow, Irene.'

'I'm reborn, Doctor.' Her obese face dimpled with self-satisfaction. 'So, of course, you do understand.' She nodded sagely.

'Understand what precisely?' Tony was nonplussed.

'I can't possibly continue the trial, Dr. Lawrence. My treatment is now in higher hands. I shall be directed in the use of herbal remedies.'

Tony finally terminated the interview when Mrs. McTavish eagerly questioned him about his own beliefs. It had become apparent that there would be no persuading her to change her mind, either about finishing the trial or attending future outpatient appointments.

'Cross me off your books, Doctor,' she said serenely. 'And Brent too. We're in good hands now.'

Ginette was covering her typewriter and turning out lights. Tony noted the deserted waiting area with enormous relief. Hugh was coming down the corridor talking to the woman whom Tony had earlier seen laughing. He hadn't realised she was a patient. Hugh must have seen her on a previous visit.

'Tony!' Hugh was looking very pleased with himself. 'This is Mrs. Bridget Gardiner.'

'How do you do?' He recognised the name and vaguely remembered Hugh's previous evaluation of her. He noticed now that her eyes were almost as dark as her hair. It was difficult to see where the pupil ended and the iris began. Her eyes were quite widely spaced and might have made her nose seem too small but the effect was balanced by a generous mouth which curved into a delightful smile.

'Very well, thank you, Dr. Lawrence. Though Dr. McGinty here has been trying to persuade me to enrol, in your trial.'

'She's a perfect candidate,' put in Hugh enthusiastically.

'Please don't feel pressured, Mrs. Gardiner.' Tony knew he sounded snappy but he'd heard quite enough about the trial for today. 'Participation is entirely voluntary.'

Hugh looked astonished and disapproving. Bridget's smile slowly subsided and left her face looking solemn. There was a hint of a frown between her dark eyes.

'I understand. I really don't have the time at present, anyway.' She tossed her mane of black hair over her shoulder. 'If you'll excuse me, there's a patient I want to visit while I'm here.'

She took her leave and Hugh eyed Tony quizzically.

'Time for a cup of coffee?'

'Thanks – I could do with one.'

They were silent until they reached the doctors' common room, situated on the fourth floor, directly below Gordon Davies' office. Hugh punched the buttons on the automatic drinks dispenser. He handed one cup to Tony who had settled himself in one of the overstuffed armchairs that dotted the room.

'Here's mud in your eye, Lawrence.' Hugh peered into his own coffee with distaste. 'Almost literally, in fact.'

'You don't have a cigarette on you, do you, Hugh?'

'I thought you'd given up again.'

Tony groaned. 'I had.'

Hugh glanced towards the ceiling and Tony grinned. 'Have you ever known him to stay after five-thirty?'

Dr. Davies was a fanatical anti-smoker. His twin passions

20

in life were the committees he served on and the lectures he gave on the subject. He had been inspired by the 'Glasgow 2000' campaign which had the rather ambitious aim of changing the world's cancer capital into an entire city of non-smokers by the start of the next century. Davies was distinctly jealous not to have thought up the idea himself and was now determined to modify the concept in some original way and apply it with equal force and publicity to an unsuspecting Newcastle. Tony and Hugh lit up now with the guilty air of two small boys behind the woodshed.

'God, that's good.' Tony exhaled with patent satisfaction. 'What a day.'

'I heard about Sharon Andrews – I'm sorry.'

'That was only the beginning.' Tony drew on his cigarette deeply, his face troubled. 'I had a terrible interview with her husband. He blames the trial and is threatening to sue.'

'That's ridiculous,' grunted Hugh.

'Maybe, but he has every right to be off the edge at the moment. I think that our celestial supervisor would like to prove him right.'

Hugh blew his smoke towards the ceiling and winked at Tony. 'Don't let it get you down.'

'And then there was Mrs McTavish.' Tony shook his head with disbelief. 'She's opted out of the trial, and any further treatment for herself or her son.'

'What?'

Tony's voice was expressionless. 'She's found God.'

Hugh roared with laughter. 'Was he lost?' he enquired.

'No,' By now Tony was laughing as well. 'But I've discovered that he's a homeopath.'

He felt much better when he finally left the hospital, having checked again on Harry in CCU. It was nearly seven o'clock as he entered the carpark. He ignored the rain falling steadily about him but was very surprised to see Bridget Gardiner there. She was struggling to untighten the nuts on the back wheel of a bright, buttercup yellow Citroën. The protruding headlights of the car gave it the appearance of an alert insect and the boot was decorated with a profusion of flowers, surrounding the neatly painted name of 'Esmeralda'.

Can I be of any assistance?' he enquired.

She glanced up. Her wet hair had the sleekness of sealskin and droplets of moisture had collected in the dark tangle of her eyelashes.

'No, thanks. I can manage.'

Tony squatted down beside her. 'Look, I apologise for bring rude to you. It was uncalled for and I have no excuse.'

Bridget glanced at him again. There was no doubting his sincerity. He grinned engagingly and she felt compelled to smile back.

'Could you get my spare out for me, then?'

Tony tugged his forelock. 'My pleasure, Ma'am.' His voice was puzzled when he spoke again a few seconds later. 'We seem to have a small problem.'

Bridget got up and peered around his arm. 'Oh, no!' She leaned against the car and laughed mirthlessly. 'I took the spare tyre in to get it fixed,' she explained. 'Weeks ago. I must have forgotten to collect it.'

'No problem,' said Tony. 'Lock up and I'll give you a lift home.'

'No, I'll catch a bus. I live miles out of town.'

'Whereabouts?'

'Grangewick – out towards Stamfordham.'

'That's not so far. Come on. I insist.'

Tony glanced at his passenger several times, considering and rejecting the conversational gambits that came to mind. Bridget stared at the road ahead, seemingly content with the silence that Tony found increasingly frustrating. Finally he cleared his throat.

'I must apologise again, Mrs. Gardiner. I hope you won't think I'm often rude to patients.'

'I'm sure you're not, Dr. Lawrence. And please, call me Bridget. I get quite enough of being called Mrs. Gardiner by my children.'

He glanced at her profile. It was a minute or two before he spoke again.

'Um . . . How many children do you have, Bridget?'

She suppressed a smile. 'About thirty.'

'That must be rather a lot to cope with.'

'It certainly is. I'm hoping to get rid of a few of them next week.'

'I can understand that.' Tony nodded seriously. They were both studiously avoiding any eye contact.

'A lot of them are Asian,' continued Bridget, 'so there are racial difficulties on top of unemployment, housing problems and of course, drugs.'

'Of course.'

Eye contact at that point made them both laugh.

'Walker's not the greatest area to teach in,' Bridget finished with a grin.

The drive out to Grangewick didn't take as long as Tony would have liked. He pulled up, at Bridget's direction, in front of a small whitewashed stone cottage, curtailing their conversation about the effects the long-term teachers' pay disputes were still having on the profession, which Tony had found quite enlightening. Bridget thanked him and paused when she had opened the car door.

'I'm sorry you had a bad day, Dr. Lawrence.' Her smile was mischievous. 'I do have time, you know – for the trial? I could come in after school.'

Tony smiled and waved her off then leaned over and unrolled the passenger side window. "Call me Tony,' he shouted after the retreating figure. 'I get quite enough of being called Dr. Lawrence by my patients.'

Chapter Four

Rain-spattered darkness and the isolation of the drive back to town nibbled at the edges of an unaccustomed feeling of contentment which had nothing to do with the fact that Tony was going home.

His satisfaction at finding a place to park only three cars away from the entrance to his apartment block was shortlived. It would be nice to own a garage, he mused, avoiding a large puddle on the pavement, but it was not sufficient reason to justify the move that his wife, Catherine, was so determined on. He liked the gracious old sandstone dwellings and felt lucky to be living in a street lined with huge and ancient Chestnut trees. From their third-floor apartment they had a view of a nearby park and a panorama of old slate roofs with the distinctive spires of several churches and the castle turrets rising in the distance. Besides, it was conveniently close to the hospital which made life a lot easier.

Tony entered the communal hallway with its clean white walls and attractive geometric patterns of coloured tiles marking the borders and climbed the stairs to his front door. Looking for his key he felt a familiar sense of gratitude that Catherine had not so far tampered with the decoration of their entranceway. He loved the solid old wooden door with the brass lion's head knocker and the fanlight of stained glass above. It was the only bit of real character left in his home now that Catherine was satisfied with the interior decoration. Not that she'd been able to alter the high moulded ceilings and bay windows of the apartment but the warmth which should have been innate in a home of this age had been nullified to a large extent by the expanse of chilly white carpet she had installed, and her choice of the palest pastel paint-work on all the walls. Even the spaciousness of the beautifully proportioned rooms had been destroyed by her collections of chinese screens which sometimes made Tony feel as if he were in the ward of some private and very expensive hospital.

He glanced into the kitchen as he walked down the hallway. The room was clinically white and spotless. A tray lay on the table set with silverware for one and a single wineglass. He entered the living room, artistically illuminated by small lamps with white silk lampshades, but nobody was there to appreciate the warmth thrown out by the gas fire. Puzzled, Tony went back into the hallway.

'Catherine?'

'In here, darling.'

He went into the master bedroom and found his wife seated in front of her dressing table mirror. She finished fussing with her hair and sprayed it liberally with a highly perfumed spray.

'You're very late tonight, Anthony.' She rose and prof-fered her cheek. He knew better than to smudge her carefully painted lips with a kiss. She wrinkled her nose in distaste when he drew near.

'Have you been smoking?'

Tony gave up on the kiss. 'No,' he said. 'Have you?'

Catherine Lawrence was not amused. She was in total agreement with Gordon Davies on the subject and it had always been a bone of contention in their marriage. She got on rather well with Davies generally, in fact, which led to the Lawrences being invited to far more social occasions at their house than Tony cared for. He knew she disbelieved him but his quick reply put the ball in her court. She chose not to argue and smiled at him tolerantly.

'I'm afraid I have to dash , darling.'

'Where are you going?'

'It's Tuesday, Tony,' said his wife patiently. 'Aerobics.'

'Oh, of course.'

'Don't wait up for me. I'll probably have a coffee with Jean afterwards, and you know how she likes to chatter.'

'I do indeed.'

She flashed him a speculative glance but ignored his remark

and turned back to the mirror. Catherine Lawrence was a very beautiful woman, with the kind of good looks only those with time, money and a great deal of self-interest achieve. Her makeup was flawless, her hairstyle a masterpiece, and her clothes were chosen with supreme skill and taste. She watched her diet with almost fanatical care and attended frequent workouts such as these aerobics classes. Advertisements for health or beauty products found a perfect target in Catherine. She used only soaps like orchid oil, vitamin E, or goat's milk with honey on her body, and cleansed her face with such products as honeyed beeswax and almond with Jojoba oil, applied with a natural sea sponge. Currently she was experimenting with white grape skin tonic, carrot moisture cream and Hawthorn hand cream.

Tony often found he had picked up a seaweed and birch or camomile powder shampoo in the shower. It was just as well he used them up, however, as Catherine rarely got halfway through a bottle before being attracted by a new variety. The kitchen had its own collection of bottles, the present favourites being Ginseng, Evening Primrose oil and royal jelly capsules. In short, Catherine Lawrence's body was an object of devotion and the majority of her time was dedicated to its wellbeing and presentation.

Satisfied with her reflection for the moment, she kissed the air an inch or so away from her husband's cheek. Have a nice evening, darling. Oh, I've left some property details from the estate agent on the coffee table. Have a look while I'm out and see what you think.'

Tony watched her fish out her car keys and followed her into the hall.

'Actually, I've been thinking of emigrating. To Canada, or maybe New Zealand.'

'Very funny,' Catherine's tone was clipped. 'See you later, then.'

The front door clicked firmly shut.

Tony had no immediate desire to investigate whatever culinary delight the daily, Mrs. McKay, might have left behind. He believed her training must have been accomplished in hospital kitchens. Had he ever bothered to investigate, he would have found the assumption to be entirely correct. He collected the wine glass and an opened bottle from the refrigerator and wandered back into the living room. Tony put on his favourite Chris de Burgh record, poured himself a glass of wine and stretched out on the couch nearest the fire. It was a relief to be alone.

In the last few years Catherine had engineered their lives so that they rarely spent any time alone together. When they weren't at the expedient social gatherings that Catherine thrived on, he was on call and at the hospital as often as not. He had the reputation of never lasting out a social gathering as he always left his number with the switchboard and had never been known to turn down a call. On other evenings Catherine was frequently out, attending classes, meetings of the local operatic society or the Physicians' Wives Association, in the company of Mrs. Gordon Davies who was the President. When on the odd occasion it looked as though they might have an evening together, Catherine would invite half a dozen or more people for a dinner party.

It hadn't always been like this, Tony reflected. They had been very much in love when they had married after a whirlwind romance eleven years ago. True, Catherine had made it clear that she had no intention of following up her training as a physiotherapist, and also that she had no desire for children, but Tony had hoped she might later change her mind. More important, she knew exactly what his career entailed, and the demands that would be made on his time, which had seemed of primary importance in a doctor's wife.

They had first met at a Robert Burns evening, organised by one of the social committees within the hospital, although Tony had been aware of Catherine's existence for some time, along with almost every other junior registrar, housesurgeon, and a fair proportion of the senior staff at the Northern Infirmary. He had been doing a brief rheumatology run at the time and Catherine was often in the ward, surrounded by a group of fellow physiotherapy students but as noticeable as if she had been a solitary figure in a deserted landscape. Her height and slenderness attracted the eye initially but a single glance at her face was never enough. She had worn her hair very closely cropped in those days, a bold, shining cap that emphasised her exquisitely sculpted features and perfect complexion.

27

Her classmates were well aware that they need not have existed when in the company of Catherine Harris. In consequence she had had no close friends, not that it had bothered her. What Tony Lawrence still didn't know was that neither friendship nor the profession of physiotherapy had motivated or even figured to any large extent in Catherine's plans. She had intended to marry a doctor which was not a difficult task. The choice offered had been wide and the process of elimination a delight. She accepted dates only from eligible contenders, politely rebuffing overtures from married staff members and generally allowing her suitors only two dates apiece. Subsequent dates were reserved only for those who reached the short list as the third date usually involved a session in bed and Catherine had no desire to be tagged 'easy.' She became the prize of that particular year. Having noticed and mentally asterisked Tony Lawrence, Catherine had ignored him, confident that she had not long to wait before he joined the favoured few. As it transpired, she eventually made the first move herself, becoming increasingly impatient for the meeting and progressively more bored with the competition.

The whisky had been circulating for some time on that January evening, the haggis was sonorously addressed by an inebriated orthopaedic consultant and Catherine had excused herself from her escort. She chatted briefly with old but still eager aquaintances, earning malignant glares from their partners as she mapped her path towards Tony Lawrence with precision. Her pause to look with interest at the disgusting and half-dissected haggis brought her seemingly accidentally to her target's side.

'Feeling hungry?' she had enquired with a smile.

Tony had grimaced. 'I'm not sure. I'm wondering whether the ingredients are fit for human consumption.'

'It's pluck,' Catherine told him knowledgeably. 'You get the lungs, heart and liver from a sheep, mix it with oatmeal, onions and blood, stuff it into a sheep's stomach, tie it up and boil it for a few hours.'

Tony's face had been a picture of distaste. 'Pluck's the right word for it. It would take more than I possess to eat it. Why don't we go and find ourselves some fish and chips?'

28

'What an irresistible invitation.'

Her hand had slipped behind his elbow as they escaped from the party. The usual reward of the third date had been conferred on the second and Tony had been clapped resoundingly on the back by his colleagues when he announced the engagement.

'Lucky devil,' they had muttered. And for a long time Tony had agreed with them.

Catherine had proved a delightful companion, devoting her time and attention exclusively to her young husband. She had moulded her activities around Tony's working hours to ensure no distraction to the pampering he received off duty. If an evening was free from on-call or other work commitments, she would often organise a night on the town with an elegant dinner and sometimes dancing after the theatre, concert or movie. In the privacy of their small apartment an evening at home was deliciously intimate. Tony had wondered in some amazement where Catherine had learned some of the exciting sexual practices she initiated. He didn't remember even reading about them in the well-thumbed, erotic paperbacks that had done the rounds of his adolescent peers. Not that he really wanted to know where his wife had become so knowledgeable. He had accepted their sex life happily, the icing on the cake of what seemed to be an ideal relationship.

Catherine had given him wonderful moral support as his career took a positive direction although it necessitated a lessening of their time together. She was delighted when he became a fellow of the Royal College of Physicians, enabling him to add the prestigious initials FRCP to his name, encouraged him through the two years of work which led to his research degree of an MD and was thrilled that he was now enrolled for a PhD. It had been a time-consuming and often difficult process and somewhere along the line Catherine Lawrence's focus of attention had changed from her husband to herself. It had been such a gradual process Tony had not been aware of it at first. He had been pleased that Catherine was finding her own interests now that they had so much less time to spend together. The passion of their early years surfaced less and less, but wasn't that normal within any marriage?

29

It was only lately that he had reluctantly recognised that Catherine's pleasure in his academic achievements was not so much in his success as in the enhanced social prestige she gained. She was not a blatant social climber but took any promotion in status as her due. She had her sights set on eventually being the wife of the chief respiratory physician and succeeding Mrs. Davies as president of the Wives' Association. Already, she was relied upon to produce original ideas for fund raising events and organise many of the administration details for wine and cheese evenings, buffet dinners and chamber music soirées. The position of secretary would be hers soon when a senior consultant took up an offered professorship in London and removed his wife from the coveted slot.

Tony sighed. Catherine knew that a consultant's position was becoming available in the respiratory department and it was the obvious step up the ladder for him. There were several contenders for the post, including some overseas applicants, but Catherine was confident of his success. He thought wryly that her own efforts at charming Davies were probably the strongest element in his favour. Tony was thirty-eight and up until now he had never questioned the direction his life was taking. His enthusiasm for medicine had been such that he had hardly noticed his career advancing through the accepted stages. It had seemed logical and meaningful, when he had bothered to reflect on it briefly, to get the qualifications, a secure job and aim for the position of senior or even chief consultant in his chosen field. Now, firmly on the way, doubts about his marriage and the end point of his career surfaced with increasing frequency. He suppressed them whenever possible, however. It was so much easier to swim with the tide and bury his doubts and frustrations in renewed dedication to immediate challenges in his work. He suspected the marriage was a disappointment for both of them.

'What I need is a friend,' he told his empty wineglass. 'Someone I can really talk to. Someone I could say 'I lost a patient today' to, and then not even have to explain how much it bothers me.'

His fingers rubbed the stem of the glass. The hospital as a topic of conversation was frowned on by Catherine. Her own medical training had confirmed her dislike of illness and she was happier not to be reminded of it, especially those disgusting respiratory patients who had to be postured and banged on the back until they coughed up foul quantities of mucus. If their conversation headed towards anything clinical Catherine would purse her lips faintly and say firmly, 'You're at home now, Tony'. In company she would smile prettily and it would be: 'No shop talk, darling,' in an amused tone of mock disapproval.

Tony rose and searched out the packet of cigarettes hidden behind the liqueur bottles in the drinks cabinet. He opened a window before lighting one. It didn't leave them much to talk about other than Catherine's activities, and the hospital politics and gossip which interested her as much as they repelled him. They didn't really talk about anything these days.

Refilling his glass, his thoughts turned briefly to Sharon Andrews again but without her notes to consider, and in the hope that the post-mortem might provide something more to go on, he suppressed the desire to begin analysing the case. He turned instead to a pile of journals which had been building up for the last couple of months. This was his first chance in a long while to do some serious reading. The escape into the fascination of some of the journal papers was a genuine pleasure and Tony was particularly keen on following up the developments in heart-lung transplants which were showing some spectacular results lately.

He automatically picked up the telephone receiver on its first ring. The brief, conditioned response of his name would have earned praise from Pavlov.

'Hullo, Tony,' said a surprised feminine voice. 'How nice to hear you.' She giggled and was instantly identifiable.

'Hullo, Jean,' he responded, also with surprise.

'Is Cathy there?'

'No.' Tony felt suddenly cold. 'I understood she was going to an aerobics class with you.'

If Jean was dismayed she covered it up superbly. 'Of course! I forgot all about it. I'll see if I can catch her afterwards. Sorry to have disturbed you. 'Bye.'

As if he could dispel the suspicion he felt by movement, Tony stood up. He felt a wave of dizziness and remembered that he hadn't eaten since breakfast. The wine was having a heightened effect. He filled his glass again, turned the record over and went into the kitchen to tackle the by now shrivelled stew and dumplings that was a favourite of Mrs. McKay's.

Chapter Five

Catherine Lawrence was still asleep as Tony let himself quietly out of the flat at seven-thirty the next morning. He felt relieved that there had been no confrontation the previous evening. Both of them seemed content not to blow on the available sparks but the inevitability of a major blaze dampened and confined communication between them. He had not mentioned Jean's call and Catherine had apparently forgotten about the property details. She had busied herself with her nightly beauty routine of shower, creams and massage, her conversation centering on the dinner they were to attend that weekend with some of the more prestigious medics, notably those concerned with the appointment of the new consultant in the respiratory department. It was obviously going to be a major task to find a suitable dress as nothing Catherine owned was remotely suitable. They did not make love but that was hardly unusual these days.

Now, thankfully, Tony shut the door on his domestic life. He positively looked forward to the stress and decision-making the day's work would bring. His first call of the day was to the respiratory laboratories situated behind the outpatient clinic area. He moved through the various rooms, deserted at present except for a cleaner who was moving a polisher with some difficulty around the machinery. One lab housed the exercise testing treadmill, banked by monitors and large cylindrical tubs containing various mixtures of gases. A corner of the room was crowded with refill gas tanks. With the boxes of tubing and the myriad attachments to the ceiling from which to suspend breathing apparatus, the laboratory had an atmosphere of barely controlled chaos to which only patients needed to be added to tip the balance. He passed through an alcove were blood testing was performed. It was a haven of tidiness by contrast, with neat boxes of assorted glass tubes and forms, locked cupboards full of syringes and needles, a couch with a crisp white linen cover and a chair with a neatly rolled tourniquet beside it. The walls displayed a bright collection of posters extolling the virtues of becoming a blood donor but Tony grinned when he noticed the new poster on the door of the 'fridge. Dracula in magnificent technicolour sweeping his cape above the words 'Time for a blood, Count?' That was more like Gwen. A motherly type in her fifties, she had a great sense of humour and the welcome skills to coax blood from the most unwilling subjects or shy veins.

Tony moved through the plethysmography lab and the computer room, noting with satisfaction the banks of sophisticated electronic technology at their disposal. It had all looked very different when he had started work at the Northern. He paused finally, knocking and entering a small office, confident that its inhabitant would be available and ready to start the day's work. As expected, Nicola Jarvis was sitting at her desk, already absorbed in paperwork. She completed tapping a figure on to her calculator before glancing up.

'Sorry to disturb you, Nicola.'

'That's quite all right, Dr. Lawrence. Good Morning.' She smiled but her tone was cool. Everyone who worked with her knew that to be the norm. Her colleagues had dubbed her 'The Icebox' but nobody disputed her ability to manage the team of technicians and ensure that research projects ran smoothly and produced results in minimum time. Her auburn hair was scraped back from her face into a severely efficient style and her large glasses gave her the classic image of the attractive but well-disguised secretary. She removed her glasses now and tucked them into the pocket of her immaculate white coat. It sported a badge proclaiming her to be Miss N. B. Jarvis, Respiratory Technician. Nobody had ever ventured to find out what the B stood for.

Tony cleared his throat. 'I need all your records on Sharon Andrews, and her notes if you still have them.'

34

'Yes, of course.' Nicola moved to a cupboard and removed a manilla folder. 'I'm afraid I sent the notes on request to pathology, yesterday afternoon. I believe the post mortem is this morning.'

Tony nodded. He opened the file and noted with satisfaction the informed consent signed by Mrs. Andrews attached to the front. He flicked through the rest of the folder.

'Your record keeping is up to its usual standard, Nicola – most impressive. Oh, I need a protocol copy, too, if you have a spare.' He noted with some surprise that all the details concerning the abrupt curtailment of the trial were already listed on an appropriate form, apart from the spaces labelled cause of death.

'What do you suppose the cause will be?' Nicola was reading over his shoulder.

'Status Asthmaticus, I expect, though what caused that will probably remain a mystery.'

'Rather a shock. She was nearly finished the trial and I certainly hadn't anticipated any problems.'

'No. I hadn't either.' Tony took the protocol from Nicola and tucked it under his arm with the file. 'I'll have to go now but I'd like a chat to review the trial later today if you have time.'

Nicola opened her diary. 'Anytime that would suit you. I'm not snowed under and anyway, I don't mind working late.'

'Thanks. Your dedication is appreciated. How about five o'clock?' Tony smiled warmly at Nicola and felt gratified to produce even a minimal response. Her green eyes and firmly controlled features softened noticeably.

'I'll be here, Dr. Lawrence.'

Nicola Jarvis sat seemingly mesmerised by the empty doorway which had framed Tony Lawrence only seconds before. Her features continued to relax until finally a gentle and knowing smile tugged at her lips. She drew in her breath, stretching her lungs to almost full capacity, and then slowly closed her eyes as she exhaled in a long sigh of pure pleasure.

Tony strode back through the labs thinking that his head technician couldn't really be as bad as some of the girls made her out to be. There was always some petty squabbling going on in the lower ranks. He managed to avoid it for the most part. Now the department was beginning to come to life. Lights indicated equipment warming up and a buzz of conversation punctuated by giggles was coming from the technicians' locker room. He could hear snatches as he passed.

'Must be a registrar, I guess.'

'Oh, hell. My coat's filthy.'

'God, he's gorgeous.'

'Who bled all over my coat?'

'Morning, Ladies,' Tony called through the door.

Sue, the leader in the beauty stakes, emerged from the room smoothing her blond curls. 'Hi, Tony. Coming to the party tomorrow?'

He raised his eyebrows questioningly.

'Jennifer's leaving. You know – from reception? We're having some farewell drinks in the library after work.' Sue widened her already big brown eyes. 'Do come.'

'I'll do my best, Sue,' Tony laughed. 'Thanks for asking me.'

The ward round was due to begin at nine and Tony had twenty minutes in hand for his usual stop in the new wing. He checked first on Harry in the Cardiac Care Unit who had had a comfortable night and seemed stable. As he jotted down some notes in Harry's file the Intensive Care Unit registrar, Jim Bradford, appeared beside him.

'Dr. Lawrence? We've been trying to contact you. I don't think your beep's working.'

Tony frowned and depressed the button used for muting the beeping noise. He held it to his ear but there was no discernible hiss.

'Batteries must be dead. Is there a problem?'

'We've just admitted a patient of yours – Bruce Matheson. Got him on Intermittent Positive Pressure Ventilation upstairs.'

'Shit,' muttered Tony in disbelief. He left Harry's file and followed Jim as he moved swiftly to ICU and into a cubicled room.

Bruce Matheson lay unconscious. A tube connected his mouthpiece to a ventilating machine. A rhythmic soft hiss and click came from the machine, corresponding to the rise and fall of Bruce's chest. An anaesthetics registrar was making some adjustments to dials which regulated the mixture of oxygen and nitrogen being driven under pressure into Bruce's lungs. A radial artery line was in place in his left wrist but the constant readout of blood pressure on the monitor was interrupted at present by a housesurgeon removing a sample for blood gas analysis. The ECG tracing on the overhead monitor looked normal.

Tony shook his head, his expression worried. Bruce was one of the more recent entrants in the oral salbutamol trial, a healthy young man in his mid-thirties whose asthma was a nuisance but had never been severe enough to be life-threatening.

'We called the department and had the trial medication code broken,' said Jim. 'He was on active phase.'

'Any clues?'

'His wife has been very helpful. She says the attack started a few hours ago but initially he wouldn't let her call help. She thinks he might have dosed himself several times with his inhaler.'

'Hell,' interjected Tony.

'Also, he's had a cold over the last couple of days.'

'Won't help.' Tony looked grim.

'And she's not sure, but she thinks he might have taken a cold preparation capsule she had in the bathroom cupboard. She's lost the box but gave me the brand name and I happen to know they contain a fair dose of aspirin.'

'He hasn't any history of allergy to aspirin,' said Tony, 'but then he's one of those macho types who prefer not to swallow anything if they can help it. His wife was the one who persuaded him to do this trial so he could have a thorough check-up.' Tony's gaze took in all the monitors and then rested on Bruce's still face.

'How long since he came in?'

Jim realised where the question was leading. 'He was still conscious when he came into A & E but looked pretty cyanosed and passed out soon afterwards. It's nearly two hours ago now.'

Tony looked from Jim to the anaesthetics registrar. 'So why is he still unconscious?'

'We had to paralyse him for ventilation, which wasn't easy. I'm afraid he had a fair period of apnoea without effective ventilation. Combined with the anaesthetic medications it could explain his present status. Worst case of bronchoconstriction I've ever seen,' he added, 'I couldn't believe it.'

Tony shook his head. 'I can't believe it myself, especially in view of his mild past history.'

Jim looked pointedly at his watch. 'It's too long now for unconsciousness to be purely the result of anaesthesia.'

The anaesthetics registrar nodded agreement. 'The suxamethonium should have worn off long ago.'

Tony rubbed his chin. 'Permanent cerebral damage, do you think?'

'Impossible to tell right now,' said Jim. 'There's probably cerebral oedema.'

'Have you got him on high dose steroids?'

'He's on intravenous cortisol for asthmatic control.'

'That won't be adequate for doing anything about oedema though. Do you think it would be worth starting something a bit more potent?'

Jim pondered. 'Yes, I think you're right. It's an hour since he had any halothane. We'll switch to intramuscular dexamethasone.'

'What about confirming brain damage?' Tony felt almost detached, the query coming from deeply imprinted automatic check lists. Part of his mind was replaying snatches of yesterday's interview with Shane Andrews. 'Only asthma for God's sake. Becomes your guinea-pig and now she's dead.' He suppressed the unwelcome thoughts and spoke to the anaesthetics registrar. 'Would computerised tomography show oedema at this stage?'

'Could well do,' he replied. 'It would be a good idea to get a series done as well so we can see what's happening over the next couple of days.'

'Do you want me to set it up?' This came from Jim.

'No.' Tony took a pen and scribbled a note to himself on the back of his hand. 'I'll get hold of Radiology and organise it.' He clipped the pen back into place. 'What about blood gases?'

'That seems to be under control at the moment,' responded

38

Jim. 'They're not too bad. I'll call you if the situation changes.'

'Thanks. I'll make sure I get a fresh beep.'

Tony hurried to the telephonist's office. The lifts weren't immediately available so he bounded down the stairs. It was now quarter-past nine and the ward staff would be waiting for him. As he sped into the office, one of the operators removed her headset and rose from her seat.

'Dead beep, I'm afraid, Louise.'

'Ok, Dr. Lawrence. I've got a spare and I'll get yours recharged.'

Tony clipped the fresh beep on to his top pocket and turned to leave.

'Dr. Lawrence? Pathology's been trying to reach you. If you go over to the phone in the admissions' office I'll put you through.'

Tony found himself speaking to a pathology receptionist.

'You asked to be told when the post mortem on Sharon Andrews was? I'm afraid it started twenty minutes ago – we've been unable to reach you.'

'That's all right,' Tony interrupted, 'I'm on my way.'

He pushed a button to reconnect him to the operator. 'Beep Hugh McGinty for me, please.'

'Hugh?' The call came through quickly. 'Can you start without me, please? The PM on Sharon Andrews is in progress and I'll have to put in an appearance.'

'Fine, Tony. Catch up with you later.'

Tony skirted the elevators and pushed open the smoke-stop door leading to the stairwell. He took the downward stairs and remembered to use his shoulder to bump open the door to the basement area which always stuck badly. It was rather eerie to be in the bowels of the old hospital. Huge pipes ran along the ceilings of the corridors emitting strange ticking and gurgling noises as though long forgotten prisoners were attempting to communicate with the outside world. Doorways stood open on unlit storage rooms where ghostly shapes of beds or equipment could be seen, out of date or in need of repair. A wave of heat enveloped him as he walked past the furnace room, the only sound the crackle of distant flames. He avoided a traffic jam of dilapidated gurneys and turned a corner into another corridor. The place was deserted and the single bulbs at intervals along the walls gave out only small pools of light into the gloom. Tony walked quickly until he paused by the entrance to the morgue that looked like the large metallic door to a safe. It had a spoked handle in its centre and temperature dials set into the wall beside it. Tony opened a door opposite, unmarked apart from a notice stating 'No Entry. Authorised Personnel Only.'

He stepped into a well lit antechamber. A forlorn-looking receptionist sat between a filing cabinet and a telephone. He recognised her as the girl who had until recently pushed a trolley through miles of corridors delivering mail throughout the hospital.

'Hullo, been demoted?' he queried in surprise.

She wrinkled her nose and nodded.

'I'm here for Sharon Andrews.'

She nodded silently again as she consulted a list on her desk. 'Table three, Dr. Lawrence.'

Tony opened another door and entered the race course-styled design of the recently renovated autopsy room. It had a clean feeling to its white tiled floors and whitewashed walls that made it a considerably more pleasant environment than previously but the pathologists were disappointed not to have been moved away from the basement. He moved around the perimeter of the room, a glassed in corridor, peering into the large central well of the room. It had four tables set into the tiled floor which sloped gently towards the drainage holes along the centre line. Today was busy with three of the tables occupied and varying numbers of personnel at each area.

The table nearest Tony was crowded and some of the observers looked like medical students. One woman was looking decidedly pale and grasped the opportunity to stare at him through the window rather than look at what lay before her. Tony could understand why. He could see the legs of the patient before her and it looked like a very young child. He flashed her a sympathetic smile before scanning the rest of the room.

The far table had only three people in attendance. One of them was Bob Matthews. Tony pushed his way through the swing door and took shallow breaths until he became used to the cloying odours assailing his nostrils. It smelled like an abattoir with a large dose of antiseptic thrown in.

The post mortem on Sharon Andrews was in its final stages. The incisions had been made to open the abdominal and chest cavities. The lungs had been removed. One sat intact on a pair of scales and the other was on a side table in a state of dissection. Bob Matthews nodded at Tony.

'What you'd expect so far. Oedema and overinflation on general inspection. Both lungs heavier than normal and gross mucus plugging of bronchi and bronchioles.'

The pathology resident completed hosing down the chest cavity and replaced the shower type head into its attachment. He also spoke to Tony.

'No evidence of bacterial infection but we'll do a culture.' He turned his attention to Sharon's heart.

'Her asthma was generally well controlled,' commented Tony, 'I wouldn't expect any evidence of pulmonary hypertension or cardiac strain.'

'Mmm,' responded the resident, 'looks normal enough. I'd say the cause of death was pretty obvious from those lungs. No reason to open the head, is there?'

'No.' Tony looked at Bob who shook his head in agreement.

'Not much else to do then.' The pathologist moved away from the table to let the attendant begin what reconstruction was possible.

'We'll do the usual checks on numbers of goblet cells, eosinophils and epithelial cells. I'll send you both a report later.' He stripped off his gloves, depositing them in a bin beside a trough, and began to wash his hands.

'Thanks.' Tony was glad to leave. 'Can you get a copy to Gordon Davies as soon as possible?'

The young female student was leaning with her back to the glass in the outer area. She didn't meet Tony's eyes but nodded in response to his query of whether she was all right. Bob walked with him along the dimly lit corridor back to the stairwell. He was first to break the meditative silence.

'I've had a change in my next run. Gillian Brown was to join your team but has opted out because of complications in her pregnancy. So, there's been a general reshuffle and I'll be working with you as from next week.'

41

Genuine delight showed on Tony's face and Bob grinned in response.

'It'll be a pleasure to work with you, Bob. You've brightened up my day considerably. Do you know Hugh McGinty?'

Bob nodded. 'I even dated his sister a few years back. I think he's forgiven me.'

'Well, come into the department or ward whenever you like and I'll introduce any new faces for you. I'll be on the ward for what's left of this morning and there's a broncho-scopy clinic this afternoon.'

Bob left Tony waiting for a lift to the fifth floor. He delivered the files to the poker-faced Mrs. Dogerty and took another minute to jot down the preliminary post mortem findings. Mrs. Dogerty sniffed.

'I hope you haven't forgotten your appointment, Dr. Lawrence?'

Tony made a questioning noise as he continued writing.

'Mr. Colin Ingram is meeting Dr. Davies at 11.30 this morning to discuss a new trial. Your presence is also required.'

Tony finished writing, clipped his pen back into his pocket firmly and smiled at Mrs. Dogerty.

'How could I forget? A new trial is exactly what I need right now. But thanks you for the reminder, Mrs. D.' He left the office hurriedly, knowing he would pay later for such mis-placed familiarity.

Chapter Six

It was common knowledge that Gordon Davies was in the pocket of the Atlas Drug company. The British base of a parent American company, Atlas had two separate divisions, one concerned with cardiological-type preparations and the other with respiratory medications. Over the years that Gordon Davies had been in charge of the Northern's respiratory department, Atlas had become increasingly prominent in their affairs, providing a large percentage of their research funding in return for the carrying out of 'bread and butter' type trials such as the oral salbutamol one that was currently running. Nowadays no other drug company even bothered approaching the department but management at Atlas needed only to click their fingers, by way of a telephone call to Davies, to receive instant compliance.

Atlas was a generous company. Very generous. Traditionally, money received from companies in return for conducting their drug trials was used to fund a department's own research interests, paying for the staff, drugs, patient co-operation, laboratory assistance and any new equipment that might be needed in the expensive business of extending medical frontiers. This had been the case when Tony Lawrence had elected to stay with the respiratory department of the Northern. Routine trials from several different drug companies were sandwiched between what everybody considered the more important original research work, exploring the etiology, mechanisms and treatments in various forms of respiratory disease. Unfortunately, things had changed. A high percentage of the funds provided by Atlas seemed not to find its way into research projects of this ilk. Instead, nowadays, the money was more likely to buy new equipment, which looked good but was often not strictly necessary, to fund lavish trips to medical conferences or simply to accumulate in various soft accounts.

Tony avoided attending conferences when possible and in particular any organised by the Atlas company. Many meetings seemed to him to be thinly disguised, all expenses paid, holiday breaks for medics and sometimes their families as well. The sideways looks and innuendos he received now, thanks to Davies' blatant and exclusive compliance with Atlas, were embarrassing but nothing was ever discussed openly. Attendance at some conferences was vital to keep up with global research trends but Tony made a point of electing a modest standard of accommodation, a choice which usually kept him well away from Gordon Davies who was a favoured guest in many of the most renowned international hotels. There were even rumours of further funding by Atlas of expenses incurred by Davies personally, such as in private entertainment of colleagues or the Rhine cruise he had taken his family on before visiting a clinic in Germany, but these were highly unlikely ever to be publicly confirmed.

When he returned to the fifth floor, Tony received a contemptuous glance from Mrs. Dogerty and a nod towards the inner office. He entered to find Gordon Davies in animated conversation with Colin Ingram, the bright new star of Atlas.

Tony disliked drug company representatives in general, with their pushy, lounge-lizard type personalities so similar to those of insurance or car salesmen. These features usually wore off to some extent amongst higher management but Colin Ingram had only recently been promoted from being a general sales representative to executive control of research drug trials and he was an excellent example of the breed. His grooming and manners were impeccable. His dark good looks and carefully cultivated charm had quickly made him a welcome visitor downstairs and Tony had wondered whether Nicola's superb record keeping was for the department's benefit or to impress Colin on one of his frequent visits to monitor trial progress.

Tony had a clear memory of his introduction to Colin

44

Ingram, four months ago, when they had set up the oral salbutamol outpatient trial that was currently running. His handshake had been firm and the warm smile revealed a set of very white and even teeth.

'I am so delighted to have the opportunity of working with you, Dr. Lawrence,' the new member of managerial Atlas staff had told him. 'I have read many of your publications and am most impressed with your work.'

Tony was immune to the type of flattery that usually preceded a sales pitch but Colin Ingram had startled him at the end of the meeting, which was why he remembered the occasion with such clarity.

'I almost didn't recognise you without the beard,' Colin had said with a smile.

'Beard?' For a moment Tony didn't understand, then a faded memory trickled through. The junior residents at Leeds General Infirmary had once taken part in a sponsored 'grow a beard' event for charity. Tony had won no prizes for the faintly gingery bristle he had accumulated but the removal ceremony had provided a memorable party. He grinned at the recollection.

'That was a very long time ago. I'm sorry, but I don't remember meeting you, Mr. Ingram. I didn't have much to do with drug companies in those days.'

'Neither did I.' Colin had not elaborated, leaving Tony puzzled, but the incident had obviously been of little importance to the Atlas man. It had not been referred to since.

Tony resented his time being taken up with trial discussions of this kind. The decisions were all made by Gordon Davies in advance, anyway. The chief consultant was in his element in this kind of liaison and was prepared to offer any promises of co-operation that could then be offloaded on to more junior staff members. When unable to avoid these meetings, Tony's eagerness to be excused was obvious and his brusqueness often interpreted as rudeness, but Colin Ingram had already learned how to handle him to their mutual advantage. He glanced at Gordon Davies for permission to initiate discussion and then quickly gathered together a sheaf of papers which he handed to Tony.

He began without preamble. 'Fairly standard trial, Dr.

45

Lawrence, comparing our new prophylactic disodium cromoglycate analogue spinhaler with a corticosteroid aerosol – Bronchotide – with a salbutamol aerosol as backup for any attacks. Standard double-blind, randomised, crossover pattern.' He paused and then came quickly to the point. 'We'd like thirty patients completed in the next six months.'

Tony said nothing, collecting his thoughts as he scanned the protocol before him. The trial involved an initial workup of physical examination, blood and lung function tests, and had a comprehensive checklist of exclusion criteria. It was pretty general and there wouldn't be any problem finding numbers of patients. Eventually. But the same source was already being tapped for the salbutamol trial. Tests for each twice-weekly visit would require probably a couple of hours testing time and several pages of paperwork. The trial could be run almost entirely by technicians. As Colin Ingram had commented, it was standard stuff. Bread and butter and exceedingly boring for all involved but necessary before a drug company could get marketing clearance for a new product. Tony mustered a protest.

'You realise we'll run into side effect problems of oropharyngeal thrush with Bronchotide?'

Colin was well briefed for any objections.

'That only occurs in ten percent of patients at the most and shouldn't present a problem in this dosage.'

Tony tried again. 'Six months is a bit ambitious, Colin. We have to consider the washout periods needed both before and between trial phases. We're stretching subject resources already with the oral salbutamol trial. To finish thirty patients will require starting up to forty-five and this –' he indicated the protocol – 'represents a considerable labour input.'

'Not necessarily by you,' Dr Davies interjected. 'You have only one trial being conducted at present – oral salbutamol versus placebo. Am I correct?'

'That's right,' replied Tony. 'But it's really only got off the ground in the last few weeks and we haven't enrolled half the required number yet.'

'Then I suggest you make a concerted effort to complete that trial, Dr. Lawrence.' Gordon Davies settled back in his chair. 'We'll aim to start this new one early next month and get the new year off to a positive beginning. That suit you, Colin?'

'That's fine with me, Dr. Davies.' Colin Ingram looked satisfied. He collected his briefcase and snapped it shut. 'I'll arrange component deliveries as soon as possible.' Colin nodded at Tony, inwardly delighted with the look of barely controlled annoyance directed at him. 'We appreciate the work your department is doing on our behalf, Dr Lawrence. I saw the technical staff earlier and it seems to be well under control.'

'Did they not tell you that we had a patient death yesterday?'

A look passed between Colin Ingram and Gordon Davies that Tony intercepted but couldn't interpret. He felt suddenly uneasy. Davies stood and moved purposefully towards the door of his office which he held open.

'We needn't delay Colin with a discussion of that unfortunate incident,' he said firmly. 'He has already been fully informed.'

When the office door had closed after the Atlas rep, Gordon Davies handed Tony back the notes and files on Sharon Andrews.

'Can't see any serious problem here. The chap's lawyer has managed to calm him down. Let's see how rapidly we can wrap this trial up, hmmm?'

His tone was unusually genial and as Tony made his way back to the ward, he found himself wondering cynically what incentives Atlas had been dangling under Davies' nose this time. It was only a matter of weeks until he was due to go on an American and European tour which would last a month. He did know that Davies had his eye on a vastly expensive computerised body plethysmography setup that would make precise measurements of lung volumes. He had heard one of the girls once refer to the well-stocked labs as 'God's toy box' and he smiled as he recalled the comment. It wasn't far wrong. His smile faded as he wondered how long it was going to be before he received any funding to start the research he planned to use as the base for his PhD.

Tony returned to Nicola's office late that afternoon in the company of Hugh McGinty. Nicola followed them in, bearing a tray with several cups of coffee. Bob Matthews poked his head around the door and Tony invited him to stay for the meeting.

'You'll probably end up with a fair percentage of the workload,' he told him. 'So you may as well have some say in the proceedings.'

Nicola raised her eyebrows and her glance flicked over Bob.

'Bob's joining us for a respiratory run,' explained Tony. 'Bob, meet Nicola. Esteemed leader of the pack in these here parts.'

Nicola took Bob's outstretched hand briefly. She looked at his name badge.

'Pleased to meet you, Dr. Matthews. If you'll excuse me, I'll just get some more coffee and round up the others.'

Hugh winked at Bob as she left. 'Don't worry, the others will make up for it.'

Sue was the first to appear, her makeup fresh and her eyes glowing as she was introduced to Bob.

'What have you done with Gillian Brown?' Sue's voice had a kind of perpetual archness which, combined with her appearance, made her a very popular staff member – at least with the males. Rumours circulated that even Davies had tried it on at some stage. Nobody knew how many of the offers she received were accepted. Sue managed to add to her appeal by avoiding any gossip and cultivating an aura of psuedo-innocence.

'Bob doesn't have complications with his pregnancy,' said Tony, watching Sue's reaction to Bob with amusement. Hugh looked resigned. His shock of red hair and ruddy though cheerful countenance had never produced results like this. Sue had no time to do any more than widen her eyes in Bob's direction at Tony's comment before Nicola returned with more coffee and three technicians in tow.

Amanda quietly selected a chair in a corner, refused coffee and opened a notebook. Barbara stared at Bob, grinned widely at Sue and sat down beside her, slopping coffee on her white coat.

'Makes a change from bloodstains,' she said cheerfully, to nobody in particular.

Jackie perched on a high stool, pointedly not looking at Bob. She glanced rather obviously at the clock and then switched her attention to a large ring that had appeared on her left hand within the last week.

'Don't worry, Jackie,' Nicola's tone was icy. 'You won't have to stay any later than we do.'

Jackie shook her head slightly, a silent and defiant gesture. Nicola B. Jarvis wasn't going to intrude on her thoughts. With a spring wedding in mind, Jackie had just ordered her off-the-shoulder Pronuptia wedding dress, with hooped underskirt. Her burning preoccupation at present was whether to have a long and flowing veil or flowers in her hair and a white, frilly parasol instead. She turned the ring to catch the light, gratified at the flash of colour she evoked. A parasol would certainly be different, and rather chic.

'Anyone else coming?' asked Tony.

'I told Alister we didn't need him,' said Nicola. 'He's not really involved with this trial.'

'Thank goodness,' muttered Barbara.

'Right,' said Tony. 'First thing is the death of Sharon Andrews which I know has upset some of you.' He smiled gently at Amanda, whose lip trembled.

'I was talking to her on the phone just the day before . . . she wanted to change her next appointment time . . .' Amanda trailed into silence and began to make meaningless marks in her notebook. Nicola glared at her. She did not approve of emotional displays during working hours.

'None of us expected it,' said Tony, 'but it underlines the fact that asthma needs to be taken seriously. Keep a careful eye on all patients that you have contact with and report anything that worries you. Nicola, how does the trial stand at present?'

She consulted a clipboard on her desk. 'We've completed three patients without problems. Number four was Sharon Andrews and there are five more enrolled at various stages and two potentials to be followed up.'

'Yes.' Tony took a deep breath. 'I'm afraid we'll have to cross off two more.'

Amanda gasped.

'Mrs. McTavish has withdrawn for personal reasons,' continued Tony. 'I'm sorry, I meant to let you know this morning.'

The groan was general. Nicola looked furious.

'Does she have any idea of what it means in wasted time and expense on our part? She was almost finished the second phase.'

'I know. I tried to persuade her to change her mind but we can't force co-operation, Nicola.'

Hugh's lips twitched and he looked about to make a quip. Tony silenced him with a warning look. It was no use trying to appeal to a sense of humour in Nicola Jarvis.

'And the other?' Nicola's expression was sullen.

'Bruce Matheson. I'm sorry to say he's been admitted after a severe attack and has, of course, been withdrawn from the trial.'

'Is he going to be all right?' Amanda asked anxiously.

'He's pretty sick, I'm afraid, Mandy.'

Bob swallowed a mouthful of coffee. 'Do you usually have problems like this with trials?'

'Sharon's death is the first associated with research in this department,' defended Hugh.

'And in Matheson's case it could be due to his overdosing himself with bronchodilator, or possibly an aspirin allergy,' added Tony. Instinctively, however, he queried both of these possibilities. Moreover, he did not believe in coincidence. There had to be some rational explanation why these severe attacks had occurred, both individually and within such a short span of time. He made a mental note of the aspects he intended to investigate himself.

'This trial is turning into a nightmare,' Nicola snapped. 'It should have been routine.'

'I'm afraid there's more,' Tony said, somewhat apologetically. Nicola looked disgusted. Jackie looked bored. Sue and Barbara rolled their eyes at each other. Only Amanda's face remained unchanged, but then she had a perpetually worried expression anyway.

'We're under pressure on time from upstairs. Another trial involving completion of thirty patients in six months is scheduled to start next month.'

Hugh scratched his head. 'How much notice do we have to take of that?'

'Some,' admitted Tony. 'But I for one would like to get this salbutamol trial over and done with as soon as possible.'

There was general agreement.

'I'll leave the new protocols for you to browse through, Nicola,' Tony continued. 'And here's one for you, Bob. I'll leave the running of it to you once you're settled in.'

Hugh put his hands behind his head and stretched, heaving a sigh of mock relief.

'Sounds fun.' Bob winked at Sue.

Nicola glared at him. 'I think we'll involve Alister in the next trial. He's getting the hang of things now and it's about time he did more than run spirometry tests.'

Tony hadn't noticed the byplay. 'OK, that's about it for now. We'll have a meeting on setting up the new trial before too long.'

Jackie was already halfway out of the door.

'Oh, one other thing.' Tony's brow creased and he spoke directly to Nicola. 'Didn't you already know about Bruce Matheson this morning?'

'No. Why?'

'Well, ICU said they rang and somebody cracked the code for them.'

Nicola moved swiftly to a cupboard and removed an envelope. She emptied its contents of smaller, sealed envelopes onto her desk and selected the one labelled 07. The seal was broken.

'I know nothing about this.' Nicola sounded angry. She looked at the other technicians. 'Who was it who took the call?'

Nobody knew. Jackie broke a puzzled silence by excusing herself. The others followed suit and presently Nicola was alone in her office. Part of her anger over this incident stemmed from the fact that she liked to reserve the code breaking for herself. It was the most interesting aspect of the otherwise routinely dull process of outpatient drug trials. A randomised trial meant that patients received two compounds in random order, crossing over after a washout period. Double-blind meant that neither the patient nor the staff conducting the trial knew in which order the drugs were being administered. In theory, this removed any bias and

51

gave objective results. The code, which stated the order the drugs had been taken in, was broken when a patient completed the trial or, under exceptional circumstances, when the participant's condition gave cause for concern. After years of experience, Nicola had become very good at preguessing the code. She enjoyed placing a bet with herself and gained immense private satisfaction on opening the tiny envelopes to find she had been correct.

Now, disgruntled, she found the manilla file on Bruce Matheson and carefully glued the scrap of paper containing the code inside the front cover. Then she picked up her pen, selected a form entitled 'reasons for discontinuation' and began to fill in the boxes in her small, meticulous handwriting.

Chapter Seven

Thursday mornings at nine saw the start of a major outpatient clinic in the respiratory department when new patients were examined and treatments started. Tony would see up to six patients, spending thirty to forty-five minutes with each one. Hugh also saw three or four people.

The first patient on the list was a sixty-three-year-old man. James McAlister was small, wiry and silent. He seemed ill at ease and avoided eye contact with Tony. He held a cloth cap which he repeatedly rolled up and then smoothed out on his lap. His lower jaw moved constantly in a methodical chewing movement, interrupted occasionally when he paused to suck his teeth noisily. The referral note from his GP stated that he was suffering from increasing breathlessness of gradual onset and a persistent cough. A chest x-ray had been taken this morning and Tony had been pleased to find in the notes that another one had been taken as part of a routine check-up five years ago. Ginette had been dispatched to retrieve it from the x-ray department's files and now Tony had them both illuminated on the wall of the examination room. There was a fine, general shadowing of both lungs which had not been present in the older film. A spirometry test had also been done that morning which showed Mr. McAlister's lung function to be well below normal.

The GP's note also stated that James McAlister was a pigeon fancier and queried a diagnosis of fibrosing lung disease. Finally, it declared that the patient was unco-operative and a heavy smoker.

Tony took his time over a history and physical examination. The verbal history taking was frustrating due to Mr. McAlister's monosyllabic replies to questions and long silences when a negative response or description of a symptom was indicated. Tony quickly changed his questioning technique and offered a kind of multiple choice whenever a silence became prolonged. It was like a game of twenty questions, he reflected, where the only answer allowable was 'aye'. The physical examination presented less of a challenge and Tony quickly came to agree with the GP's diagnosis. He found some bilateral loss of chest wall movement, evidence of early finger clubbing, and fine, widespread crackles could be heard at the end of indrawn breaths.

When his patient was dressed again and seated before him, Tony spoke directly.

'You have a lung disease which is causing your shortness of breath, Mr. McAlister. It is most likely to be what's known as "pigeon fancier's disease" and is an allergic reaction to your pigeons which has developed over a long period of time. The advisable course of action would be, first, to get rid of your pigeons.'

James McAlister was shocked into eloquence. 'Ah canna do that, Doctor.' His gaze met Tony's directly. 'Pigeons' all I got.' He sucked his teeth and added an end to the discussion with quiet pride. 'Best racing birds in district.'

Tony had expected this response. According to the notes, McAlister's wife had died twenty years ago and his only son emigrated to Australia. Probably his only social contact was with the club where he would take his birds early on racing days to be loaded on to their truck for the journey to a release point and where he would return later in the day for the serious ceremony of clock reading and a pint or two. He tried another tack.

'Have you tried to cut down on your smoking?'

His patient looked disgusted. 'Aye,' he muttered and began a lengthy tooth sucking session which put paid to any further discussion of that subject.

'We can give you drugs which may help, Mr. McAlister,' continued Tony, 'Penicillamine and corticosteroids. But they're not without side effects.'

James McAlister shook his head. 'Don't hold with no pill takin'.'

'I'm afraid there's not much more advice I can offer, Mr. McAlister,' said Tony. 'Is there anything you'd like to ask me?'

There was a long silence. McAlister's eyes roved the room and finally met Tony's briefly.

'How long?' he queried gruffly.

'Will you live?' Tony needed clarification.

'Aye.'

'No doctor can ever say that with any certainty, Mr. Mc-Alister. Even if you gave up the pigeons and smoking and took the drugs your condition might continue to get steadily worse. On the other hand you might be lucky and have another ten years just as you are now.'

James McAlister unrolled his cap for the final time and fitted it snugly over his thinning hair, standing ready to leave. He paused to collect his thoughts and then smiled at Tony for the first time.

'Thanks, lad,' he said, 'but there's nae much point living longer if ye canna enjoy it.'

Tony returned the smile. 'I'd like to see you again in six months or so.'

'Aye.' The tone was resigned but Tony doubted that Mr. McAlister would ever return to outpatients. Privately he wished him luck.

The next patient was a middle-aged woman, a chronic asthmatic who was becoming less responsive to her treatment. Tony arranged for a comprehensive series of lung function tests, a new drug regime and weekly OP follow-ups until she was better managed.

The clinic was interrupted at this point by a phone call from the ward. A woman had arrived with a request for direct admission into hospital from her GP and there were no medical staff available for the admission procedures. Tony muttered about the nuisance of gaps created by the changeover of runs in junior staff. Hugh had just begun an interview with an outpatient so Tony asked him to see the next on his own list and hurried up to the ward. The patient was another middle-aged woman, Florence Murdock, who was presenting with a seemingly straightforward early pneumonia. Tony gave her a thorough examination, arranged for chest x-ray and blood tests, and charted an immediate course of penicillin. By the time he got back downstairs there was only one patient remaining for him to see.

His last patient for the morning was a thirty-year-old male, William Chalmers. The note from the GP sounded puzzled, listing symptoms as a persistent non-productive cough, shortness of breath on exercise, and night sweats of several weeks' duration. No findings on physical examination but temperature had been raised on the last two visits. Previous history had included an attack on glandular fever some three years ago but otherwise the patient had a clean record and had been exceptionally healthy. Tony checked the x-ray which had been taken that morning. At first glance it appeared perfectly normal but on closer examination Tony could detect a suggestion of a faint, fine shadowing in both lungs.

William Chalmers was a good-looking, cheerful young man. He spoke with a broad Geordie accent and apologised to Tony for probably wasting his time.

'The cough's driving me crazy though, Dr. Lawrence,' he explained, 'and more importantly it's driving my wife crazy. She's pregnant and generally irritable, and lack of sleep isn't helping either of us.'

Tony smiled, noting the shadowing under William Chalmers' eyes and his rapid breathing even while seated.

'It's certainly not a waste of time, Mr. Chalmers.'

'Please, call me Bill.'

'OK, Bill, tell me about these symptoms you've been getting.'

'Well, the cough's the most annoying one. Apart from that I feel quite winded after things like mowing the lawns and lately it's getting to be an effort to get anything done.'

'How long have you been coughing?'

'Oh, a good six weeks now. I kept waiting for it to clear up but finally went to my doctor a couple of weeks ago.'

'Losing weight at all?'

'Yes, I have a bit, come to think of it.'

'Tell me about these night sweats.' Tony was making rapid notes.

'Well, that upsets Caroline too. She says it's like sleeping with a frog.'

'How long have you been married?'

'Nearly three years,' said Bill proudly.

'Notice any unusual sweating during the day at all?'

'Not really,' replied Bill. 'I do get sort of hot flushes and then feel cold again sometimes.'

Tony interrupted the history taking with a physical examination but could find nothing abnormal apart from the more rapid than normal rate of respiration. His diagnosis was made but he felt a vague disquiet about the case and continued his questioning.

'Tell me what you can remember about the glandular fever you had, Bill.'

'That was years ago, Dr. Lawrence. Felt pretty grotty for a while and had a sore throat. Haven't had it since.'

'How long did it last?'

'Only a few weeks. Mild case, my doctor said. I was lucky.'

Tony chewed the end of his pen for a moment. He knew what was bothering him now. Bill appeared to have pneumonia – an unusual variety. With the warning bell sounded by the symptom of glandular fever, even years previously, Tony was alerted to the possibility that Bill was suffering from Acquired Immune Deficiency Syndrome or AIDS as it was commonly known. Tony had never diagnosed a case but knew that the commonest presentation was a form of pneumonia called Pneumocystis Carinii pneumonia – PCP. He knew also that the initial contraction of the virus could result in a glandular fever-type illness and that it could be several years before full-blown AIDS developed. Now was not the time to make inquiries concerning Bill Chalmer's sexual practices, however.

'I'd like to admit you into the ward for a few tests,' he told his patiently calmly.

Bill raised his eyebrows. 'But I'm not sick enough to be in hospital.'

'I think you have a type of pneumonia, Bill, and we need to run a few tests to find out exactly what sort of bug we're dealing with and what the best treatment will be.'

'What sort of tests?' Bill asked anxiously.

'We'll take another x-ray and a few blood tests. We'll also do a bronchoscopy and take a small sample from your lung.

57

Don't worry.' He smiled at Bill's horrified face. 'It's a very straightforward procedure – not all all alarming.'

His patient still looked frightened. 'Taking a sample, does that mean . . .' He swallowed hard. 'Have I got cancer, Dr. Lawrence?'

'No, Bill. Cancer is extremely unlikely to be the problem,' Tony groaned inwardly at the look of relief his statement produced. If he was correct in his suspicions, Bill's prognosis would probably be worse than if he did have a malignancy.

'I'll have to call Caroline.' Bill sounded almost cheerful again. 'I'll need my toothbrush.'

The arrangements were made concerning Bill Chalmers and Tony had warned the staff of the possible diagnosis and the need for special precautions. There was nothing more he could do until some test results came back. Tony stayed sitting at the desk in the examination room as the outpatient area emptied, the staff hurrying off for their lunch break. Hugh poked his head around the door. Seeing Tony alone, he entered and deposited an armload of patients' notes on the desk.

'There are Bridget Gardiner's notes, and two more I saw this morning that are definite possibilities for the trial and quite willing to co-operate. How did you get on?'

Tony smiled ruefully. 'It was quite a morning. A fibrosing lung disease chappie who'd rather enjoy his pigeons and smokes than live a bit longer, an asthmatic . . . No. Tony shook his head in response to the lift of Hugh's bushy red eyebrows. 'Too severe for inclusion in the trial. Then an early pneumonia I saw on the ward. Final case I've also admitted. I'm pretty sure it's a case of AIDS – presenting as PCP.'

'Was it that young guy?'

Tony nodded. 'I haven't asked about any drug taking or sexual practices but he had a bout of glandular fever a few years ago.'

Hugh clicked his tongue sympathetically. 'It was only last week that we were saying we hadn't seen a case of it here yet.'

'I know,' said Tony. 'But, as we said, it was only a question of time. With the projection of figures being bandied around at the moment we could well be overrun with cases within the next decade. Mind you, that's still a bit hard to believe. I'd like to confirm this particular diagnosis as soon as possible, though.' He smiled hopefully at his registrar. 'Could you fit in a bronchoscopy on him this afternoon?'

Hugh shook his head sadly. 'There goes my game of golf. No – ' he added hastily, seeing Tony's stricken expression – 'that shouldn't be any problem. I'll jack it up after lunch.' He bent to pick up the pile of notes. 'Coming?'

'No thanks, Hugh. Leave those notes and I'll have a look at them. I'll grab a sandwich later.'

'I'll bring one back for you, if you like,' offered Hugh.

'Great. Don't pick any of those squashed pea ones, though.'

'You're supposed to think they're asparagus and a treat.' Hugh chuckled and wandered down the corridor, the handles of his stethoscope flapping idly against his leg.

Tony spent a few minutes scribbling some extra notes about the patients he had seen that morning with instructions for himself concerning the follow-up of those he had admitted. He would go and check up on them again this afternoon. He chewed the inside of this cheek. Thursday afternoon was theoretically time set aside for his own research work, his current interest and potential PhD material being the mechanisms rather than causes or treatment of bronchoconstriction. As often as not, however, the afternoon had become an essential period in which he could catch up on other things. His inspiration was at a low ebb at present anyway, and until his protocol and fundings were approved by Davies things were pretty much at a standstill.

Tony left his room and went into the small kitchen attached to the outpatient area, the main purpose of which was the brewing of cups of tea for waiting patients. It was ruled by Muriel McKenzie, a short and rather stout woman with a slightly vacant expression, whose accent was often totally incomprehensible to everyone. Muriel had come back to nursing ten years ago, after twenty years away, when her husband had died leaving her financial position somewhat precarious with two teenage sons still at home. It was soon obvious to all that her knowledge was so far out of date as to make her a danger near patients. She had been kept on, her duties gradually being made lighter and, while the butt of some unkind jokes, she had made herself indispensible within a clearly defined set of duties, the demarcation of which she guarded more jealously than any trade union official. Muriel provided and arranged flowers in the waiting room, kept cupboards stocked, made the tea, provided toys and magazines for those waiting and also provided a counselling service for nervous or bored patients. She had the ability to talk to anyone and her cheerfulness was appreciated even when she was not understood.

Muriel entered the kitchen just as Tony had finished making himself a cup of coffee.

'You make sure you bring that cup back,' she ordered.

'Oh, I will, Muriel.'

'And wash it, mind.'

'Of course.'

She glared at the dirty spoon Tony had placed beside the sink. Hastily he rinsed and dried it, placing it back in the drawer before escaping back to the office. He reflected that if he was Davies, Muriel would have found it no bother to delve into her secret supply and find biscuits to go with the coffee.

Sipping his coffee, Tony surveyed the pile of notes. His eye caught those of Bridget Gardiner at the bottom of the pile and he eased them out, folding back the front cover and scanning the personal details on the first page. Her age was thirty-two, occupation a primary school teacher, and she was a widow. He noted with some surprise the word 'none' in the space provided for next-of-kin. She had had two admissions into the Northern. One had been three years ago for infertility investigation and the other two years ago for an acute asthmatic attack. Tony had a vague sense that he was invading her privacy by reading further, but he reminded himself that she was a patient in his department, not to mention a possible candidate for a trial he was responsible for. He turned quickly to the pink summary sheet of the first admission, halfway through the file.

It stated that Mrs. Bridget Gardiner was a slim, attractive young woman of twenty-nine years of age. She had been admitted overnight to undergo the procedure of a laparoscopy as previous investigations of the cause of a two-year history of infertility had proved negative. The laparoscopy findings had also shown no abnormality and the recommendation was that the couple should continue to attend the infertility clinic with the possibility of starting fertility drug treatment and perhaps going on the waiting list for an In Vitro Fertilisation treatment at a later stage.

Tony wondered what had happened to Bridget's husband. He was a general practitioner, and described in the summary as very supportive and their marriage as stable and happy. He turned to the pink sheet nearer the front of the notes which was concerned with the more recent admission. He frowned as he read both the typewritten lines and what lay between them. It stated that Bridget had been in a severe state of depression since the death of her husband in a car accident some weeks earlier. She had miscarried in an early stage of pregnancy. When she had had an attack of asthma she had failed to treat herself with her bronchodilator or call for help. She had been found some hours later in a distressed state by a friend who immediately called an ambulance. Her condition had been stabilized in casualty without too much difficulty. She had been admitted for observation and psychiatric evaluation, being discharged a few days later with prophylactic medication for asthma and a course of antidepressants, to be seen in a psychiatric outpatient clinic at a later date.

Tony flicked through some pages of lab results and found the outpatient summary sheet with notes by a psychiatric registrar who had seen her. There was only one entry, a month after the discharge date. The registrar considered Bridget to be coping normally with grief, more positive about the future, and in his opinion able to cope without further medication. No follow-up was deemed necessary. Her asthma had been monitored from then on by her GP, apart from a six-monthly visit to respiratory outpatients for lung function tests.

Tony looked up the outpatient sheet for the respiratory department and was reading the last entries when Hugh came back in. He deposited a plastic-wrapped cheese and pickle sandwich in front of Tony, peering over his shoulder at the notes.

'What do you think?'

'Stretching the inclusion criteria a bit far, Hugh. She only uses a bronchodilator once or twice a week on top of prophylactic dosage.'

'Mmm. Well, winter's really arrived and she'll probably use it a bit more now. I'm sure I could persuade her to do the trial and we need to muster enough to get the damned thing off our backs.'

Tony nodded. 'You're right. See what you can do. I'll be as happy as you when it's finished.'

The afternoon was hectic and Tony felt dissatisfied at the end of it. The normal hassles of clinical work had made themselves manifest and he seemed to spend his time chasing his own tail: searching for notes that had mysteriously vanished, ringing for lab results that should have arrived but had also vanished, equally mysteriously, en route, and dictating the discharge summaries that had accumulated until they could no longer be ignored. Almost every task had been interrupted by the insistent beeping of his page and all the calls had been trivial.

He had been to see Bruce Matheson at one stage who seemed stable but was showing no signs of improvement. There was nothing Tony could suggest that might make his treatment more effective. Another worry was that the pneumonia case he'd admitted that morning was worsening. Her temperture was up and she had pleuritic pain on inspiration. To top it off, he'd only just remembered that he had to catch a shuttle flight to London at nine that evening to attend an early morning session of a large display of medical equipment being run in conjunction with a small conference. He would liked to have cancelled the trip but unfortunately he would be accompanying Gordon Davies and his absence would not be appreciated. The arrangements had been made some time ago and he knew his invitation was only to provide support for Davies' decision regarding the computerised body plethysmography setup he coveted.

It really was a bit much to have to participate in the process, Tony thought bitterly. It would be yet another large chunk of available funding being directed away from the serious research he wanted to initiate. It wasn't simply that Tony desired a PhD. The main attraction of joining the Northern's respiratory department all those years ago had been its reputation of being involved in front line research, and the acclaim that papers produced within the department had received. The papers he had published himself from his MD material had been amongst them but over recent years, under the direction of Davies, funding and approval for research projects had gradually dwindled to the point that the only experimental work being conducted at present were the damned drug trials. The knowledge Tony had gained from his years of training and experience served to underscore vast areas of medical ignorance. It wasn't enough for him to be simply an excellent physician. Tony needed the stimulation of identifying and participating in the investigation of new fields that offered the promise of increasing both knowledge and available methods of treatment.

He turned his thoughts to more immediate concerns. If he drove straight from the hospital to the airport he should have enough time to organise things for Hugh to cope with the next morning, and maybe even finish the paperwork he had collected this afternoon. There was no need to go home as he kept a clean shirt and shaving gear in his office for nights on call which necessitated remaining in the hospital. He rang Catherine to explain the situation.

'That's fine, darling,' she replied. 'Have a good trip and I'll see you tomorrow night. Can you try and make it home by seven tomorrow, Tony? I've arranged for us to be shown around a house in Darras Hall which sounds superb.'

'I'll see what I can do, Cat, but you know I can't make any promises.'

'I'm sure you'll make it, darling. For me.' Catherine was at her most persuasive but Tony had always found that tone exceptionally irritating. He almost blessed his beep for sounding at that instant.

'Must go, love. Be good and I'll see you tomorrow.' He hung up without waiting for her reply and rang the operator to find that Hugh was trying to catch up with him.

'I'll meet you upstairs in five minutes for a coffee,' Tony told him. 'Bring a wheelbarrow for the list of things I've got lined up for you to do tomorrow morning.'

As Tony walked towards the lifts a few minutes later he saw Hugh talking to Bridget Gardiner near the front door. He quickened his pace to join them.

'May I be of assistance, Mrs. Gardiner?' Tony intoned in his most professional manner. 'I do a very good line in second-hand tyres.'

Bridget giggled and Hugh looked astonished.

'I just about need some wheels to get to the car park,' complained Bridget. 'After what Dr. McGinty here's put me through.'

Hugh grinned. 'I caught Bridget on her way in this afternoon and persuaded her to make a quick detour into our interrogation chambers.'

'Quick?' exclaimed Bridget. 'I've only just got out.'

Hugh looked at Tony smugly. 'Bridget hasn't been on any contradictory treatment so we didn't need a washout period. Thanks to the foggy weather the last couple of days, her lung function tests were just bad enough for her to scrape into the inclusion criteria. We did the physical and blood tests and a week zero exercise test.'

'I'm a fully paid up member.' Bridget patted her handbag. 'Patient ten, complete with little bottle of mysterious pills, diary for recording of asthma attacks thereof, new nebuliser, appointment cards and tired legs,' she added finally, looking accusingly at Hugh. She grinned at Tony. 'I'm not a great fan of exercise at the best of times and I felt like a sort of giant hamster on that treadmill.'

She bent down to retrieve a bag resting at her feet. A handle gave way as she lifted it and a battered old teddy bear with one eye missing fell on to the floor. Tony picked it up and handed it to her gravely.

'Who's your friend, then?'

'That's Sebastian. The reason I came in in the first place was to bring some get well cards from the school to a pupil of mine who's in here. His mum couldn't get in tonight and asked me to bring in Sebastian as Christopher claims he can't sleep without him.'

'I can understand that.' Tony nodded.

'Anyway, I'll have to hang about for a bit as he'll be having his tea at the moment and the staff aren't too keen on interruptions.'

Hugh had been feeling excluded from the conversation. He broke in abruptly. 'Come and have a cup of coffee with us while you wait.'

'Oh, no.' Bridget was hesitant. 'I'd better not.' She glanced at Tony.

'Please do,' he invited. 'We owe you something for your exhausting afternoon of being a guinea-pig.'

'Hamster,' corrected Bridget. Other inhabitants of the foyer stared in the direction of the trio at the burst of laughter they produced. Such sounds did not seem quite right in the oppressive infirmary environment.

Bridget wasn't deterred by the coffee.

'We have the same sort of machine in our staffroom,' she said. 'It kind of grows on you after a while.'

'I try not to spill any on myself, actually,' smirked Hugh. 'But I can believe it.' He barely sipped at his cup before his beep sounded. After speaking on the phone he came back and excused himself.

'Duty calls, I'm afraid. I have to make an appearance on the ward.'

'Problems?' queried Tony.

'Nothing major. I'll catch you again later.'

Tony nodded. 'I'll be here till about seven-thirty – have to head out to the airport then.'

'Airport? Oh, that's right. God's off to the toyshop, I'd forgotten. Are you going to make an appearance in the library to farewell Jennifer?'

'I'll do my best.'

Hugh turned to Bridget. 'Thank you for your assistance. I'll look forward to your next exercise test.'

Bridget wrinkled her nose. 'At least someone will, then.'

Hugh emptied his coffee down the sink, shaking his head sadly. 'Shame,' he commented. He crumpled the polystyrene cup into a ball and fired it at Tony as he went out the door.

They sipped coffee in silence for a minute or two. Bridget broke it with a query.

'Who's God?'

Tony grinned. 'Assuming you don't want to initiate a lengthy debate on religious philosophy, he's Gordon Owen

65

Davies. Chief respiratory physician. My boss.'

Bridget smiled. 'My headmaster's got a bit of a complex himself. Do you suppose it's a necessary requirement for being a boss?'

'Could well be. I haven't checked out any application forms yet.'

A companionable silence fell between them again. They glanced at each other and smiled when their eyes met, then Bridget transferred her gaze to her coffee. It was Tony who spoke first.

'How's Grangewick as a place to live?'

'OK. Better than Newcastle, anyway.'

'You don't like the city?'

'I hate it,' she replied with feeling. 'I hate the weather, the horrible grey suburbs, the poverty, litter and tramps.' She paused and Tony smiled placatingly.

'It's not that bad, surely?'

'Oh, parts of it are lovely, the wealthy areas, but Walker is just so depressing. Row after row of grey little houses, the only difference between them probably the types of problems and misery inside. The kids have so little. I couldn't imagine having their lifestyles, and there's so little hope for the future for them.' She shook her head.

'I'm not that struck on Newcastle as a place to live myself,' said Tony. 'I've been here for twelve years and often thought I'd like to go back down south, but now I'm seriously considering getting out of Britain altogether and emigrating to New Zealand.'

'Really?' Bridget's face lightened. 'I have a girlfriend who went there five years ago. She writes every Christmas and is trying to persuade me to go. She lives in the North Island, somewhere in Hawke's Bay.'

'Hastings? Napier?' Tony named the two towns he could think of easily.

'No. But close to Hastings I think.'

Tony's brow furrowed. 'I know where you mean. I can't think of the name.' A second later he snapped his fingers triumphantly. 'Havelock North?'

'That's it.' Bridget looked delighted. 'They have an old farmhouse and four kids. They love it. In summer they can plan a barbeque a month ahead and know that it won't rain. This Christmas they're going to celebrate with a beach party. Imagine that!'

'Sounds great.' Tony grinned at her enthusiasm.

'And on Guy Fawkes night they drive into Napier. There's this road that goes for miles beside the beach – Marine Parade and everyone has driftwood bonfires and lets off their fireworks on the beach.'

'I'm sold,' said Tony happily. 'When shall we go?'

Bridget flushed, and finished her coffee quickly. 'I'd better go and deliver Sebastian. Thank you again for rescuing me the other night.'

'Anytime.' Tony watched her leave appreciatively, her slim legs neatly encased in blue jeans and the lovely hair swinging in a smooth curtain which just overlapped her jeans' waistband. It was several minutes before he could concentrate on writing a list of tasks for his junior registrar to attend to the next day.

Chapter Eight

The bright yellow Citroën beetled through the roundabout at Westerhope and increased speed as it left the city outskirts behind. Bridget was humming happily to herself and a smile played around the corners of her generous mouth. She was reliving the earlier conversation with Tony Lawrence with such clarity that the memory of his laughing query of when they would go to New Zealand brought an instant return of her blush. She laughed aloud, feeling the warm flush suffusing her cheeks, and then bit her lip thoughtfully. It was not until the little yellow car chugged to a halt outside the cottage that she realised she had passed that point in her journey without a single thought of Peter. Surprised, but not totally displeased at herself, she searched for her key and gave herself over to a vociferous welcome from Jody, the mostly Otterhound.

Crouching to hug the large, shaggy brown dog, Bridget's face was thoroughly washed.

'Yes, I'm pleased to see you too,' she told Jody, laughing. 'I know I've been away a long time today.'

Straightening up, she held the front door open. 'Be quick,' she directed the dog. 'It's too cold to hang about.'

She watched as Jody obediently performed in the usual place, shaking her head as she wondered how long the climbing rose was going to survive such treatment. Still wagging his tail happily, Jody padded after his mistress into the bedroom. He knew the routine and automatically leapt smoothly on to the bed, his vantage point for observing the transformation to old dungarees and sweater – the dog-walking ensemble. He whined softly, hoping to speed the process up a little, but to his consternation he was ignored. In fact, the whole routine seemed to be going awry, for having made a start by removing her shoes, Bridget was simply standing still, staring at her bedside table. Jody thumped his tail encouragingly when she moved again but it was only to pick up one of the photographs she had been looking at. The old brass bedstead creaked as she sat down and absentmindedly stroked the dog pressed against her. Jody sighed, rested his chin on her leg and patiently closed his eyes.

It was an old photograph, black and white, typical of studio portraits done in the forties with the lighting, expression and probable retouching designed to flatter. Not that her mother's portrait would have needed any retouching. She had been an extraordinarily beautiful woman and no amount of hard work or suffering could have altered the fine features or the set of those wonderful dark eyes. Bridget had inherited the lovely eyes, so dark they were almost black, as well as the matching hair colour, but her mouth had definitely come from her father's side. The mobile and expressive lips were now pressed together ruefully and Bridget started unseeing at the photograph in her hand as the memories crowded in.

Her earliest memories were happy ones. Born in the village of Blaenau Ffestiniog in Northern Wales, she had been the only child of Aled Morgan, a miner in the nearby Llechwedd slate mine, and Bronwyn, who had worked in the village post office. Those early days had seemed full of music and laughter. Snatches of the lilting Welsh language, only half remembered, brought the shine of unshed tears to Bridget's eyes. Aled Morgan had been a huge bear-like man, six foot three in his stockinged feet, with a bushy black beard and a laugh to raise the rafters. He was immensely popular and not only for his jovial good humour. Aled had been blessed with the finest singing voice in the village. The best in the whole of Snowdonia, some claimed. He was in demand constantly, always there to lead the singing in the pub, church or village hall. A clear memory, in spite of long suppression, was the thrill of hearing rich male voices weaving a complex and perfect harmony as she sat curled in her father's lap, feeling the swell of his chest and the almost solid vibrations of sound around her.

There had always been a pint or two to wet the whistle on singing evenings but Aled Morgan had been able to hold his drink. One night, after a particularly long and fine effort on Aled's part, the publican rewarded him with a shot of whisky. It soon became a nightly tradition and gradually the beer was delegated a chaser. Villagers shook their heads in dismay at the change in Aled that became more pronounced as the months went by. The laughter that had always been his badge of identity was heard less and less often. The miner still led the singing, but while the volume increased, the words were often slurred and the harmony shaky. Aled did not notice the friendliness of his friends and neighbours waning, but then he was more irritated by problems at home. Times had always been difficult financially for the small family and now, with so much of the hard earned money being used on whisky, things were becoming unbearable. Aled sought refuge from the obvious misery of his wife and daughter by spending more time and money in the local.

He had been ashamed of himself the first time he had beaten his wife, but the silence it produced had been a relief. It became a habit. He had been horrified the first time his fist had flown into the face of his daughter. The silence that blow had produced had been an accusation, not relief. It did not become a habit. When Aled Morgan came home the next day, he found himself, drunk and bewildered, in a deserted house.

The courage that had enabled Bronwyn to flee was born of the determination to ensure survival and happiness for her child. She took the seven-year-old Bridget to Cornwall where she stayed initially with her sister in the town of Bodmin. A succession of jobs, usually manual and exhausting, meant that her daughter was well clothed, fed and educated. The values of love and loyalty, mingling without apparent diffi-culty with a fierce pride and independence, were woven into the fabric of Bridget's soul. The cracked cheekbone and bruised face of the seven-year-old healed without a scar but the mark of that blow had been more deeply imprinted and its shadow haunted and undermined her early attempts at relationships with men. She and her mother never spoke Welsh again.

With her mother's support and encouragement, Bridget Morgan applied for and was accepted into a London teachers' training college. She lived in a small bedsit on the outskirts of the city, relying for company out of college hours on the frequent letters from her mother who often wrote two or three times a week. It was a wintry February morning in her last year at college that the early mail had brought an unusual letter from Bronwyn. The brevity had surprised her but the ending of the letter had been even more of a puzzle. *'Gofal, Cariad.'* 'Take care, love.' Not a rare sentiment, but in Welsh?

Concern made Bridget search out all the ten pence pieces she could find and stop off at the phone box on the way to the station. There had been no reply from home so she had transferred her attention to the day ahead, using the coins to purchase her Underground ticket. She was by now running late. By the time she reached Victoria station, where she needed to change from the District to the Victoria line, it was a quarter to nine and the Underground station was swarming with people at all levels. Standing on the right hand side of the long downward escalator Bridget tucked her handbag under her arm to protect it from pickpockets and pondered her mother's strange letter. She had been unaware of the buildup of the crowd and nearly panicked as she stumbled off the end of the escalator to find there was no room to move forward. She was pressed into the crowd by people still spilling off the moving staircase behind her and had to fight for breath as her face was pushed against a prickly tweed jacket. The escalator shuddered to a halt as someone pushed the emergency stop button but it took a few minutes for the tangle of bodies to sort themselves out. No one could move forward as the platforms were jammed and there was no train due for some three minutes yet. Bridget freed her face and gasped for air. The back she had been pressed into turned with some difficulty and a pair of steady grey eyes regarded her with concern.

'I say, are you all right?'

Bridget had nodded and smiled a little shakily, hoping that the situation would not bring on one of the asthmatic attacks she had been periodically prone to since childhood. The stranger smiled back but continued to watch her as they shuffled forward a few feet. The sound of a train hurtling into the station caused a wave of forward movement which again pushed Bridget forward and this time the owner of the grey eyes put his arm around her shoulders for support. She had been embarrassed to realise that the press of humanity around them then made it impossible for the arm to be removed. She glanced up at him to be met with a smile reflecting her own embarrassment.

'Dare I say we've got to stop meeting like this?' he enquired. They both laughed and suddenly found they were enjoying what should have been an intolerable situation. In the ten minutes it took for them to reach the platform and board a train they had learned each others names and even agreed to meet for a drink on the way home. Bridget had nearly not turned up for the meeting, wondering what had possessed her. It turned out to their mutual amusement that Peter had shared identical emotions and had even walked around the block twice before entering the pub. They were both very glad that they did decide to have that drink.

Bridget's brown study was interrupted by a wet nose edging under her hand where it lay on her lap, still holding the photograph. She placed it carefully back on the bedside table and smiled gently as she looked at the one of Peter which stood on the other side of the lamp. She had trusted him from almost that first moment when his arm had encircled her in that frightening crush of people in the Underground, but the depth of his compassion had startled her only a few days later when she discovered that her mother's letter had been a farewell. Bronwyn Morgan had died of a cancer she had been fighting for months without giving her daughter a hint of any problems. It had been a traumatic beginning to a relationship but the trust and friendship had deepened to a love they had both recognised as a guiding force for their lives. They had married the day after Bridget graduated with commendation from college and had taken their honeymoon of a weekend in Paris six months later, after Peter had graduated MBChB with distinction from medical school.

The first years they had remained in London. Bridget

happily taught in an infants school locally and Peter distinguished himself by his hard work and application in his house-surgeon years. He chose the areas thought to be of most use in general practice, covering obstetrics, paediatrics, psychiatry and geriatrics. For another year he was apprenticed to two GP trainers for a period of six months each. With a lot of dedicated slog and the staunch support of Bridget, Peter sat and passed the MRCGP, becoming a member of the Royal College of General Practitioners. With the increasing unemployment amongst doctors, the added qualification was beneficial and it was with a spirit of optimism that the Gardiners began the hunt for a practice and a place for them to settle and start the family they both wanted. They had both felt some trepidation about a move north when the Grangewick opportunity presented itself, but they took it without too much soul searching. No place could really be as bad as they'd heard Newcastle was, Grangewick was several miles out of the actual city, and anyway, they had each other so what difference could the place they lived really make.

The young couple tackled the initial problems with enthusiasm and surprised even themselves with the results. In looking for a place to live that they could afford, Bridget had fallen in love with a derelict cottage, a little way out of Grangewick village, on the road towards Stamfordham. It stood amongst the dense jungle of a badly neglected garden, the whitewash peeling off the stone, slates slipping from the roof to collect in the gutters or lie half buried under weeds, and many of the leaded window panes were broken. The inside was in an uninhabitable condition but the cottage had two great advantages. One was the magnificent Weeping Elm tree that grew beside it, giving the property an aura of stability and peace. The other, more important, advantage was that they could afford it.

It took a month of intensive effort before they could even camp inside the cottage but gradually they repaired and redecorated as time and money allowed. The slate roof and crumbling stone chimney were restored professionally and a glazier replaced all the panes of broken glass. Bridget had tried to persuade Peter that they should strip off the whitewash and reveal the natural stone of the exterior, and obligingly he helped her make a start one weekend. At the end of an exhausting day of chipping, scraping and wirebrushing to little effect they compared their broken nails and bruised fingers and admitted defeat. After getting rid of the worse flakey patches the cottage then received several new coats of whitewash. Bridget had painstakingly stripped and then painted the intricate wooden surrounds of the arched windows a gleaming black, and polished each of the tiny diamonds of leaded glass. Peter dug holes on either side of the front door so Bridget could plant the old-fashioned Albertine climbing roses and then they had both cleared the weeds from the front brick pathway to stand and admire the stage they had reached.

Bridget had wanted to call their home by its former name of 'Weeping Elm Cottage' but Peter had screwed up his nose and suggested they needed a name to reflect the recreation they were effecting. Amidst a lot of laughter they decided on the title of 'Phoenix Cottage' and confounded many of the villagers when they attached the small engraved brass name plate on the front door above the fox head door knocker.

Redecoration of the interior of Phoenix Cottage was a slow process, mainly due to the fact that the Gardiners were both exceptionally busy. Bridget eventually gained a teaching position at a Walker school and commuted into town each day. She found the area and school a little frightening after the middle-class serenity of her London suburb job but she hoped she would not be there for too long. As she had stopped taking the Pill shortly before applying for the position, they were both confident of her becoming pregnant in the near future. When nothing had happened after a year of trying they worried a little but then shrugged the concern off in favour of trying a bit harder. They both had other worries at the time. Bridget was becoming increasingly involved with the problems faced by her pupils, with the local drug crisis and the skyrocketing level of unemployment amongst the parents of the children. Peter had a major problem that threatened to dominate his life unpleasantly. His problem was the partner in his new practice – a fifty-eight-year-old Scotsman, Dr. James Lewis.

Very much a part of the village scene after thirty years'

74

service, Dr. Lewis was genial, popular, lazy and dangerously incompetent. Peter had been unaware of anything amiss in the beginning. The practice seemed to be well run, with an efficient part-time receptionist, neatly kept drug supplies and records. Dr. Lewis was genuinely concerned about his patients and always made them feel welcome in the surgery, giving the impression that their problems were of paramount importance. He never appeared bored with the trivia that comprised the bulk of the work load: sore throats, arthritis, colds, sinusitis, athlete's foot, indigestion, chronic bronchitis, fatigue, sore backs and depression. The patients all received treatment and kindly assurances.

Peter had been impressed and didn't complain about having to shoulder ninety percent of the night calls. After all, that must be a major incentive in taking on a younger partner. He may not be so keen to be dragged out of bed at all hours when he was approaching sixty either. Come to think of it, he wasn't all that keen on it now.

It was on one of these night calls that Peter had the first inkling of trouble. The ten-year-old child he was called to see was comatose and the mother explained in nervous detail that she had taken the boy to see Dr. Lewis earlier that same day because he was suffering from constipation. Dr. Lewis had prescribed a laxative and patted both the boy and his mother on the back, saying with a wink that it might not be a bad idea to keep some California Syrup of Figs in the house. 'Old-fashioned it may be – effective it definitely is,' he had chuckled.

As Peter quickly checked the child's vital signs he was only half listening to the mother's agitated chattering. He paused on opening his bag, however, and gave her a sharp glance.

'What was that you just said, Mrs. Geddes?'

'It's just what I told Dr. Lewis.' The woman looked worriedly towards her son. 'It seemed odd that he was having the trouble when he was up to the toilet to wee so many times in the nights.'

'How many times does he usually get up?'

'Five or six. Sometimes even eight.'

Peter frowned, but checked the comment he would like to have made about James Lewis' treatment of the boy. He held up a plastic bag of fluid and spoke to the woman.

'Can you stand over here by his head and hold this up for me, please?' Peter had inserted a butterfly cannula into the lad's limp arm and before connecting the saline drip, collected a few drops of blood on to a Labstix. He shook his head in disbelief on reading the level of sugar in the blood and immediately gave a lifesaving injection of insulin before ringing for an ambulance. Peter had accompanied young Iain Geddes into hospital and it was not until three o'clock that he reached his own bed, satisfied that things were going to be all right. The next day he had found his senior partner having a cup of tea before the morning surgery.

'You're looking a wee bit weary, lad.' Dr. Lewis' brogue was tinged with obvious concern.

'Yes, well, I was up most of the night with Iain Geddes.'

'Oh?' James Lewis seemed to be reading his tealeaves.

Peter watched him closely and weighed his words carefully. 'Did you have any reason to suspect he might be a diabetic?'

The elder doctor cleared his throat as he shook his head lightly. 'What makes you think he is?'

'I found him in a ketoacidotic hyperglycaemic coma last night,' Peter said quietly.

Lewis tutted with a paternal concern but avoided meeting Peter's intense gaze. No mention was made of the visit to the clinic by the Geddes the day before and Peter managed the case from then on without complication but a seed of doubt had been sown. A chance encounter with an old medical school friend which led to a drinking session in a Newcastle pub with a group of young registrars one Friday evening, caused the seed to blossom and threaten to choke Peter's working relationships both in the clinic and the community who liked and trusted their known practitioner and were not yet ready totally to accept a young stranger in their midst.

Peter had been on the outskirts of the group that evening in the pub, listening to a discussion about some of the horrific errors made by GPs, obviously a favourite topic of conversation. At one point he placed his beer carefully down on the bar and cut in.

'Did you say Lewis?' he asked the speaker.

'That's right. Chap out in Grangewick.' Without pause, the

young doctor eagerly continued with his story. 'And this chap goes to his GP and complains of the most awful headache that had come on, completely out of the blue while he was at work. Absolutely splitting, pain down the back of his neck and into his shoulders, dizziness and vomiting. Worried as hell, as he'd never had a headache before in his life.'

The listeners nodded wisely.

'Classic,' one of them muttered. Peter stared into his beer, guessing with a sinking sensation what the ending of this story was likely to be. The speaker refreshed himself with a long swallow of beer and wiped his mouth on the back of his wrist.

'The old codger saw him the day after this sudden onset: splitting, totally out of the ordinary headache. Did he take the guy's blood pressure? Did he hell! Gave him some aspirin and made an appointment to give him a check up in three months!'

Pete shut his eyes briefly. 'Christ,' he muttered silently.

The point of the story having been made, the ending was something of an anticlimax, the group waiting morosely to hear the worst.

'Poor chap goes home and takes his aspirin. Sure enough the headache gets better. Thinks his doctor is bloody wonderful and a few weeks later drops dead at the age of thirty-two from a massive rebleed from his berry aneurysm and a subarachnoid haemorrhage.'

Peter confided his fears to Bridget and she supported and comforted him. She confided her fears about the length of time it was taking for her to conceive and he comforted her and made an appointment for her to see a specialist. They drew closer together and relied totally on each other's companionship to provide the relief they both needed from worry. The stress inevitably led to strife. A major row broke out at one point when Bridget was depressed during a period, having received a letter from a girlfriend announcing her pregnancy, and Peter was trying to sort out all manner of minor discrepancies he was discovering in Lewis's treatment of cases without alienating any of the parties concerned. It had been a bitter few days they both regretted. Miraculously, it had been forgotten when Peter had arrived home carrying a cardboard box which he had placed carefully on the floor in front of his wife. She opened it to find a ball of brown fluff with legs and sharp little teeth that gnawed happily at her fingers and toes.

'He's almost pure Otterhound,' Peter had announced proudly.

The puppy had been a delight and altered their lives immeasurably. They seemed to be laughing constantly for months afterwards as they watched Jody's antics, rescued him from the innumerable disasters he initiated, and tried to save their feet from the danger of toe loss.

As though he knew she was thinking about him, the large shaggy dog raised his head from Bridget's lap and barked quietly. She scratched the spot between his rather woeful brown eyes.

'OK. I've certainly wasted enough time dwelling on the past today. It's time for our walk, and then we'll get a nice fire going.'

She stood and stretched, then shivered as she removed her top layer of clothes to don ancient, patched dungarees and Peter's old fishing sweater, which came right down over her hips and was beautifully warm. It was good to distract herself because memories of the times after that were still distressing. Even as she tried to close her mind to them now, as she changed and chatted to Jody, she could feel the old horror hovering at the edge of her thoughts. She had been through it all too many times already – that terrible night when Peter had rushed to an emergency call, the delivery van which had been carelessly speeding downhill through the acute turns of the notorious approach to Grangewick. The sound of the impact had been loud enough for Bridget to hear at the cottage but she had thought nothing of it until their village policeman stood on the doorstep, white-faced and stammering. For months afterwards she had burst into tears on hearing even a door slam. That black period of nearly a year after Peter's death held a dreamlike quality now, shades of a nightmare she would prefer but was never quite able to forget. She could remember the asthma attack clearly enough. Normally a terrifying and rare experience, she had welcomed the onslaught, feeling angry and somehow cheated later at finding herself in hospital, recovering.

Bridget buttoned up her oilskin snapped a lead on to her dog's collar. The bite of the chilly wind brought her back into the present. She set off towards the village for a change, with Jody capering joyously beside her. Their mutual devotion to each other had grown over the last couple of years and it has been the only close relationship that Bridget had felt comfortable with. But it was time to look ahead. The future seemed more hopeful at the moment than it had for a very long time. That conversation with Tony Lawrence had sparked a feeling of instinctive trust in someone which Bridget had been convinced she could never recover. She detached Jody's lead as they reached a grassy patch and bent to pick up a convenient stick for him. Bridget grinned as she watched him bunch his muscles in anticipation.

'Go for it, *Cariad*!' she shouted with enthusiasm, hurling the piece of wood with all the strength she could muster.

Chapter Nine

'You need a haircut,' Dr. Anthony Lawrence told his reflection firmly. 'And just where do you think you're going to find the time to get one?'

Alone in the staff toilet he paused thoughtfully and ruffled his hair. A sprinkling of grey was beginning to show amongst the sandy brown waves but if anything, it was vaguely pleasing. Tony Lawrence had the type of boyish looks that had always belied his years. It had been a definite handicap in his twenties. Patients never said anything to his face but the message might as well have been a printout on their foreheads – 'You're too young to be a proper doctor. Are you sure you know what you're doing?' Yes, the grey was pleasing. The fringe beginning to flop towards his eyebrows was not.

Tony rummaged through his pen pocket and somewhat guiltily removed the double sharp stainless steel suture scissors that had accidentally made a new home there some weeks previously. He applied himself to the task with enthusiasm and the enamel of the basin rapidly became coated with a layer of clippings. He grinned lopsidedly at the mirror as he rinsed the basin, clogging the drain with a plug of hair that was to puzzle the cleaner the next morning. Catherine would have a fit, he thought, combing the much shortened fringe to one side. Never mind, they say the difference between a good haircut and a bad one is only a few days.

The muted sound of alcohol-sodden merriment met Tony well before he reached the departmental library. The party had been in full swing for some time. He knew from experience that it had probably been a quiet affair until about six, when Nicola Jarvis would have finished her single paper cup of wine and excused herself. Tony was just in time to wish the girl from reception, Jennifer, all the best in her new job, before she also left. He accepted a cup of wine that Amanda had coaxed from the box by dint of careful tipping with the button depressed and bit thankfully into the sausage roll that would most likely be his dinner. He watched the technician begin to clear away some of the debris from the table.

'Don't you get enough of that at home, Mandy?'

'That's quite true, Dr. Lawrence.' Amanda brushed the crumbs from her hands. She smiled brightly and her cheeks dimpled. The wine had erased the spaniel-like creases around her eyes and Tony realised how rare it was to see the girl enjoying herself.

'How are things at home?' he asked gently, not wanting to spoil her relaxed mood.

'I've got the night off.' Amanda swallowed another mouthful of wine. 'Mind you, I'd better not be too late. Dad won't be too happy at coping by himself.'

'How is your mother?'

Mandy's nose wrinkled slightly as she considered. 'Just the same. You'd think she'd make up her mind either to die or get better after all these years but she just goes on and on, driving me and Dad slowly round the bend.' She flushed abruptly at her admission. 'It's not that we don't love her, it's just . . . Oh, I don't know.' She lapsed into her more customary silence, suddenly ill at ease in the atmosphere of spirited conversation going on around them.

Bob was looking very much at home to one side of them, one arm resting on shelves of recent periodicals, the other outstretched to create an arc that Sue was happily cornered in.

'We've been married a year,' he was saying a trifle wistfully. 'Alice is fifteen months old. I wouldn't have called it a shotgun wedding exactly, but the writing about my career prospects was pretty well on the wall – her father's a renal consultant over at the R.V.I.'

Sue was nodding sympathetically. Tony wished he hadn't overheard. Amanda appeared not to have.

'What would you do if you didn't have to run things at

home, Mandy?' He tried to draw her away from her preoccupation.

'Hangliding,' she said with a shy smile. 'Or karate. Something nobody would ever think of me doing.'

'How 'bout sky-diving?' Hugh had surfaced beside Amanda in time to hear her. The response was obvious embarrassment. She stammered slightly as she made excuses and slipped away.

'Now I've done it,' Hugh sighed.

Barbara offered them the last of the sausage rolls.

'What Amanda needs is a boyfriend,' she said seriously. 'But she never gets the chance to meet anyone, the way she's kept running around after her mother.'

'It's pretty Victorian,' commented Hugh. 'Her shyness won't help even if she does manage to meet someone.'

'Mmmm.' Barbara glanced over Hugh's shoulder to see Jackie showing off her ring to the motherly Gwen.

'That doesn't help either.'

Hugh turned his head at her nod.

'There's Jackie, only eighteen, spouting forth all day about rings, weddings, dresses and honeymoons, and poor Mandy at twenty-two has probably never spent a night in the back row at the movies.'

'What happens there?' asked Hugh innocently.

Barbara giggled. 'Why don't you ask him?' They both looked in Bob's direction. Sue peeped out from under his arm and winked at them. Tony refused the cigarette Hugh offered him and watched sadly as his registrar lit Barbara's and then his own.

'Given up again?' asked Barbara sympathetically.

Hugh chuckled. 'Probably for the third time today.'

Tony raised an eyebrow. 'Someone needs to set degenerates like you a good example. I plan to last at least a week this time.' He washed down the last of his sausage roll with the oversweet wine. 'Still, enjoy your iniquity while it lasts. I'm afraid I'll have to tear myself away. See if you can behave yourselves at least until I get back from London.'

The weather had deteriorated and a foggy drizzle enveloped Tony as he hurried towards the carpark shortly after seven-

82

thirty. With only half an hour before his check-in time he drove the six miles to the airport in some frustration as visibility was poor and traffic slow negotiating the numerous roundabouts on the route. Relieved to find a space in the long-term carpark without difficulty, Tony sprinted into Newcastle International airport and joined the queue at the British Airways check-in desk only to be informed of a delay in his departure time to London due to a hold-up from the connecting flight. He would have to wait at least an hour.

The upstairs bar was well populated but Tony found a seat in the adjacent lounge area. He looked around briefly on the offchance that Gordon Davies was nearby, knowing as he did so how unlikely that was. Davies would have taken a much earlier flight in order to dine expensively and probably take in a West End show, courtesy of the drug company whose conference he was gracing with his presence.

Tony opened his briefcase resignedly. He discarded the journals he had brought to read on the plane and removed Sharon Andrew's case notes, the front cover of which was stamped with the message that they were not to be removed from the hospital. He spent the next thirty minutes reading discharge summaries, outpatient notes and laboratory results that spanned the fifteen years since Sharon had first been seen at the Northern. Aside from a concussion from a cycling accident and having her tonsils removed, her history was entirely respiratory. Her family history showed a tendency towards asthma and Sharon's early childhood had been plagued with recurrent episodes of wheezing usually associated with infections, flexural eczema and seasonal rhinitus. By the age of ten she had persistent problems and was avoiding all forms of exercise which exacerbated the breathing difficulties. At the time of her first admission at the age of thirteen, the list of recognised allergies was receiving frequent additions. Sharon was allergic to pollen, feathers, fur, house dust and mites, sensitive to changes in temperature, atmospheric conditions and exposure to cigarette smoke. Over the next few years she had accumulated several admissions. Tony made particular note of one slightly cryptic discharge summary.

The registrar concerned had taken the trouble to conduct a

lengthy interview with Sharon's parents and had unearthed a nest of resentments. Both parents smoked and were unwilling or unable to stop in spite of their daughter's sensitivity to the habit. They had also been unwilling to meet the expense of providing synthetic bedding for Sharon, and as her mother worked full-time she could not accept the extra burden of vacuuming mattresses or even floors daily. Sharon's younger brothers also resented their sister's condition. Desperate for a pet they were forbidden to have they took our their frustration by encouraging the neighbour's dogs into the house at every opportunity.

What was more interesting was that in the opinion of the registrar concerned, Sharon had learned to manipulate those around her by her asthma and could, in fact, turn on the symptoms to obtain what she wanted. The doctor had witnessed this ability himself when trying to talk to Sharon cautiously about psychological factors. She had not wanted to discuss the matter, becoming immediately wheezy. The symptoms had faded equally rapidly when the registrar changed the subject. He thought that the reaction was probably subconscious and that her frequent admissions, in spite of what should have been effective therapy, could be the result of her initiating symptoms in a stressful family environment and then losing control of the situation. Certainly, following her marriage at the age of eighteen and the move away from her family, her admission rate had dropped markedly. Over the last four years she had had only two attacks resulting in hospitalisation, the last one having been eighteen months ago. Her asthma seemed generally very well controlled, even to the extent that she could exercise without problems after first dosing herself with a bronchodilator. A perfect candidate for the drug trial, in fact.

Tony closed the notes thoughtfully. There were a lot of possibilities for what might have precipitated her last asthmatic attack. Exercise without prophylactic treatment, exposure to allergens or perhaps an argument with her husband. The thought of Shane Andrews prompted Tony to return the notes to his briefcase. He was the only person who may be able to help but contacting him at present might only rekindle Mr Andrews' anger and decision to cause trouble for the department, a situation that Davies appeared to have defused.

Tony glanced up at the overhead monitors to see that as yet no departure time for his flight was being advertised. The weather looked worse. The control tower, only a hundred yards from the terminal, was now only dimly visible in spite of the powerful outside lighting. The bar was doing a roaring trade, its customers becoming progressively more jovial and noisy, seemingly enjoying their situation. Considering his briefcase again, Tony selected the DHSS booklet of December 1984 as the case of Bill Chalmers claimed priority in his thoughts. From the advisory committee on dangerous pathogens, it contained interim guidelines on Acquired Immune Deficiency Syndrome that Tony wanted to revise. He read with a practised rapidity, using a Glo pen to highlight sentences by giving them a lurid yellow background.

The first formal report of AIDS in the UK had appeared in 1981. By October '84 there had been 88 cases, 37 of whom had since died. Well, that figure is well out of date, Tony thought. There must be twice as many cases just amongst the heroin community of Edinburgh, judging from recent news reports. He scanned quickly through the lengthy detailing of precautions which seemed to cover everything from being spat in the eye by an infected patient to having to dispose of a contaminated body. He turned to the more recent publications of May and October 1985 which unfortunately had been the most up to date he could unearth in the department. Someone else must have borrowed the latest material. Not that the basic information had changed dramatically, just the statistics leaping upwards, and the focus on public education through media advertising. By February '85, only 132 cases of AIDS had been reported in the UK: 126 males, 6 females, 58 of whom had died. A drop in the ocean compared with American figures but Britain was following the same pattern and apparently only needed a year or two to catch up on the present US rate.

He recognised the sentence which had tolled in his mind during the interview with Bill Chalmers – probably the most important factor in making a diagnosis of AIDS was to think of it. He scanned the list of patient groups, wondering which one Bill might belong to. Perhaps he had used intravenous drugs at some stage, or was bisexual. There was always the useful category of Insufficient Data or Unknown to fall back on. Tony was not looking forward to hearing the outcome of the tests done on Bill, dreading the painful interviews that would be forthcoming if the results were positive and feeling a nagging certainty that they would be. He highlighted the section on available counselling. He wasn't going to be very much help on his own with this one.

Tony was roused from this depressing thought by the muffled tones of an airport announcement. There was a collective groan at the news. All flights in and out of Newcastle were now cancelled due to adverse weather conditions. Passengers were advised to call at the check-in areas to make arrangements for accommodation on flights the next day. Tony shook his head in annoyance and abandoned the idea of attending the conference. Davies couldn't blame him for this, anyway.

He considered ringing Catherine to let her know the change of plan but there was a long queue by the telephones. Another queue held him up as he left the airport carpark and in the freezing, almost solid, fog the traffic moved at a crawl as he headed back to town. It was after midnight as he neared the flat and he had to park half a block away from home. In spite of the cold, Tony paused for a moment to stare at the car parked in his favoured position. It was very distinctive, a late model Porsche with pale pink paintwork. What an incredible colour for a car, he thought. It struck a faint chord in his memory but he didn't bother trying to pursue it as he quietly made his way up the stairs. He hoped Catherine hadn't put the chain across the door as he didn't want to have to wake her by ringing the bell.

He inserted his key into the lock, turning it and the handle carefully as he gently pushed the door open. The chain was not on and a faint light from the bedroom indicated that Catherine was still awake.

Suddenly Tony froze. A distinct murmur of voices reached him. Then he heard Catherine clearly.

'Don't move, my love.' Husky and sensual, it was a tone he knew so well but hadn't heard in a very long time. The voice became even clearer. 'I'll go and get the rest of that superb wine of yours, darling.'

A murmur of a male voice then, his wife's throaty laughter and sounds of movement.

Instinctively, Tony closed the door and removed his key as silently as he had opened it. Quietly he retraced his path down the stairs and along the street. He slumped into the driver's seat of his car.

Tony felt completely numb. The scene replayed itself endlessly before his eyes, his mind adding a different ending each time. He could clearly imagine what the confrontation might have been had he continued into the flat. Equally, his mind tortured him with graphic scenes of what was happening now, in his bed. *His* bed, for Christ's sake! An edge of anger began to form and he was tempted to return and force the confrontation. But mixed with the anger there was also a sense of guilt and shame for having allowed his marriage to deteriorate until this was the inevitable result. Catherine was a lovely woman who enjoyed male company and needed admiration and attention. She got neither from him.

Tony watched the door of his apartment block. He was convinced that Catherine's lover was the driver of the pink Porsche. He wanted to see who it was, as racking his memory had failed to produce the owner's name. He sat for an hour which crept into another. No hint of fatigue overcame him but eventually he decided that it was going to be an overnight visit. Not wanting to be seen still sitting there in the morning, he started the car and automatically drove towards the hospital. He welcomed the sense of temporary refuge produced by the greeting of the night porter at the main entrance and entered the familiar subdued night-time atmosphere of the Northern. His presence would be unremarked due to his frequent responses to night calls.

Tony walked towards his office but then changed direction abruptly and made for ICU. Bruce Matheson's condition was worrying him and he needed someone else's problems to focus on right now.

Chapter Ten

Staff nurse Clare Murray sat with her feet up on the desk of the ICU nurse's station, surrounded by a bank of small screens which relayed the information appearing on the patients' bedside monitors. She swung her feet to the floor with guilty haste on hearing the ante-room door open but relaxed as she recognised Tony. She greeted him warmly before rubbing her eyes and yawning.

'Don't wake up on my account,' Tony grinned half-heartedly as he took a seat beside her.

'Sorry,' Clare apologised with a giggle, stifling another yawn. 'It's my last stint on nights for a while and I'm afraid I celebrated by staying up all day. Margaret's away getting me some coffee.'

'Quiet night?' asked Tony.

'I'll say,' she responded. 'Deadly, in fact, if you'll pardon the expression.'

'How's Bruce?'

'Not so good, I'm afraid. They tried him off the respirator earlier but there were no signs of any spontaneous attempts to breathe himself. No reflexes to be found either. The neurology boys are making noises about brain death. The blood gases aren't bad, though. I'll find the lab report for you.'

'Won't be much use without a brain,' Tony said gloomily. He idly flicked through the pages of a magazine lying in front of the monitors as Clare looked through the recent laboratory reports awaiting filing in patient notes.

'His wife's in there with him at the moment,' Clare commented. 'Neurology says they'll repeat the checks in twenty-four hours and if there's no change they'll declare brain death and switch off. Someone else to approach about organ donation. Never rains but it pours as they say, and I . . .'

Tony interrupted her as an advertisement featuring a Porsche triggered the query: 'Can you imagine anyone painting a Porsche pale pink?'

'Clifford Barrington does.' Clare's tone was offhand as she sorted out the results she wanted and handed them to Tony. 'So I suppose it's the most expensive colour you can get,' she added with a touch of sarcasm.

He had difficulty keeping his voice expressionless. 'Who's Clifford Barrington?'

'You must have heard of him.' Clare snorted. 'He's that plastic surgeon there was all the fuss about a couple of months ago.'

Tony stared at the reports in his hand without seeing them. Yes, he had heard of Clifford Barrington all right. A plastic surgeon with a heavy financial interest in the private hospital he favoured, and a reputedly heavier interest in seducing the female patients who consulted him. There had been minor complaints over the years of questionable examination procedures but nothing serious until recently when a young lady had claimed she had been sexually assaulted.

The case had received a lot of press coverage and might even have resulted in a conviction had not a second witness, prepared to testify as to what really went on in that consulting room, declined to give evidence at the last minute. The young woman who had initiated the case had been referred to Mr. Barrington for a possible breast reduction as her Dolly Parton-style endowment was making her life a misery. It was her word against the surgeon's that he had done anything more than examine her breasts, and she became so confused under cross-examination that the case was dismissed due to lack of evidence. Clifford Barrington had coolly nodded at the judge's admonition that a nurse should be present during future examinations and had then gazed at the public gallery, where several well-dressed, middle-aged women were looking vaguely alarmed by the prospect.

Clare's voice filtered through to Tony.

'. . . not that I've been invited for a ride in the fabulous vehicle, but I must be one of a select few amongst females in this vicinity. I hear that the seats are covered in imitation mink.'

'I don't believe I've met him,' Tony said wearily.

'You haven't missed much.' Clare was delighted at this unexpected opportunity for a spot of gossip. 'Personally, I think it's pathetic for a man of that age to go for a playboy image. Grey hair and diamond rings, would you believe? Seems like a lot of women go for it, though. I . . .'

Tony cut off the stream by standing up abruptly. He remembered that Hugh had once taken Clare out on a date. He understood now why he had since referred to her as 'motormouth'.

'I think I'll check on Bruce while I'm here,' Tony excused himself. 'Do you have his notes handy?'

Effectively silenced, Clare handed him the notes and watched him leave with mild regret. Perhaps Margaret would be more interested in an in depth discussion of Clifford Barrington and his sexual prowess.

Tony paused by the door of Room Three and glanced through the large window which ran the length of the room on the corridor side. The still, blanket-covered shape of the patient seemed almost incidental alongside the mass of equipment. A woman sat beside the bed, her head resting on her arms. She looked to be asleep, but as Tony watched she slowly raised her head and gazed at her husband. Tony entered the room quietly.

Lyn Matheson watched silently as Tony shone a torch into Bruce's eyes, felt his pulse and checked readings and settings on various monitors. She spoke in a whisper.

'He's no better, is he?'

Tony shook his head, his face concerned as he noted Lyn's exhaustion. 'You need some rest.'

'I can't sleep.' Her face crumpled and she fought to control her voice. 'They said that . . . that they might have to consider switching the machine off –'

Tony put an arm around the woman's shoulders. 'Come and have some coffee,' he said firmly.

They sat in the small staff kitchen attached to the Unit. Lyn sat with her eyes shut until Tony handed her the mug of strong sweet coffee she had requested. She squinted slightly as she focused on her surroundings.

'I don't suppose I'm allowed to smoke in here?'

'Of course you are.' It was not allowed but Tony welcomed the chance to create a more relaxed atmosphere. He rose and shut the door, collecting a saucer to use as an ashtray.

Lyn held the packet tentatively towards him. 'I don't suppose you – ?'

'Thanks, I'd love one.' Tony accepted the cigarette gladly, although he never normally smoked her menthol variety. It was like smoking toothpaste. He lit hers, then his own, sitting beside her and positioning the saucer on the arm of her chair.

'Does Bruce smoke at all?'

'Heavens, no.' Lyn drew deeply on her cigarette. 'I try not to smoke around him. I feel so guilty if he gets wheezy.' She sipped her coffee gratefully. 'I have tried to give up but it's not easy.'

'I know.' Tony's reply was heartfelt. 'Have you noticed other things affecting Bruce's breathing particularly?'

'He used to get very bad in the summer with pollens and things. I could never have fresh flowers in the house either.'

'Has he ever reacted to aspirin?'

'The other doctor asked me that.' Lyn shook her head. 'I honestly don't know. I'm always the one to run for pills. Bruce never seems even to get headaches. I don't think I've ever known him to take anything.'

'But you think he may have taken a cold capsule before this attack?'

'I'm not sure about that, either. The pills were out of the cupboard when I went into the bathroom but I didn't think to ask him. I should have, but the kids were both sick with their colds and I was fussing around, trying to look after them and get breakfast. I should have asked,' Lyn repeated miserably.

'Don't worry about it,' Tony reassured her. 'It wouldn't have made any difference to his treatment, it's just that I'd like to find out what caused the attack. His asthma has been so well controlled lately.'

Lyn nodded. 'Do you think it might have been an allergy to aspirin?'

'It's possible. Bruce had a history of hypersensitivity to pollen and other substances in skin prick tests, and problems with eczema. Patients like that are more susceptible to drug or food allergies. Had he eaten anything unusual or had a lot of alcohol, or chocolate, or maybe something containing yellow food colouring?'

'No.' Lyn smiled sadly. 'He was feeling so awful with his cold, he hadn't eaten anything at all the night before. He didn't have a chance to have breakfast . . .' Her lip trembled.

'A cold could have triggered the attack as well,' Tony said. 'Or it may be a combination of things. Do you know whether he took his trial capsule?'

'Yes, I'm sure about that. He always took it first thing in the morning. I've got the bottle. I thought someone might want them back.' She reached for her handbag and gave the bottle to Tony. She extracted and lit another cigarette, watching as Tony read the label and then put the bottle into his pocket.

'Do you think he might have been allergic to those pills?' asked Lyn.

'No. He was on the active phase of the trial and these capsules contain salbutamol – the same drug as the inhaler. They should have helped, if anything.' He smiled at Lyn. 'Would you like some more coffee?'

'No, thanks. I'm feeling a lot better. I think I'll go home for some breakfast and check that Mum's coping with the kids.'

'That's a good idea,' Tony nodded. 'We'll call you if there's any change here. Before you go, though, do you know how many doses Bruce might have given himself with his inhaler?'

Lyn groaned. 'I knew that was dangerous. He had three puffs while I was there. He wouldn't let me call for help, kept saying he would come right. Then he got pretty frightened, I think, and may have had more while I went and called for the ambulance and took the kids next door.'

Tony nodded. 'Have you ever known him to react like that previously?'

'No.' Lyn ground out the cigarette on the saucer. 'He was usually very calm. There was something different about this attack, though – it seemed to come on so suddenly and get bad so quickly . . .' Her voice trailed into silence and she bit her lower lip.

92

'See if you can get a bit of rest when you get home,' Tony advised gently. 'I'll be here for a while and I'll keep an eye on Bruce.'

Alone in the kitchen, he emptied the saucer of butts into the rubbish bin and washed the coffee mugs. Then he sat and flicked through Bruce Matheson's notes, trying to find any common denominators that might link this case to that of Sharon Andrews.

Their early histories were similar. They were both prone to extrinsic attacks though Sharon showed a much wider range of sensitivities. They were both also liable to exercise-induced asthma but recent histories indicated effective treatment and stable conditions causing no undue concern. Two perfect trial candidates.

Tony stood and paced the small kitchen. Something had to be wrong. In Bruce's case, obviously the respiratory tract infection was a factor, possibly the only one needed to cause the attack, but it didn't feel right in view of the sudden onset of symptoms and rapid deterioration. There was no way of checking whether it could have been an allergy to aspirin unless Bruce recovered enough to be tested. That possibility seemed highly unlikely. And what of Sharon Andrews, the other perfect trial candidate? Any number of possibilities existed for the cause of her attack but there was only one avenue through which to investigate them. The outstanding common denominator in the two cases was the unexpectedness, swiftness and severity of the attacks. Coincidence had to be rejected, at least until every effort had been made to find a more satisfactory explanation.

Tony Lawrence's pacing of the ICU staff kitchen was only one of many pockets of activity in the Northern that night. At two o'clock the nurse on duty in ward A7, men's general surgical, rang the hospital operator and asked her to page Dr. David Laing, the surgical housesurgeon on call for the night.

David Laing took nearly sixty seconds to answer the phone and almost fell asleep again as he waited to be connected to the ward. He didn't bother to question the nurse thoroughly before agreeing to come to the ward as he knew from experience that she only called when absolutely necessary. He took another sixty seconds to summon the energy to get out of bed. He reckoned he'd only had about half an hour's sleep so far tonight and he felt distinctly under par. He splashed some cold water on his face but failed to dissipate the woolly sensation in his head. The light hurt his eyes even when they'd had time to accustom themselves after the initial shock and he noticed the ominous tickling when he swallowed that heralded a sore throat. He realised he was another victim of the virus that was doing the rounds of the staff at present. The thought was not a cheering one.

The nurse lit his way through the ward with a torch beam pointed at floor level. She stopped at a screened off bed and switched on a small overhead light at the end of the bed. The patient was a Mr. Ray Higgins, a querulous sixty-five-year-old gentleman who had until now been making good progress after surgery for a duodenal ulcer. As the nurse had already explained to Dr. Laing, Mr. Higgins was now running a temperature, complaining of a sore throat and nausea and had been unable to sleep due to a persistent cough. His incessant calls for attention and then the rise in his temperature had prompted the nurse to page the housesurgeon.

'I know how he feels,' David had said ruefully.

He checked Mr. Higgins' temperature again, which was now 39°C, and noted the inflamed throat and rapid respiration rate. He laid the middle finger of his left hand along the line of a rib and struck it with the middle finger of his right hand. One side was distinctly dull. On listening with his stethoscope he could hear harsh bronchial breath sounds over the dull area with crackles in the adjacent areas. Mr. Higgins coughed repeatedly during the examination and complained in a hoarse whisper that it caused pain on his left side.

Keeping his voice lowered, David explained to Ray Higgins that it looked as if he probably had pneumonia and that he was going to start him on a course of antibiotics immediately. He got his patient to cough up a sample of sputum which made them both feel queasy. He then shut off Mr. Higgin's intravenous line and took a sample of blood. He dispatched the nurse to call for the portable x-ray machine so that a chest x-ray could be taken without Ray being moved or waiting around in drafty corridors.

Rubbing briefly at his gritty eyes, David sat on the bedside chair as he turned his attention to the patient's notes to check for any history of allergy to penicillin. There was none, so he charted one gram of ampicillin six-hourly to be given intravenously. He also asked for four-hourly checks to be made on Mr. Higgins's temperature, pulse and respiration rates. The nurse had brought the requested drugs by the time David completed his notes, so he administered the initial dose himself and reconnected the IV flow. A grumpy x-ray technician arrived and trundled his trolley noisily into the ward as David prepared to leave, knowing that it would be some time before the plates would be ready and that it wouldn't alter the immediate treatment in any case. A few patients woke up at the commotion and called for attention.

David escaped thankfully and made his way back to the housesurgeons' quarters. He was living in as this was his first year, both on the wards and in Newcastle. He could feel the virus taking a firmer hold and his head throbbed dully. He made his way past his room and into the kitchen, hoping that the packet of soluble aspirin he'd seen in one of the cupboards was still there. Another housesurgeon was sitting at the table, drinking black coffee.

'Hullo, David,' she said. 'You're not looking too good.'

'I'm at death's door, Kay,' David stated seriously. 'Maybe you should examine me.'

'Fat chance,' grinned Kay. 'Take two aspirin and call me in the morning.'

'You doctors are all the same,' grumbled David, running some water into a glass to dissolve the tablets. He swallowed the mixture and grimaced.

'Thanks for waiting up for me.' David wiggled his eyebrows suggestively. 'We can go to bed now.'

Kay rolled her eyes and then sighed. 'That's almost an attractive invitation, even from an egghead. Unfortunately an imbecilic night nurse, who can't even wipe a bottom without calling a medic, has prior claim on my services.'

As if to punctuate her sentence, Kay's beep sounded. Wearily she pushed herself out of her chair and moved to the telephone.

David headed for the door. 'You know what they say,' he

said over his shoulder.

'Mmmm?' Kay picked up the receiver and paused with her finger in the dial.

'Housesurgeons are like mushrooms. Keep them in the dark and shovel shit at them occasionally.'

David's final thought before drifting into sleep was that Kay's peal of laughter had made him feel much better than the aspirin.

Chapter Eleven

It was more by luck than desire that Tony Lawrence arrived home on the Friday in time to accompany his wife to view the property in Darras Hall.

Even through a daze of fatigue he registered the chic of the modern, assiduously interior-designed dwelling. He remembered in mild alarm having read of a house in this area recently selling for a record £250,000. He followed his wife and the estate agent through room after room but his thoughts centred wholly on Catherine and her bland, totally normal behaviour. How practised she must be in the art of deception to show no hint of the events of the past twenty-four hours.

She was dressed in a tailored black suit and cream cashmere sweater. He noted with amusement that both his wife and the female estate agent, who sported a similar suit in iron grey, wore black seamed stockings and gleaming stiletto heeled shoes. It was obviously the correct outfit to view houses in and they might well have purchased their ensembles in the same shop, but while Catherine looked elegant in the extreme, the agent's skirt was too snugly fitted, gathering into creases behind her knees as she walked, and the seams of her stockings had twisted slightly, making her calves look as though they had corkscrewed into badly fitting shoes.

'The master bedroom has bathroom en suite, of course,' the agent was saying to Catherine. She dismissed the bedroom with a wave and strode across the room to throw open the french windows with an air of a chef uncovering an exquisite cordon bleu creation. She said nothing as Tony and Catherine walked past her.

The room they entered was large and oblong-shaped. It had no windows but the walls were lined with mirrors. The floor was tiled in a green and white mosaic and a profusion of plants filled the perimeters of the room. Boston ferns topped the white wrought-iron plant stands, white Impatiens spilled from hanging baskets and an enormous indoor palm tree dominated the far end of the room, the top branches pressed against the ceiling. With mirrors reflecting greenery and everywhere, the effect was that of instant transportation into a tropical jungle. The steamy atmosphere heightened the illusion and was caused by the huge circular jacuzzi pool in the room's centre. The water level of the pool was below that of the floor and the wide recess between water and floor was a seating area. Large, soft white vinyl cushions printed with a green leaf pattern were grouped invitingly.

Catherine's quick intake of breath and shining eyes were noted with satisfaction by the agent who stood beside her and spoke softly. She had assessed her client well.

'Invitations to this house will be *the* most sought after. Imagine the impact as you open a door from the hallway that looks as though it belongs to a wardrobe, and lead your guests through the ferns to enjoy their pre- or after-dinner drinks in this unique setting.' The agent moved to the edge of the pool and with her foot depressed a button set into the tiles. The water in the pool began to move, small ripples worried the surface and then it settled into a myriad of whirlpools each expanding to merge with those surrounding. The agent eyed Tony shrewdly.

'A consultant's life must be *so* stressful. A room such as this in your home could be your greatest investment in future health and happiness.'

'Speaking of investments,' replied Tony, 'you haven't mentioned the price.'

He received a cool look. 'Offers over £150,000 are invited and I can assure you that there will be a great deal of interest. This is possibly the most superior property I've had the privilege to put on the market.'

'Good grief,' Tony muttered to himself. An icy look from his wife silenced the protest that sprang to his lips. He felt a mischievous urge to enquire whether the agency might per-

98

haps have any small whitewashed stone cottages on their book that they could view instead.

Catherine turned to the agent with a brilliant smile. 'We'll be in touch,' she promised.

'There is absolutely no way we can even consider that house, Catherine,' Tony said with finality as they drove home. 'It's too far away from the hospital, not to mention the fact that the mortgage would cripple us financially for the next twenty years.'

'Let's just think about it for the moment, darling,' she said serenely. 'We'll talk about it tomorrow.'

Catherine wanted that house, and she was going to get it. She had known that from the moment she had entered it. In her mind she possessed it already. The details of arranging the legal and financial transactions might present a hassle but they were not beyond her abilities, not by any means.

Tony dropped her back at the flat, explaining that he had a patient he wished to check on and that he would be home for dinner within an hour. Catherine was happy enough. The evening she planned required special preparation.

Alone in the car, Tony opened the window to dissipate the cloying remnants of his wife's perfume. Taking a street map from the glovebox he searched for the address he had taken note of before leaving the hospital. Apprehension over the consequences of any interview with Shane Andrews had been overruled by concern about the trial patients. There was no home telephone so the only option was to pay a visit.

Curtains in neighbouring windows twitched as Tony rang the doorbell of the Andrews' house for the third time. He was about to leave when the door opened slowly.

Shane Andrews was dressed in a crumpled dark suit. His shirt was stained and the collar was open, a loosely knotted tie hanging like a necklace. He was unshaven, smelled strongly of alcohol, and gazed blearily at Tony for several seconds before recognising him. He turned then and walked wearily into the house, leaving the door open. Tony hesitated and then followed, closing the door behind him.

Glasses and bottles littered the surfaces of furniture in the living room that Tony entered. Shane was filling a glass with whisky. He offered it to Tony.

'Would you like something to drink?'

'No, thank you.'

Shane shrugged and sat down heavily on a red vinyl-covered couch, taking a long swallow of the drink.

'What can I do for you, Doctor? The party's over, I'm afraid. We had the funeral yesterday.'

Tony eyed the remnants of food and the bunches of flowers, none of which had been put in water and all of which were badly wilted.

'I'm sorry to intrude on you at this time, Mr. Andrews,' Tony said quietly. He took a seat facing Shane Andrews. 'I needed to talk to you about Sharon. It's worrying me that she had such an attack and I'd like to find out whether you know of anything that might have caused it.'

'What difference would it make?' Shane asked bitterly. 'It's not going to bring her back.' His hand trembled and he raised the glass it held shakily to his lips, draining it in a single draught.

'It may help the other asthmatic patients I have in my care at present, Shane,' Tony said gently.

He was silent.

'Sharon had a lot of allergies,' Tony continued. 'I wondered whether she might have been exposed to something the night before or the morning of her attack.'

Shane shrugged. 'Could have been, I guess. The neighbour's cat is a real nuisance – comes inside if the back door's left open. She usually gets problems after that. Got,' he corrected himself grimly, reaching for the whisky bottle again.

'Did she ever get attacks if she was at all depressed or if you had an argument?'

Shane spoke reluctantly after several seconds of silence. 'Yeah. Sometimes. But we hadn't had a fight that day if that's what you're getting at. She was a bit upset but that was because her mother stopped in on her way to work. She had a go at Sharon because we hadn't been to visit last week, on her father's birthday.'

'Was her mother smoking?'

Shane looked startled. 'Yeah. She always is. I left for work then myself. Me and her mum have never got on.'

100

Tony nodded. It was more information than he'd hoped for, more than he'd really wanted as it provided several possible explanations without any proof. Not wanting to keep Shane dwelling on the matter any longer, Tony rose to leave.

'You've been a help, Shane. I'm sorry if my visit's upset you.'

Shane looked at him wearily. 'I'm all right.'

'Before I go, would you possibly be able to give me the diary Sharon kept of her attacks for the trial? It's a small, folded cardboard sheet.'

'I already gave it to the other bloke.'

Tony was stunned. 'Who was that?'

'The guy from the drug company. He came here with my lawyer on Wednesday.'

'What did he want?'

Shane looked away. 'They decided to settle out of court. Said Sharon's death wasn't anything to do with their trial but they wanted to avoid publicity and court costs. My lawyer advised me to accept.'

Tony couldn't believe he was hearing this. There was something very odd about it. He tried to sound casual as he paused at the front door.

'How much did you settle on?'

Shane's voice had become slurred. He supported himself against the wall and waited until Tony was through the door before mumbling 'Five thousand pounds – that's what my wife was worth.'

Tony realised that he was receiving the full blast of Catherine's charm when he returned home but was unmoved, knowing that her intention was simply to manipulate him into agreeing to buy the property in Darras Hall. She had cooked dinner herself, something she normally only did when they were entertaining.

Catherine was justifiably proud of her talent for cooking. She knew every specialist food shop in Newcastle and could happily spend an entire day tracking down unusual ingredients. She would search out tofu, dried mushrooms and exotic spices for her oriental dishes. Italian food was a speciality and only fresh pasta was used. Catherine took

101

delight in using green, pink and sometimes even blue fettucine, linguine or tagliatelli. She loved to find cheeses that could provide a conversation point and dinners often ended with such varieties as Mascherpone with Gorgonzola, Satersleigh Goat, Bleu D'Auvergne or Swiss Appenzell. The beverage to accompany them might be Brazilian Bourbon coffee or Tanzanian Chagga, or a tea such as Assam or Formosa Oolong. In Catherine's special dishes, colour, shape and texture were combined with a skill that made her dinner parties famous, culinary *tours de force*, though Mrs. McKay was not always thrilled to have to cope with the clearing up the next day.

Catherine ignored Tony's quietness this evening and filled silences with the kind of light and amusing chatter that made her a sought after guest at other people's social functions.

At midnight, she drained the last drops from her liqueur glass, running the tip of her tongue sensuously around the rim. Her eyes glowed.

'Coming to bed, my love?' she asked Tony huskily.

He winced inwardly at the endearment and his voice was unusually cold. 'Not right now.' There was no way he could even contemplate entering her bed at that point. His lips tightened as he wondered in disgust whether she had even bothered to change the sheets. He forced the grimace into a smile. Catherine was watching him with what seemed a faintly contemptuous air of self-confidence.

'You go ahead, Catherine. I have some reading I really must catch up on.'

He entered the bedroom silently the next morning to collect a clean shirt. Catherine was deeply asleep. She was never troubled by insomnia and might well not even realise that her husband had spent the night on the couch. It had been a sleepless night in which the disclosure at the end of the interview with Shane Andrews had vied with the despair with which Tony contemplated his marriage.

The Saturday morning ward round and conference with the other members of the firm did not provide a respite from the depression dogging him. At one stage he made a telephone call in an attempt to dissipate one of the previous night's worries.

The call was to Colin Ingram at the Atlas drug company headquarters.

'I'd like to know just what the hell is going on,' he informed the drug company representative angrily.

'I'm sorry, Dr. Lawrence,' Colin said, unruffled but cautious. 'Could you be a bit more specific?'

'I certainly can! I'd like to know why your company has paid compensation to Shane Andrews.'

There was a short silence then Colin said calmly: 'That really doesn't concern you, Dr. Lawrence. It was a decision –'

'Like hell it doesn't concern me,' Tony interrupted. 'She was my patient. Are you trying to tell me you consider the trial responsible for her death?'

'Certainly not,' said Colin Ingram crisply, with a hint of anger. 'Which is why you were not informed of the matter. The compensation, as you call it, was paid simply because the young woman was involved with the trial of one of this company's products at the time of her death. We admitted no liability whatsoever, but simply wanted to avoid the adverse publicity that would have resulted from any legal proceedings. Our management and legal advisers considered it to be a reasonable course of action. If you wish to discuss it further I suggest you contact the head of my department, Dr. Greene.'

'I might just do that.' Tony was still not convinced. 'It seems to me like a peculiar thing to do.'

Hanging up the receiver, he felt dissatisfied. He debated calling Gordon Davies at home to try and clarify the matter but was prevented by the arrival of the call he had been dreading. Blood tests and bronchoscopy results from William Chalmers confirmed infection both by PCP and by Human T-cell Lymphotropic Virus Type 111. There was no excuse left to postpone the interview.

Colin Ingram stared at the now silent telephone on his desk. He toyed with a pencil, his expression unreadable. The pencil snapped with a sudden crack and he sniggered softly. Then his eyes glazed and the pieces of pencil slipped unheeded from his fingers as the snigger developed into a shrill and decidedly bizarre giggle.

103

Tony unhooked the chart from the end of Bill Chalmers' bed, taking refuge in the action as he searched for a starting point to the interview. The persistent dry coughing from the bed filled the awkward silence. Tony wondered where to position himself. If he sat on the visitors' chair, he would have to look up at his patient, which would be disconcerting. If he stood, a safe but impersonal barrier was created. He compromised and perched on the end of the bed.

'Can you remember clearly that attack of glandular fever you had, Bill?'

The patient nodded. 'It's the only illness I've had in more than ten years. . .' He coughed and shook his head with annonyance. 'Until now, that is.'

'Think back to the weeks just prior to that attack. Were you having a sexual relationship with anyone at the time?'

Bill looked taken aback. 'I guess so.'

'Can you remember who it was?'

'Yes, of course I can,' Bill said indignantly, punctuating his words with a bout of coughing. 'Look, what's this got to do with anything? It's ancient history.'

Tony took a deep breath. 'Right now, you're suffering from a form of pneumonia called Pneumocystis Carinii pneumonia – PCP. It's treatable and nothing to get alarmed about at this stage, but . ..' He paused. 'It's the commonest presentation of Acquired Immune Deficiency Syndrome and –'

'Acquired what?' Bill interupted worriedly.

'Immune deficiency syndrome. AIDS.'

Bill laughed with obvious relief. 'So that's what's bothering you. No, Doctor Lawrence,' he stated firmly. 'There's no way I'm gay.'

'It's possible to be infected outside of homosexual relationships, Bill, and I'm afraid your tests confirm the presence of the virus which causes the syndrome.'

'It's not possible.' Bill shook his head. 'The results have to be a mistake.'

'It's possible to contract the virus through sharing needles in drug taking, blood transfusion, possibly an accident involving contact with infected blood, or even a sexual relationship with a female who's had an infected partner. That's why I asked you about your partner earlier. An attack of glandular fever-type illness can indicate the initial contraction of the virus. It may take years to develop into AIDS.'

'How many years?'

'Maybe up to four or five. Perhaps longer, we don't really know yet.'

Bill Chalmers had paled noticeably. 'Oh, my god.' He rubbed the palm of his hand across his forehead. 'Jesus,' he muttered.

Tony waited, frowning slightly. Bill looked up, his eyes shadowed by fear.

'The girl, the one I was sleeping with before I met Caroline? It only lasted a couple of months. Well, she – Susan, her name was, she . . .' Bill coughed again and swallowed painfully. 'She had just left her husband because she found out he was bisexual. But it was so long ago. I haven't even thought of her in years.' Tony began to speak but Bill continued wildly. 'I just don't believe this. How the hell am I going to tell Caroline?'

Tony said quietly, 'I'm afraid she's going to have to be tested as well, Bill.'

Bill gazed at him in horror. 'You mean she . . . Oh, God! What about the baby?'

'It's possible that your wife may have been infected but has not contracted AIDS but there has been a case in the States where a haemophiliac contracted AIDS, passed it on to his pregnant wife and the baby contracted it as well.'

The sick man was silent, his eyes tightly shut.

'That doesn't necessarily mean it's happened in your case,' Tony said calmly. 'But we'll have to check. I'll be around the hospital this afternoon so I'll come back when your wife comes in to visit you. I'd like to talk to you both.'

Bill remained silent.

'Is there anything you'd like to ask right now?'

He shook his head, turning his face to the pillow. Tony rose, ready to leave and give him some time alone.

'It's not the end of the road. Not by a long shot. I'll bring some information when I come in later and we'll talk some more. Get the nurse to call me if you want to see me before then. OK?'

At the patient's resigned nod, Tony left. Nicola Jarvis had

105

stayed on to discuss the department's research work, also a regular Saturday meeting. She was confident that the salbutamol trial could be wrapped up within the next eight weeks. Tony could relax about that pressure at least. She assured him she had everything under control.

Bruce Matheson was no better and Tony left instructions with the ICU staff to notify him of any change over the weekend, leaving several telephone numbers at which he might be contacted. His depression increased a degree as he went to his office to catch up on some more paper work.

The afternoon sped by, interrupted only by the predictably difficult interview with Caroline Chalmers. She was shocked and frightened, her immediate reaction anger at her husband for endangering both herself and their unborn child. Tony spent an hour with them both but didn't feel he'd provided anything but the destruction of their hopes for the future. He knew it would all have to be repeated, as neither Bill nor Caroline would have completely understood his explanations and prognosis in that emotional climate. He had taken the blood test from Caroline himself, knowing there was little hope that she might have escaped infection.

Chapter Twelve

Catherine had a gin and tonic waiting for Tony when he arrived back at the flat. She sat down beside him.

'I was hoping you'd be back in time for us to talk before we go out to dinner, darling. I'll have to get ready soon, though. You're going to love the dress I found.'

'I'm sure you'll look as gorgeous as always, Cat.' Tony felt a palpable weariness enfold him as he swallowed a mouthful of his drink.

'So, darling.' Catherine's voice sparkled with contained excitement. 'Have you had time to think about that wonderful house?'

'I don't need time,' Tony said patiently. 'It's way out of our price range, and what on earth do we need six bedrooms for anyway? To have them ready for the children we'll never have?'

Catherine's eyes narrowed and she moved to a seat opposite Tony. Her voice echoed her husband's patient tone. 'I'd like to be able to give weekend parties, Tony. They would be well used as guest rooms.'

'Is that how you see your future, Catherine? As hostess supreme of the Northern Counties?' Tony's voice held an edge of bitterness.

She eyed him coldly. 'What exactly is that supposed to mean?'

'Well, what exactly do you want out of life? Are we headed for an endless round of parties, dinners, and group jacuzzi sessions?'

'It shouldn't bother you too much,' Catherine snapped.

'You're never at home long enough.'

'Perhaps when I am in my own home, I'd prefer it not to be inundated with strangers,' Tony countered with rising anger.

Catherine's lips tightened. 'I'm going to get dressed. I suggest you finish your drink and try to cultivate some sense of your social obligations before we go out.'

Tony was furious. 'The social "obligations" I have,' he said, enunciating his words with icy precision, 'are generated solely by you. And, what's more, I don't give a tinker's shit about them! Take a good look in the mirror while you're getting ready, Catherine. You're thirty-five years old, and what have you got to show for it but a collection of your precious social obligations? Oh, yes –' he added sarcastically – 'there's all the superbly suitable clothes you've spent years collecting, and the cream of the cosmetic industry's preparations to hide any presumptuous wrinkles.' He slammed his glass on to the coffee table and strode to the drinks cabinet, removing the packet of cigarettes and a box of matches.

Catherine's fingers had involuntarily moved to her eyes for an instant, gently touching the surrounding skin. The urge to reassure herself with a glance in the mirror sent her out of the room.

Tony had noticed her instantaneous reaction to his taunt. He felt an incredible wave of contempt mixed with an urge to inflict pain equal to that he was experiencing. His words were unleashed at his wife's retreating back like poison-tipped spears.

'Not that wrinkles will present a problem, will they, Catherine? I'm sure you'd be able to find an eminent plastic surgeon you could persuade to give you a discount. Or perhaps he might even prefer an alternative form of payment.'

Catherine had reached the door. She glanced back, her face white, and mouthed an inaudible retort.

She reappeared in the room an hour later and seated herself calmly on the couch, without looking at Tony who sat beside an ashtray crowded with butts. Her face betrayed no emotion whatsoever as she clicked open her black satin evening bag to check on its contents. Her voice was as expressionless as her face.

'The taxi will be here in ten minutes.' Catherine preferred

to use taxis on social occasions to avoid any problems with either parking or the amount of alcohol consumed.

'Fuck the taxi. I'll take my own car, thank you,' said Tony. When his words produced no reaction he angrily stubbed out the cigarette he was holding. 'Jesus Christ,' he seethed.

The Davies' elegant reception room was packed with notable medics and their wives. Catherine was warmly welcomed and soon conversing animatedly with acquaintances, carefully avoiding any group which included her husband. Tony eyed the scene with displeasure and gritted his teeth as the head of Cardiology in the Northern congratulated him on his charming wife.

He listened abstractedly to a monologue about the disastrous effect the weather was having on farmers this year. The speaker owned a farm that was being managed for him so Tony guessed that he was more worried about the profit margin from his investment than the effect on the farming economy or families in general.

His eyes roved over the collection of expensive trophies Davies had collected on his travels. A flash of wry amusement came as he noted the antique Lewis chess set displayed on an onyx and marble board. The only pieces in their correct positions were the pawns. The back rows were a jumble of placements intolerable to the eye of anyone who played the game. Tony itched to rearrange them. He was distracted by Mrs. Davies and selected a stuffed olive from the dish she was offering him.

'I wonder how long you will be with us this evening, Anthony,' she smiled.

Tony smiled back. Mrs. God was really a very pleasant person. She had a genuine warmth which survived despite her husband's domination but was apparent only so long as she wasn't in his company.

'It would take an acute emergency to force me to miss your wonderful cooking, Jane.'

'It's not a patch on Catherine's, as you well know. But thank you.' She placed the dish of olives on the centre of the chessboard. 'I'd better go and see what chaos is brewing in the kitchen, if you'll excuse me.'

Tony found himself isolated between two conversations, neither of which appealed to him. One concerned the merits of various local boarding schools, comparing the degrees of excellence in education the participants felt their offspring were receiving. The other was exploring the probable outcome of a fatal accident inquiry on an even more local disaster. The heart of a middle-aged woman had been punctured during a procedure to insert a tube to drain a chest infection.

'Of course, the heart shouldn't have been where it was,' explained the speaker. 'It had shifted considerably and attached itself to the chest wall after the removal of a lung twelve months ago.'

'How inconsiderate of it,' Tony muttered to himself. He wasn't in the mood to dissect the case. He had enough ongoing personal disasters without dining out on someone else's. He sipped at his sherry and thought longingly of being in a pub with Hugh, a pint in one hand and a cigarette in the other. He eyed a dignified-looking gentleman wreathed in a cloud of cigar smoke, taking in the view from the large picture windows. He obviously didn't know Davies or, more likely, was important enough not to give a damn about the small 'Thank You For Not Smoking' signs arranged at intervals around the room which contrasted oddly with the objets d'art. Tony had just decided to go and introduce himself and at least do a bit of passive smoking, when Jane Davies reappeared by his side.

'Telephone call for you,' she whispered.

The Northern's operator was on the line. 'ICU calling you, Dr. Lawrence. I'll put you through.'

Clare's voice was agitated. 'Tony? It's Bruce Matheson. He's had a grand mal epileptic seizure and arrested. They're working on him now.'

'I'm on my way.' Tony replaced the receiver and glanced back towards the reception room. Jane Davies stood in the doorway. She smiled sympathetically.

'I'll give Catherine a doggy bag for you.'

As Tony left the party and sped towards the Northern, Nicola Jarvis finished drying her dinner dishes and poured herself another glass of wine. She checked that the door to her apartment was firmly bolted and locked, switched off the

110

lights and went into her bedroom. Her breathing quickened as she began the elaborate ritual that was her Saturday night. It was the highlight of her week and always awaited with eager anticipation.

She drew the curtains, turned down the bedclothes and dimmed the lights to a soft glow from her bedside lamp. She banked up the pillows and spread a large, soft towel over the sheet covering the mattress. Then she opened the locked drawer under her bedside table. She removed a photograph set in a silver frame and positioned it carefully under the lamp, turned towards the pillows. She stroked it lightly with her fingertips and smiled gently. She then removed a bottle and cylindrical object with a smooth, tapering tip from the drawer, placing them on either side of the photograph.

Nicola left the bedside and sat in front of the large central mirror of her dressing table, tilting the wing mirrors so that her profiles were visible. She removed the pins imprisoning her hair and brushed it into a fine cloud that settled on to her shoulders. Discarding the brush, she picked up her wineglass, eyeing her reflection as she sipped. Her reflection revealed a seductiveness nobody at the hospital had guessed at as her head tilted, her lips pouted slightly and she glanced at herself with lowered lids. The pout became a smile.

'Why, thank you,' she whispered huskily. 'I didn't think you'd noticed.'

Seconds later, she giggled. 'Really?' she asked a profile.

She looked down at her lap and her eyes were serious as they met themselves again.

'But I've always loved you. I always will. There will never be anyone else.' She shook her head gently in response to the unspoken question. 'It could never be too soon for me.'

Her eyes shut and her lips parted for long seconds. Her breath was a shudder and her eyes remained closed as she rose from her seat and slowly eased herself out of her clothes.

Naked, Nicola moved with the grace of a cat towards the bed. She pulled the stopper from the crystal bottle and poured some of its contents into her palm. She shivered with excitement as the scent surrounded her. Musk oil. This smell, for Nicola, was synonymous with sex and fulfillment. She dipped a finger into her cupped palm and touched it to her nipples, already hard and burning with expectation. Then she dribbled the oil down between her breasts. Her hands gently chased the rivulets, smoothing them across her belly and between her thighs.

With her eyes closed, Nicola lay back on her pillows, spreading her thighs by bending her knees and touching the soles of her feet together. She lay for a moment, revelling in the pure sexuality she was exuding, then she opened her eyes and gazed into the face set within the silver frame. Her right hand moved towards the object resting beside the beloved face and as her fingers clicked the switch on its base, a humming sound filled the heavily perfumed air.

'Oh, God,' Nicola moaned. She couldn't wait. Even the sound was too much. Her nipples ached and her hips undulated gently with desire. She held the vibrator for only a second against the opening of her vagina and then slowly, with the gentlest touch, moved it up towards her clitoris.

The release her body screamed for came within seconds and she moaned with joy at the exquisite sinking sensation that heralded her climax.

She shut off the hum as she lay waiting for her breathing and pulse rate to subside to normal levels, enjoying the tingling sensation running through her limbs. She smiled. The whole wonderful Saturday night lay before her to coax her body again and again to physical rapture. And there was so much to tell her lover when they rested.

In the early hours of Sunday morning came repletion at last. The name on her lips, as her exhausted body jerked convulsively with the final orgasm she had the strength to generate, was the name of the face within the silver frame, still softly illuminated by the burning lamp: the name and face of Dr. Tony Lawrence.

Chapter Thirteen

Irene McTavish eased her bulk into the armchair which, over the years, had moulded itself to accommodate her generous curves. She was tired and her breathing was wheezy and uncomfortable. She knew why, however, so wasn't too worried about it.

Last week, to her delight, she had been invited to join the 'Women for Christ' prayer group at her church. They held weekly meetings to pray together, particularly for their more unfortunate acquaintances who had not yet seen the light. Irene intended to focus initially on Dr. Lawrence. They met at each others' houses and Irene was due to welcome the group in two weeks' time. Her enthusiasm for anything connected with the church had led to her decision to spring clean the house in preparation for the occasion. She had also decided to repaint the kitchen cupboards to cover up the years of gouge marks left by Brent's penknife. She had chosen a lovely bright shade of pink and had been working hard at the task for much of the day. The gouge marks hadn't vanished but at least they were less obvious now, being the same colour as the rest of the paintwork. Perhaps another coat of paint would do the trick.

It was the fumes from the paint which had caused the present upset to Irene's breathing. She took a deep breath and expelled it with some effort and a loud wheeze. Whenever Brent heard her like this he asked, with a snigger, who she intended making the obscene 'phone call to? It had been funny for the first few times. Irene sighed noisily. Brent was on her mind rather a lot lately. She supposed he was just going through a difficult phase but she wished he was easier to handle. Irene had been encouraged when he had not resisted attending the church but now she wished he would stay at home. He had taken to sitting at the back of the hall, loudly shouting 'Hallelujah' at inappropriate moments. The tolerance of the congregation was beginning to wear a little thin and Irene feared her own standing might be affected. This was why it was so important to make a good impression on the women's group. Her desire to get back into the kitchen and complete her painting turned her thoughts away from her present discomfort.

'Lord, guide me,' she said aloud, holding her pudgy hands with the sausage-like fingers palm upwards.

She shut her eyes and sat back, confidently expecting a message as she cleared her mind. It came with a clarity that surprised her. The message too was a surprise so she waited a while longer, not really questioning what her mind told her to do but wanting to make sure no countermanding order would arrive. No other ideas occurred to her so she gripped the arms of the chair and heaved herself to her feet. She went into the kitchen, wading through the thick layer of newspaper on the floor. Another layer covered the kitchen table where the paintpot and brush sat in the midst of a sea of pink dribbles and spots. Irene eyed her work so far with satisfaction. It was a very pretty colour and she still had time to run up some curtains to match before the night of the meeting. Laura Ashley was bound to provide a perfect fabric in the right shade of pink.

She made her way over to the bench which was littered with the objects that usually lived on the kitchen table. Irene paused to remove the sections of newspaper which had glued themselves to her shoes due to the sticky pink spots she had been unable to avoid. She eased the kettle from behind the breadboard, knocking the half loaf into the sink along with the breadknife. She filled the kettle with water and placed it on the stove, turning up the gas beneath it. Then she sorted through the various pots of jam, salt and pepper shakers and sauce bottles, looking for the packet of herbal tea. She found it finally, wedged behind the large plastic tomato that held the sauce she and Brent loved to pour over their chips every night. The water was still a long way off boiling so Irene decided to attend to the second and more puzzling part of her message while she waited.

She sat in her armchair again while she rummaged through her cavernous handbag. She removed a dozen or so used tissues and discarded them on the floor. After adding a handful of bus tickets, several outpatient appointment cards, numerous chocolate bar wrappers and two as yet unopened packets of crisps, she found what she was searching for. Irene read the label on the bottle. Patient 06, Week 7, Double-blind, crossover trial, Salbutamol vs Placebo. Gazing at the bottle, she wondered why it had occurred to her to take one of these capsules now. The guidance to withdraw from the trial and to avoid doctors in favour of spiritual and herbal remedies had been very strong only the week before. While puzzled, however, Irene was not going to dispute the message. She had complete faith that when she asked for guidance and cleared her mind, whatever first occurred to her was the only course of action.

Irene unscrewed the cap of the bottle and tipped its contents into her hand. There weren't very many left. Both halves of the capsules were a plain white. They looked identical to the other capsules at all the previous stages of the trial but Irene knew that this was done so that no one knew whether she was taking the medication or the sugar pills.

'These are probably sugar pills,' she told herself, poking through them with her forefinger. One capsule dislodged itself from her palm and caught in her lap on a fold of her skirt. This seemed a good indication to Irene that this was the one to take so she put the others back into the bottle and swallowed the errant capsule with the water she had brought from the kitchen. She waited a few minutes, eyeing the bags of crisps speculatively. Cheese and onion, her favourite, but she didn't feel very tempted. Perhaps with the cup of tea. Irene listened in vain for the squeaks the kettle made as it came to the boil, its whistle having long since broken. Her breathing was becoming more difficult.

'Bloody sugar pills,' she said angrily. That was it, she decided. Her guidance had been to take medication but the pills were fakes. She must be supposed to use her inhaler.

115

Another search of the handbag proved futile and Irene groaned as she levered herself out of the chair again.

Climbing the stairs to the bathroom required a concentrated effort. Irene paused on each step to try and catch her breath, wheezing so stertorously she failed to hear the squeaks emitted by the kettle. Reaching the bathroom was an achievement and she felt encouraged as she sorted through the small cupboard on the wall. She moved bottles of hand-lotion and makeup, the cough mixture Brent had had last year and the half empty bottles of antibiotics. Irene had never believed in finishing a course once she began to feel better. Some of them were years old now but she was a bit of a squirrel and never liked to throw out anything which might be useful later. She switched her attention to the cupboard beneath the basin and finally found the plastic canister she was seeking, behind the Tampax.

Irene perched on the edge of the bath, removed the cap from the inhaler and gave it a shake. She forced some air out of her lungs, then placed the mouthpiece of the inhaler to her lips and pressed the canister as she inhaled. Tasting it on her tongue and around her lips, Irene was aware that her technique had been poor, so she tried again. Twice.

Expecting imminent relief from her symptoms, she placed the inhaler beside the soap in the basin and decided to relieve the tension in her bladder before returning to the kitchen to make her tea. Attending to the calls of nature was a task she disliked and did as little as possible, especially in the winter, and she wanted to avoid having to mount the stairs again in the near future. The layers of clothes were awkwardly time consuming, and the toilet seat icy cold. It was bad enough even in the summer, as Irene's ample buttocks considerably overflowed the area of the moulded plastic seat and the toilet roll holder on the wall bit painfully into her thigh. As she urinated, Irene was pleased to note that even in these circumstances she was feeling a little more relaxed. She had been aware earlier of her heart beating faster than normal, as it usually did when she had an asthmatic attack, but now it had slowed so as to be barely noticeable. Her breathing was no better yet, though, and she was gasping as she struggled to rebutton her spencer and reattach the surgical stockings to

116

her suspenders, the fasteners of which always popped under strain.

As she straightened, Irene felt a new constriction in her chest. Her lungs just seemed to refuse her body's command to expel the air contained in them. She gave a desperate grunt as she gathered up her abdominal muscles for extra push.

'Don't panic,' she told herself, but it soon became an impossible order to follow. She gripped the sides of the handbasin and hunched over it. Irene felt an edge of terror creeping rapidly towards her. In her worst asthmatic attacks, and there had been many over the years, she had never felt anything like this. She could feel her face filling with blood as she struggled to breathe. She was shifting a small amount of air but she knew it was not enough and she would soon be exhausted by the effort. She felt a wave of dizziness, and trickles of perspiration on her face and her back. She had to get help. Her neighbours would probably be at home and could 'phone an ambulance for her. They were only a few steps away from her front door but the stairs presented a very unwelcome obstacle.

The water had long since evaporated from the kettle on Irene McTavish's stove but the flames still licked at it relentlessly. The metal blackened and the flames crept further up the sides. The black plastic handle began to melt in the intense heat and as a drop of molten plastic dripped off, it passed through the edge of a flame and ignited with a joyous spurt on its journey to the floor. The pink paint-spattered newspaper it landed on responded instantly and flames spread themselves quickly across the floor, lapping at the legs of the table and the bottom of the cupboards, freshly pink and still damp and sticky. As the new paint heated and caught light, it emitted a pungent black smoke which filled the room, pressing itself initially to the ceiling but rapidly reaching lower levels. The paint can on the kitchen table exploded, adding a huge belch of poisonous smoke and forcing the kitchen door wide open.

Irene heard the explosion as she descended the first few steps of the stairwell. She gripped the bannister and stared in horror at the thundercloud of smoke billowing towards her. She had time only to turn and throw herself towards the landing before the smoke reached her. She covered her face

117

with her arms. The condition her lungs were in already prevented the release of the primal scream echoing in her head. She felt the burning of the smoke penetrating her nostrils, throat and lungs and all efforts at breathing ceased. Irene McTavish was fully aware that she was suffocating and panic obliterated any faith she may have had in an afterlife. She dimly heard the shouts from below as neighbours broke open the door to confront the inpenetrable barrier of heat and smoke. She knew it was too late and almost thankfully felt her panic fade into oblivion.

The men of the Tyne and Wear fire department controlled the fire with relative ease. It was with more difficulty that four of them manoeuvred Irene's body down the stairwell and on to the waiting ambulance stretcher. A valiant resuscitation attempt was made, as no flames had actually reached, her, but Irene McTavish was pronounced dead on arrival at the hospital they took her to and no further attempt was made. Cause of death was listed as smoke inhalation and no inquest was ordered.

Chapter Fourteen

The Monday morning ward round was interrupted when the ward clerk approached the group of doctors and other staff surrounding the bed of only the second patient they were reviewing.

'Telephone call for you, Dr. Lawrence,' she said apologetically.

Tony had ignored the beeping of his page a few minutes previously while examining the patient and now he looked irritated.

'Take a message for me, will you please, Mary?' he asked.

'It's Mr. Harrison,' she said in explanation. 'He said he was sorry to interrupt your round but it was urgent.'

'OK.' Tony replaced the chart, fitting the clip over the hook on the foot of the patient's bed. He smiled in resignation at his colleagues. Hugh looked sympathetic but Arthur Stewart, the senior consultant, looked annoyed.

Tony listened to what the chief general surgeon, John Harrison, had to say with a curiosity tinged with dismay. He left the respiratory ward immediately and walked swiftly to men's general surgical ward, A7. He was met by John Harrison and led into an office where the door was closed firmly behind them. David Laing was huddled over the radiator at one side of the room. Although the office was overheated to the degree typical of hospital interiors, he was shivering visibly. Mr. Harrison ran a hand through his greying hair as he spoke.

'Thanks for coming so promptly, Dr. Lawrence. I'd like a word before you see the patients I mentioned. I didn't like to say too much on the phone.' His smile of welcome flickered only briefly.

Tony nodded. John Harrison was a highly respected surgeon in the Northern and Tony knew his reputation although he had not had any personal contact with him previously. He was well liked as well as respected, which was unusual for a surgeon, but Mr. Harrison was noted for a calm and genial temperament, even when under stress in theatre. At present he was looking very worried and his introduction of Tony to David was abstracted. Tony noted the shivering and clammy feel of David's hand as he shook it but kept his concern silent as he listened to what John Harrison was saying.

'We've had several cases of pneumonia in the last couple of weeks. Two deaths of elderly patients which weren't entirely unexpected and the chappie I mentioned to you earlier who's pretty sick right now. He's a sixty-five-year-old that David started on penicillin last Thursday.' John Harrison nodded towards David and then looked grimly at Tony. 'Because of the previous outbreaks of Legionnaires' in the past year, it's routine for any case of pneumonia for a series of antibody titres to be done.'

Tony raised his eyebrows expectantly as Harrison continued. 'One of the initial patient's results were confirmed by the lab this morning. It seems we have our own outbreak of Legionnaires' Disease on our hands.'

Tony said nothing and Harrison continued worriedly, 'So, you can see why I didn't want to say too much on the phone. We've put the wheels in motion for testing the water supplies and so on and have closed the ward to new admissions. Of course, we have no idea whether the outbreak is confined to this ward or where the source is. We've called you in to help with examination of all patients here now but Administration wants it kept quiet for as long as possible. This will be the third outbreak in the North in twelve months and the press will have a field day as soon as they get wind of it.'

'That's true enough,' agreed Tony. 'We'd better get started. The priority is obviously this critical chap of yours but after him I think I'd better give Dr. Laing here an examination.'

'It's only a cold,' protested David.

'You should know that Legionnaires' is most likely to be contracted by anyone in an already weakened condition,' Tony reminded him. 'A virus of any sort and contact with Legionella pneumophila makes even young people susceptible. What's more, you look pretty unwell from where I'm standing.'

John Harrison agreed. He rested a hand on David's shoulder as they left the office. 'No arguments, young man. I don't want you out of action any longer than necessary.'

Ray Higgins had deteriorated considerably since David had first seen him. His temperature had skyrocketed in the last twelve hours and he was now having a lot of difficulty breathing. His breath sounds dominated the room and his face had a bluish tinge. Tony picked up his chart. The temperature recordings looked like the profit margin graph of an enormously successful company.

'What about titres?'

David sounded hoarse. 'We took one off initially but it wasn't too out of the ordinary. The results are here.' David handed Ray's notes to Tony. 'A second sample was sent off this morning.'

Tony nodded. A rise in numbers over the last few days would indicate an active infection. He quickly scanned results of other tests done and clipped the chest x-rays on to the viewer in rapid succession. His examination of the patient was thorough but swift. Ray Higgins was exhausted, the effort of dragging air into his lungs almost too much. His level of consciousness was slipping. By the end of the examination his only response to Tony's commands was to force his eyelids open briefly.

Tony charted and gave the first dose of Erythromycin, the antibiotic which should have been given initially with the slightest suspicion that the pneumonia could be other than pneumococcal. Even changing the treatment now was unlikely to benefit Ray Higgins. Tony authorised his immediate transfer to Intensive Care as ventilation was already necessary and possibly overdue. He ordered a repeat of all tests done in the last few days and added arterial blood gas measurements to be done at once. He paged Hugh and asked him to be in ICU to supervise admission and to have the anaesthetics registrar there, ready for the ventilation procedure.

When that was organised, Tony took David into an unoccupied side room and examined him carefully. He had a raised temperature and cough and admitted to pleuritic pain. He could feel a distinct 'catching' when he took a deep breath. Tony listened to his chest, took some blood samples and ordered David off to x-ray with instructions to bring the film back to the ward as soon as it had been developed.

The next two hours were spent checking the other inpatients of A7. One patient was found to have had symptoms for a week though had not complained about them.

'Didn't want to be a nuisance,' he explained. 'And I've always had a bit of a cough from the smoking, anyway.'

Another two patients were found to be feeling generally weak, with diffuse aches and pains and off their food, and a further case had been suffering from diarrhoea for several days, all indications of possible infection. A wide spectrum of tests were ordered including antibody titres to be done on all patients, and nursing staff were instructed to monitor all patients carefully.

David Laing returned with his x-ray which showed a faint patch of consolidation in one lung. Tony injected him with the initial dose of an Erythromycin course and ordered bed rest. David protested strongly but Tony was adamant and threatened to admit him if he didn't comply.

'You're living in, aren't you?' he asked.

David nodded with resignation.

'Well, you can stay in your own room. I'll come up and check on you later today. If you're no worse tomorrow, I might let you up again as long as you don't overtire yourself.'

'Great,' David muttered glumly, his face totally dispirited.

'Is there anyone else living in who would be able to keep an eye on you?'

David's face brightened. 'There's Kay Patterson. She might spare me a minute or two.'

Tony grinned. 'I'll call her and let her know that a large dose of TLC is your only hope of survival.'

'Thanks, Dr. Lawrence.' David's smile was cheerful. 'I'll invite you to the wedding.'

As Legionella pneumophila is a water-borne bacteria, tests were already in progress around the ward fixtures. The most likely cause was the air-conditioning system which meant that other wards could well be affected. Staff were alerted and Tony knew that the hope of delaying exposure of the outbreak to the press was a forlorn one. Television and newspaper journalists were probably even now converging on Administration in response to a helpful phone call from someone on staff who had a friend in the business that they wanted to provide with a 'scoop'.

When Tony returned to his own ward, the round was still in progress. Arthur Stewart, his registrar, housesurgeon and the senior nursing staff were gathered around a bed in one of the last rooms. Tony ignored them, however, and made his way to the bed of Florence Murdock. The lack of any improvement in her condition since her admission last Thursday had been a worry. Tony was now mildly alarmed. If Legionnaires' showed up in recent admissions, then the source of the outbreak was going to be much harder to trace and a certain amount of panic would be instilled in the general public. Tony asked whether this admission had been the first visit Florence had made to the hospital recently.

'Oh no,' she replied. 'My father-in-law was in the week before last having his gall bladder removed. I was in to visit him every day while he was in here.'

Tony wasn't sure whether he felt relieved or not. 'What ward was he in?'

'A7,' replied Florence.

Tony was already changing the chart orders and writing out a request form for an antibody titres test. 'I'm going to start a different antibiotic for you which should clear up these bugs a lot faster. We'll do a few more tests as well.' He smiled at his patient who smiled back. She was perfectly confident that this charming young doctor would have her cured in no time.

As Tony had feared, it didn't take long for the press to get wind of the outbreak of Legionnaires' Disease at the Northern. Having left Florence Murdock he paused on the way to his office to join a knot of staff watching Gordon Davies being interviewed for television, his white coat firmly buttoned as usual. Tony decided it made him look like a factory supervisor or perhaps a cleaner. He listened to the well-modulated voice of an accustomed public speaker.

'As I'm sure you are well aware, Legionnaires' Disease is caused by a water- or mist-borne bacteria. It was named after a 1976 outbreak at an American Legion function which claimed, I believe, twenty-nine lives.'

Gordon Davies spoke directly to the camera which the interviewer found intensely irritating. He interrupted the monologue.

'The death toll in the Staffordshire outbreak in May 1985 was . . .'

'Ah, yes.' Davies glanced at the interviewer briefly, then turned to face the camera again with a confident smile. 'The main problem with Legionnaires' is that it is very difficult to diagnose in its early stages. In the case of that particular outbreak, it took nearly three weeks to discover that it was not, in fact, a virus causing a severe type of influenza. Largely thanks to the unfortunate outbreaks in Britain recently, we have managed to make the diagnosis very early on and appropriate treatment has been instigated.'

'How much of the hospital is affected, Dr. Davies?' The interviewer took advantage of the consultant's pause for breath.

'That's impossible to say at present. However, I am confident that the situation is under control. We have a team from the Communicable Diseases Centre investigating the source and all possible precautions are being taken.'

The interviewer tried again. 'In an earlier outbreak in Glasgow, two staff members – a consultant anaesthetist and a student nurse – died of Legionnaires' Disease contracted in a new ward . . .'

Davies interrupted smoothly. 'That bears no relation whatsoever to our situation.'

Tony thought of David Laing and felt thankful that the young doctor now had a hefty dose of antibiotics circulating. He left the swelling group of people, knowing that Davies could handle anything the press cared to come up with and disliking watching the physician's obvious enjoyment of being the centre of attention, and was then caught himself by a newspaper reporter who had somehow found out about his involvement in the situation.

He hoped they would not sniff out the AIDS patient upstairs to add to the pressure. There was more than the usual interest in AIDS at present, owing to the statistics relating to the disease amongst the heroin addicts in Edinburgh. The latest concern was for the future of the high number of babies born infected with the virus to addict mothers. The fear of the general public, of potential contagion, now on the increase due to advertising campaigns, made any news of cases worth reporting and Tony dreaded seeing a headline of 'First AIDS case in Newcastle's Northern Infirmary.' With so many reporters milling about and talking to anyone who would give them a minute or two, it was quite possible that one would ferret out the case.

Hugh McGinty had been due to present the case of Sharon Andrews at the monthly death review of the respiratory department held over the Monday lunch period which alternated with normal 'conference' which presented cases of interest for review and discussion. The monthly death review came up too often for most concerned. It was a depressing business picking over unsuccessful cases at the best of times but, to add insult to injury, these sessions were dominated by the senior pathologist, an exceedingly boring man who conducted expressionless and lengthy monologues that were of little benefit or interest to the listeners.

It was with some relief that he read a memo posted outside the conference room. The review had been postponed in favour of a staff meeting concerning the outbreak of Legionnaires'. The meeting was packed and a reporter who had managed to sneak in was requested to remove himself which he did reluctantly, to hover in the hallway outside, hoping for a later interview.

Guidelines on observation and management were given. The alert would be hospital wide until the source of the outbreak was confirmed which might take several days. Referral of suspected cases was to be to Tony Lawrence or Arthur Stewart and pressure from the media was to be directed to Gordon Davies. Severe cases were to be transferred to ICU and the respiratory wards could handle any overflow of ventilator cases if pressure on ICU facilities made it necessary.

Leaving the meeting, Tony caught his chief consultant's eye.

'What is it, Lawrence?'

'I'm concerned about this salbutamol trial we're running.'

'In what connection?' Gordon Davies was obviously impatient to continue his role as a media star.

'I think we should abort the trial.'

'What?' Davies' anger was instant and threatening.

'We've had two patient deaths,' insisted Tony quietly. 'I don't like it and –'

'What you like or don't like, Lawrence,' the consultant's tone was menacing, 'has little or nothing to do with what *I* say is done in this department. *My* department. If you are incapable of supervising this trial I'll get Arthur Stewart to do it or do it myself, but it will be completed. Do you understand?' Davies turned to leave, not waiting for a reply.

Tony grimaced mentally at the thought of either Arthur Stewart or Gordon Davies becoming involved in the physical running of an outpatient trial, or any research for that matter. Gordon Davies' only publications in the last six years had been those papers of Tony's that he'd insisted on taking first authorship on. Arthur Stewart's only contribution to these papers, that he'd also appeared as co-author of, had been to provide suitable patients when they became available. Gordon Davies' dependence on the finance provided by drug trials was exceeded only by Arthur Stewart's total lack of interest in the field.

Tony raised his voice slightly. 'There was another matter, Dr. Davies.'

The physician's slowly straightening spine reflected extreme irritation. Without turning back to face Tony he snapped: 'Yes?'

'I was wondering why Atlas had paid a substantial amount of compensation to Shane Andrews, unless they felt that the trial was in some way responsible for her death?'

Davies turned deliberately, meeting Tony's stare with ill-concealed fury. He spoke softly, aware that other people could be within earshot.

'I don't know what you are talking about, Dr. Lawrence. What's more, I don't think you do either. Any matter relating to Shane Andrews ceased to be any of your business when Sharon Andrews ceased to be your patient. I can assure you that you will regret meddling in matters that do not concern you. Do the job that you're paid to do, Lawrence, or I'll find someone else who will.'

Gordon Davies' voice rose as he finished his sentence, attracting the attention of some reporters hovering nearby. One raised an eyebrow to his companion and made a beeline to try and intercept Davies as he strode away. He was unsuccessful and, disappointingly, by the time he returned the younger doctor had also left.

Tony didn't manage to catch up with Hugh again until late that afternoon. He found him with Bob Matthews who had started his new run with their firm that day. They were having a cup of coffee in the doctors' lounge on the fourth floor and both had newspapers spread out before them. Tony got himself a drink as he greeted them.

'Are they the evening papers?'

'Yep. We're starring on the front page.' Bob folded the paper back to show Tony.

'Well, we like to give the new firm members a bit of excitement to start them off. How's it going, Bob?'

'Flat out. This is the first break we've had all day – and I thought A & E was tough.'

Tony turned to Hugh. 'That reminds me – what happened to our new housesurgeon scheduled to start today?'

Hugh groaned. 'Oh, God, he's just what we need right now. Looks like a refugee from the sixties. Didn't turn up on time 'cause he overslept. No apology. He's followed us round like a puppy all day and seems incapable of moving without specific direction. I've got rid of him for the moment so I don't go round the bend. He's in the library reading up on Legionnaires'.' Hugh turned the page of his newspaper and was scanning it as he spoke. 'Hey, look at this,' he exclaimed, handing the paper to Tony.

Tony glanced at the small item Hugh's finger was indicating. 'Woman Dies in House Fire,' the headline read. It conti-

127

nued for only a few lines. 'Mrs. Irene McTavish, aged 43, of Flat 2, 97 Naseby Lane, Heaton, Newcastle, died yesterday as the result of smoke inhalation. The fire is believed to have started in the kitchen of her home and is not considered suspicious.'

Tony shook his head. 'What a horrible way to go.'

Hugh grunted. 'At least it didn't happen while she was on the trial. Our statistics are bad enough as it is.' I couldn't believe it when I heard about Bruce Matheson this morning. The girls downstairs are pretty upset about it. Amanda doesn't want anything more to do with the trial.'

Tony sighed. 'I know how she feels. I'll speak to them later.'

Hugh stood up. 'I'm going back to ICU to check on Ray Higgins. Coming, Bob?'

Tony stood as well. 'And I've got a staff member with suspected Legionnaires' to check on. I'll see you later.'

He folded the newspaper he was still holding and placed it on the table. He paused to reread the item on Irene McTavish before leaving the room, unable to pinpoint the cause of the distinct uneasiness he felt.

Chapter Fifteen

Tony arrived home that evening to find the flat deserted.

It was no great surprise. When he had returned in the early hours of Sunday morning after Bruce Matheson's arrest, he'd found Catherine had not come home after the Davies' dinner party. The hours she had been present on Sunday evening had been silent for the most part. Any necessary conversation had been formal, as though they were two strangers forced to share accommodation. Without comment, Catherine had slept in the spare bedroom.

As Tony now ate the meal Mrs. McKay had left for him and relaxed for a while, listening to some music, he wondered if anything could be done to salvage their marriage. He already felt a sense of loss for the wasted years in which they had drifted apart, years that should have been spent cementing their relationship with friendship and understanding. Yet even if they did ride out this crisis, Tony could see little joy in the future. Their goals in life were so different and a future with Catherine, combined with a continued scramble up the academic ladder at the Northern, seemed a bleak prospect. Tony didn't want to contemplate it. He felt tired and depressed.

As usual, he turned his thoughts to a professional problem. He had brought home reports on a beta-lactam antibiotic, imipenam, used with success on patients with Legionnaires' Disease. Exhaustion crept over him as he read which, combined with the glass of wine he had poured to make his dinner of chops more palatable, caused him to doze off. He awoke with a start at the sound of the front door clicking shut.

Catherine was also looking exhausted. Her make up failed to conceal the shadows under her eyes, outlined by uncharacteristic creases. She sat opposite Tony, giving him an almost wistful half-smile. He indicated his glass. 'Can I get you something to drink?'

'Thank you.' Her gaze was fixed on one of the dragons in the Chinese screen near the fire. Tony handed her a glass of her preferred red wine and sat again, sipping at his own glass of dry white.

'We have an outbreak of Legionnaires' Disease at the Northern,' he said conversationally.

'So I heard. You're going to be kept very busy.'

They both fell silent. Eventually Catherine sighed lightly. 'I'm leaving you, Tony.'

He was stunned. Even though expected, and possibly desired, the imminent reality of the breakup was a painful blow. He wanted to crawl away and try to absorb the shock but Catherine's quiet voice continued relentlessly. 'Clifford has asked me to live with him and I've agreed. He's going to buy that house in Darras Hall. She paused and then looked briefly at her husband. 'I'm sorry, Tony.'

'Congratulations,' he said dryly. 'Was the house the prime incentive, or was it Clifford Barrington's money?'

'I have no intention of fighting with you, Anthony.' Catherine's voice was cold and tired. 'I've had enough. It's clear that any ambition you once had to rise in your profession has been lost, unlike Clifford Barrington. I don't want to continue running a boarding house for someone who's only interested in grassroot medicine and research.'

'What on earth do you mean by that?' Tony was incredulous.

'I mean that you could have been somebody if you didn't deliberately destroy all your chances. Do you think Gordon Davies will even consider you for that consultant position now, after your prize performance the other night? Walking out without even an apology, for God's sake.'

'Oh, I'm sorry,' Tony said sarcastically. 'I should have asked Bruce Matheson to die at a more convenient time.

'Perhaps grassroot medicine is the only worthwhile thing I have in my life,' he continued angrily, before pausing to light a defiant cigarette. Catherine sniffed in disgust. Tony expelled the smoke forcefully and pointed the cigarette at her. 'Perhaps this place has felt like a boarding house because of the never ending stream of guests you've filled it with. As far as I'm concerned, it's been like living at the back of an exclusive restaurant.' He fell silent and drew smoke deeply into his lungs.

Catherine was examining her nails and he felt he might as well have been talking to the brass lion which stood guard on the hearth. When he spoke again it was with less hostility.

'I loved you when we married, Catherine, and I thought you loved me. There must have been something more than habit keeping us together all these years, surely?'

'Yes, there was.' Catherine spoke without looking at her husband. 'I didn't marry you just for love, Tony. You must realise that by now, if you're honest with yourself. I wanted to be a doctor's wife. I wanted the respect and position my mother could only dream of.' Catherine glanced at Tony and bit her lip at the sight of his ashen face. 'Oh, I did love you at first,' she said sadly. 'It wasn't purely ambition. And you were great in bed in those days.' She paused as she smiled at the memory.

Tony's voice was bitter. He tried to ignore the pain he knew he would have to deal with later. 'Do you think Barrington's reputation is likely to give you this "position" you want so much? I think you've become confused between ambition and avarice, Catherine. Do you suppose for one minute that he even intends to be faithful to you?'

Her face tightened angrily. 'That needn't be any concern of yours, Anthony. I've consulted my lawyer and he'll be contacting you. If we both sign a separation agreement now, the divorce will be automatic in two years time.'

'Fine.' Tony controlled the fresh burst of anger her calm tone invoked. So few words needed to wipe out so many years.

'I'll collect what I want from the flat over the next few days. I don't think there's much to be gained from our meeting again at present.'

'Fine,' repeated Tony heavily.

Catherine rose to leave. 'I really am sorry,' she said with sincerity.

Tony said nothing. As the front door shut behind her he rose, hurling his wine glass into the kitchen with such force that fragments of shattered glass and droplets of wine spread themselves over the entire floor surface. He stood motionless for a second, then savagely picked up Catherine's glass, still full of red wine, and hurled that as well.

Mrs. McKay was informed of the situation the next day, when Catherine met her at the flat while filling suitcases. She was unsurprised, having been aware of Mrs. Lawrence's clandestine activities for some time.

'I'm sure Dr. Lawrence will want you to continue working for him,' Catherine told her. 'I know he appreciates your cooking.'

Mrs. McKay promised to stay on and to increase her hours if necessary. She did not mention that her sympathies had always been with Dr. Lawrence. She cleaned up the fragments of glass in the kitchen as best she could and found herself tut-tutting aloud at intervals over this latest development as she went about her afternoon's duties. She called in for a cup of tea with her sister-in-law on the way home, something she often did but not usually with such excitement at the news she had to impart.

Jean McKay was met at the door of the small terrace house by her brother's widow – Muriel McKenzie. She waited until she was comfortably settled in front of the heater with a steaming cup of tea and a large sticky bun. Muriel could sense her excitement and waited expectantly, sipping her own tea.

'Well, I told you so.' Jean announced cryptically and then sank her teeth through the pink icing of her bun. Muriel had to contain her curiosity until the bite of bun was slowly chewed and swallowed. She knew from experience that there was no point in rushing Jean, who obviously intended to spin out the enjoyment of imparting her gossip as long as possible. Jean sipped her tea noisily and gave the second installment with relish.

'The trollop's run off and left him – just like I always said she would.'

Muriel clicked her tongue with disapproval, but her eyes sparkled.

132

'Who with?' she asked breathlessly.

The heads of the two women drew closer together and the day's news was dissected with relevant past history and future prognosis probed until both were entirely satisfied.

Muriel went to work early the next day. Her popularity amongst the outpatient staff that day was to reach an unheard-of peak as the hospital grapevine was injected with such a juicy morsel.

Tony was unaware of his aura of the wronged hero as he went about the hospital that day. Being unaware of the relationship between his housekeeper and Muriel McKenzie, the thought that the developments in his private life were everyone's main topic of conversation was inconceivable. He was too preoccupied with attending to all the extra duties concerned with the Legionnaires' outbreak on top of his normal routine to notice the sympathetic glances he received, or even the unprecedented co-operation from staff everywhere.

Two incidents did penetrate his awareness and surprise him mildly, however. One was that, unasked, Muriel produce a cup of coffee for him when he had a break between outpatients and in the saucer rested a chocolate biscuit, albeit already melted against the side of the hot cup.

The other incident was the warmth of the smile with which he was greeted by Nicola Jarvis and, even more, the fact that she called him by his given name for the first time in their five-year association.

Tony Lawrence's ability to handle smoothly the enormous increase in pressure that the crisis of the Legionnaires' outbreak entailed was being threatened by more than the active hospital grapevine. His scientifically ordered thought processes were being annoyingly disrupted and undermined by the thread of unease he was still aware of surrounding the routine drug trial in his department, and also by his dissatisfaction over Davies' response to his concerns.

Something had to be done.

It was a foregone conclusion that Gordon Davies would not co-operate if Tony formally requested an investigation or, as he felt like doing, demanded that the trial be aborted. He was not going to risk antagonising Atlas and losing his source of

133

profitable bonuses. Colin Ingram was the logical contact but since the conversation about the questionable compensation paid to Shane Andrews, Tony didn't really trust the drug rep. Besides, Ingram probably didn't have the authority to abort a trial.

But something had to be done.

Tony closed the door of his office behind him. He ruffled through the tray of recent correspondence on his desk. The letterhead on the communication from Atlas concerning the delivery of components for the trial planned to start in January gave him the information he needed. It was a telephone number in the Edinburgh district which meant a toll call placed through the switchboard operator. Charged to the department, it would eventually mean a query and possible confrontation with Davies, but Tony was too worried to consider the consequences of such an encounter.

The call was answered swiftly by the musical tones of a well-paid member of the drug company's switchboard personnel.

'Atlas International. May I help you?'

'It's Dr. Lawrence speaking,' answered Tony. 'I'd like to speak to the head of your respiratory division, Dr. Adam Greene.'

'I'm sorry, sir.' The voice reflected extreme disappointment. 'Dr. Greene is unavailable at the present time. He has just left to attend a managerial meeting at our offices in Washington. Would you like me to put you through to his secretary to make an appointment for next week when he returns?'

'No.' Tony thought quickly. 'Would I be able to contact him in Washington? The matter is rather urgent.'

'He only left this morning and I don't know his travel arrangements. His secretary would be of more assistance, Dr. Lawrence. I'll put you through –'

'No, wait,' Tony changed his mind. 'Have all your senior staff left to attend this meeting?'

'No, Dr. Hughes, the head of our cardiology division, is available. Would you like to speak to him?'

'Yes, thanks.'

The operator sounded relieved. 'Putting you through now.'

Dr. Lionel Hughes was a worried man. He had been with Atlas for thirty years, all of his working life and he was now faced with the awful prospect of redundancy. Awful, because it would mean amputating a large percentage of the lavish lifestyle he and his family had grown to accept as essential.

Atlas International was planning to close one of the divisions of its British base and concentrate resources on expanding the single interest remaining. The choice between closing the cardiology or respiratory divisions was to be based on marketing and drug trial records over the next six months. Respiratory was doing well, Dr. Hughes was informed by his sources in the rival department. Very well indeed.

When his secretary buzzed the intercom on Lionel Hughes' desk, he was wondering sadly whether it might be prudent to cancel his order for the 1987 five speed, 3.6 litre XJ6 Jaguar, the 130 mph high performance luxury saloon car, promised to be their most exciting model ever. He depressed the switch on his intercom.

'What is it, Miss Warren?'

'I have a Dr. Lawrence on the line, from the Royal Northern Infirmary in Newcastle. He would like to speak to you.'

'I don't know any Dr. Lawrence,' said Hughes. 'Did he say what it was about?'

'It concerns a respiratory drug trial being run in his department.'

'Tell him he's got the wrong division.'

'I did, Dr. Hughes. It seems that Dr. Greene is unavailable and Dr. Lawrence says the matter is urgent.'

'Oh, very well. I'll speak to him.' Lionel Hughes did not particularly want to discuss any of the successful trials being rushed through by Greene to impress Washington staff. His own reps were having difficulty in initiating any cardiology trials at present. He listened to Tony introduce himself.

'I'm calling in connection with an oral salbutamol drug trial being run in our outpatient department,' continued Tony.

'I'm not sure I'll be able to help you, Dr. Lawrence,' Dr. Hughes responded. 'I know very little about the trials in our respiratory branch.'

'I realise I should be speaking to Dr. Greene about this,'

Tony said, his anxiety obvious. 'But I think it's urgent that this trial is aborted, or at least investigated thoroughly.'

'Really?' The calm tone belied a sudden and intense interest in the call. Lionel Hughes pulled a memo pad towards him and lifted the fountain pen from the silver desk tidy. 'What exactly is the problem, Dr. Lawrence?'

'We've had two deaths from asthmatic attacks amongst the patients enrolled in this trial.'

'You think the deaths are connected to this trial?' The Atlas manager's tone was incredulous.

'I couldn't say that, exactly,' said Tony. 'But something has to be wrong. We've never had a single death in this department associated with research previously and our record is suddenly alarming to say the least.'

'Perhaps you could give me a few more details, Dr. Lawrence?'

The engraved silver fountain pen made soft scratching sounds as Hughes took rapid notes, encouraging or sympathising briefly with Tony at appropriate intervals. The pen was abruptly dropped as Hughes changed the hand holding the telephone receiver and transferred it to his other ear.

'I beg your pardon?'

'It may well be none of my business,' Tony said apologetically, 'but it seems odd that a drug company would pay compensation to a patient's relative while denying any liability.'

'I would have to agree with you, Dr. Lawrence, if indeed that is the case. It will need looking into.' Dr. Hughes sat back in his chair. 'I can also understand your concerns over continuing this trial but I'm afraid I have no jurisdiction over trials being run by our respiratory division. Who's the chief of staff in your department?'

'Gordon Davies.'

'Ah, I believe I've heard of him.' Hughes suppressed the beginnings of a smile. He'd heard of him all right! There had been rumours circulating that this Davies was not averse to doctoring results to make both the trials and his own department look good. So, there was trouble brewing in Adam Greene's tame hospital department. Couldn't have timed itself better, in his rival's opinion.

136

'And he's not willing to abort the trial?'

'No.' Tony's reply was curt.

'Yes, I understand. I'm glad you've brought this matter to my attention, Dr. Lawrence. Very glad indeed. I've made notes of your concerns and I promise to deal with this matter immediately.' Lional Hughes' tone was reassuring.

'Thank you.' Tony sounded immensely relieved.

'My pleasure, Dr. Lawrence.'

Lionel Hughes stared at the memo pad on the desk before him for several minutes. He picked up the telephone receiver without removing his gaze from the notes then slowly replaced it. He shook his head in disbelief. Whether or not the trial was somehow contributing to these patient deaths, it was going to be a major catastrophe for Adam Greene and the whole respiratory division of the company. The doctor was right. Something *had* to be done about it.

After several motionless seconds, Hughes' lips twitched and gradually settled into a satisfied smile. He peeled the top page from his memo pad, screwed it tightly into a small ball and dropped it decisively into the waste paper bin at his feet.

He wondered if the 1987 XJ6 might be available in a metallic shade of quartz silver.

Chapter Sixteen

The promise from Lionel Hughes had been reassuring. Atlas had the facilities to investigate Tony's concerns and the authority to abort the trial if necessary. Thankfully, with increasing confidence over the next week, he concentrated on the more pressing crises in both his professional and personal life. In many ways it was fortunate they had occurred simultaneously. He devoted his energy and time totally to dealing with the crisis at the Northern, free of the nagging guilt that Catherine's reaction to his neglect of her would have engendered. The exhaustion and preoccupation his work produced served in turn to cushion the initial shock of his wife's departure.

Tony became accustomed to the idea of Catherine being out of his life far more rapidly than he would have believed possible. The few hours he spent back at the flat at first seemed painfully empty.

Catherine had been remarkably efficient and had removed all trace of her existence there within thirty-six hours of her declaration. It was as though the plan of action had been worked out well in advance and then carried out with military precision. Her wardrobe was deserted. The hundreds of bottles, tubes, brushes and mysterious plastic cases which comprised her wealth of beauty paraphernalia had vanished. The kitchen shelves were bare of her library of exotic recipe books. Numerous ornaments and the Chinese screens had also been removed.

Tony didn't mind. In fact, he found himself enjoying it. He could find his shaving gear in the bathroom without knocking over half a dozen objects, and he noticed with astonishment the lovely wood grain in the antique oak dressing table which had belonged to his mother and had for years been hidden by a collection of perfumes, hair spray, silver-handled brushes and a tribe of tiny porcelain birds that Catherine had collected with zeal. He had been struck by a childhood memory. Once upon a time he'd thought he could discern the shape of an animal in the grain of the wood, but when he looked for it again his imagination was too rusty to rediscover it.

The living room minus its screens had become a room again, rather than a ward, and Tony couldn't quite believe the spaciousness and sense of peace to be found there. Catherine had left Jasper, the brass lion, by the fireplace but had removed the large expensive books of art reproductions from the coffee tables. Tony caught himself smiling when he noticed she had also removed the stack of Mills and Boon she kept in her bedside cabinet.

The absence of tension in his home was so obvious that Tony finally realised just how long they had been unhappy together. He raised a wineglass and wished Catherine well in her future, feeling at the same time, a tiny seed of hope for his own.

The media's initial excitement over the outbreak of Legionnaires' faded, although reporters were still at the Northern in force every day for updates on the situation. Tony thought of them as vultures, just waiting for another death to produce a new headline. One female freelance reporter, with the unlikely name of Jemima Pride, was particularly obnoxious. She had shoulder-length, straight brown hair that never looked clean. Her fringe should have been trimmed weeks ago and continually flopped in her eyes in lank strands that looked damp and potentially sticky. She had a beanpole figure usually encased in a tight-fitting knitted skirt and an oversized sweatshirt emblazoned with the female symbol accompanied by an exclamation mark. Tony thought a question mark might have been more appropriate.

She seemed to be everywhere, wire-rimmed spectacles glinting as she glanced from whomever she was interviewing to her clipboard. Jemima had been banned from the press conferences held daily by Dr. Davies as a reprimand for having been caught inside a ward office, on the point of reading a patient's notes she had extracted from the trolley rack. Now, undeterred, she lurked in waiting rooms and prowled corridors, pouncing on visitors, porters, cleaners and even kitchen staff, some of whom unfortunately were only too happy to talk to her. She spent her days and evenings stalking the Northern, filling in her foolscap pages with her individual and peculiar form of shorthand, waiting for the break she was sure would come.

The source of the outbreak of Legionnaires' had now been traced to a particular air-conditioning system. The cooling towers and water supply had been chlorinated and three wards had been re-opened. The press had been delighted with the discovery that the usual six-monthly checks and chlorination of the cooling towers had not been carried out for over a year and that on the last occasion no chlorine had been added to the cooling water. This had been due to the fact that nobody was specifically responsible for the task and delegation had become sub-delegation and then disintegrated into inertia. The call had gone up for a committee to be formed and personnel employed for this purpose alone which had opened the can of worms that comprised hospital funding and unearthed several political factions within the Northern, quite prepared to give interviews and participate in panel discussions to air their grievances.

The press went from one extreme to another in its coverage of the hospital. The public were fascinated to read lurid details of past cases, like that of the previously healthy young man who was sent home from work one day feeling unwell, developed searing pains in his chest and stomach, later suddenly collapsing, his eyes fixed and staring and all power of speech gone. His wife, convinced he had suffered a stroke, rang for an ambulance and then spent the next two weeks watching him fade to a living skeleton, kept alive only by a ventilator. Then there was the woman treated with Erythromycin who became totally deaf until the drug was withdrawn.

There were warnings for anybody who had visited the hospital recently and was feeling unwell, to contact their doctor immediately. Many people, the reports stated, could

140

have Legionnaires' Disease without realising it. A young, fit person who contracted the disease might suffer only mild symptoms, similar to an attack of 'flu.'

The less interesting news items detailed the need for anti-scaling compounds and algicides with a twice-yearly draining, cleaning and disinfection by chlorination of cooling towers, shower heads and re-circulating water systems, and guidelines for the temperatures at which both hot and cold water should be stored and distributed.

The possibility of further people contracting the disease had been removed but the incubation period meant that new cases could continue to appear for the next two or three weeks. Already the number of victims had increased to fourteen and seven deaths were attributed to the outbreak – including Ray Higgins. Resources in ICU were being stretched with five ventilator cases currently being maintained. On the brighter side, David Laing was feeling fine and working his normal hours and had even managed a night out with Kay. Florence Murdock was well on the road to recovery and a nurse from A7, who had also been found to have contracted Legionnaires', had received early treatment which had meant her duties were uninterrupted.

Tony's workload had almost doubled, keeping him stretched to full capacity for twelve or fourteen hours a day. The normally minor irritations of clinical life assumed larger proportions, increasing the pressure and dominating any potential quiet periods. One of these irritations was his new housesurgeon, pony-tailed Calvin Jones. He annoyed the senior staff by his familiarity and disreputable appearance. The ward staff, who had closer contact with the new arrival, were appalled by his incompetence, Calvin was not good with needles of any description. Having observed the housesurgeon's initial forty-five minute marathons to insert even an intravenous line, the staff now went out of their way to avoid using him. Tony didn't have time to berate staff for summoning him to do the task when Bob or Hugh were unavailable. Calvin's incompetence in other fields was much more of a problem. Tony was cornered at frequent intervals or beeped by an enthusiastic but bemused Dr. Jones who wanted advice on drug dosages, explanation of chart orders, or ideas on the

141

significance of basic clinical signs he had discovered on his examination of the unfortunate patients who met him on admission.

One incident had succeeded in making Tony and Hugh laugh. Calvin had contacted Tony in some alarm having found breath sounds on only one side of the patient's chest. Had he bothered to read the notes prior to his examination, Dr. Jones would have discovered that this patient had had a lung removed some time previously because of a malignancy. Calvin's current obsession was with one of the Legionnaires' cases whom he had decided must have a leukaemia underlying the bacterial infection, due to the high count of white blood cells. Tony had pointed out that the levels of neutrophils made this unlikely but Calvin was being very persistent. Overall, the young doctor was a first-class pest and the staff in general were thankful that his run was only going to last three months.

Another irritation, that of delayed or lost laboratory results, became a real worry when Tony's efforts to trace the blood test for the HTLV-111 on Bill Chalmers' wife were unsuccessful, and the young AIDS victim became so depressed he refused to co-operate with the treatment for his pneumonia.

'What's the point?' he asked angrily of Tony, summoned from a half-eaten lunch. 'We're all going to die, so I may as well get it over with.'

'Do you want to throw away a possible two years and the chance that a treatment may be found, Bill?' Tony asked quietly. 'There's an enormous amount of research going on at the moment and drugs could be found to inactivate the virus or boost the immune system. We're treating your pneumonia primarily at the moment but there are drugs currently available, such as types of interferon, which may help improve you immune system and prevent new infections.'

'For what?' Bill asked bitterly. 'To watch my wife and child die?'

'We don't even know that they've contracted the virus, Bill.' Tony mentally cursed the laboratory staff responsible for the cock-up over these results. 'I've been trying to trace the results but I'm sorry, I think we're going to have to repeat the test. We should know within a few days, even if I have to sit on the test tube and hatch it myself. There's no point crossing that bridge until we do know.'

'Even if they don't have it, there's nothing much left for me, is there? I won't even be able to live with them.'

'That's not true,' Tony said firmly. 'The idea that AIDS can be caught by sharing bathrooms, cutlery and so on is just a myth. The virus can't exist outside living cells, so it's contact with blood and semen that spreads the infection.' Tony's beep went off at that point but he ignored it. 'It means you'll have to take some precautions around home and your sex life will be significantly altered, but there are many worthwhile things you're going to miss out on if you just give up now.'

The beep sounded again and this time Tony rose from his seat on the end of the bed.

'I'm going to arrange for a counsellor from the North East AIDS Monitor to come and talk to you and Caroline.' Tony made a note on his hand.

'She won't come,' Bill said miserably.

'I'll give her a call too.' Tony made another note. 'She'll have to come in for a repeat blood test in any case. Now, I'm going to answer my call and send the sister back in with your medication and lunch.'

Tony waited for several seconds until Bill nodded reluctantly. He smiled at his patient with sympathetic encouragement. Bill twisted a corner of his mouth in response.

'I guess it might be worth having a go at beating this,' he said wearily. 'But only if I know that Caroline and the baby are going to be OK.'

The call from Gordon Davies to remind Tony of the time limit on the salbutamol trial had been an unwarranted aggravation. Tony tried to immerse himself in the mass of paper work awaiting his attention but later in the afternoon he walked out and shut the office door on it all. He spoke briefly to Colin Ingram who was hanging around the exercise laboratory, secretly pleased when the drug rep excused himself, and he refused to feel guilty about taking the time to have a chat to Bridget Gardiner who was recovering from the exercise test Colin had been observing. He waited while she received her next week's supply of capsules from Sue. Bob had filled in his comment on the exercise test which he had supervised and was now hanging around waiting for a chance to speak to Sue. Tony ignored the not very subtle non-verbal communication going on between Bob and Sue who was filling in the dates in a diary for Bridget's coming trial week. She handed it to Bridget, along with the small glass bottle of white capsules.

'Just the same procedure for this week, Mrs. Gardiner,' she said quickly. 'One capsule morning and evening. Use the bronchodilator inhaler if you need to but record it in the diary along with any other symptoms you experience.' The patter was practised and delivered with a smile, then Sue excused herself and Bob immediately put down the journal he was flicking through and followed his willing prey out of the lab.

Bridget was packing her supplies into her handbag. Tony leaned on the railing round the front of the treadmill.

'How did it go?'

'Really good,' said Bridget. 'Twelve minutes – running for the last three. Didn't produce any symptoms other than tired legs.'

'Does running usually give you symptoms?'

'I wouldn't know,' she laughed. 'I don't indulge very often.' She picked up her bag. 'I must go, or I'll miss my bus.'

'Bus?' queried Tony.

'Poor Esmeralda's in the garage. Some sort of transplant required, I believe.'

'Let me give you a lift.'

She looked pleased. 'That would be great. Sure you're not too busy?'

'I'm finished for today. At least, I've had more than enough of this establishment for the moment. Come with me while I grab my jacket.'

Jemima Pride was sitting in the main foyer and noticed Tony and Bridget leaving the building. Her eyes narrowed slightly. She knew that Dr. Lawrence was one of the central characters in the drama she was desperate to probe and she didn't like him. He had snubbed her rudely when she had pressed, politely for her, for an interview when she had caught him the day Davies was being interviewed for tele-vision. Jemima was convinced that he had also been the one responsible for the complaint about her and her subsequent exclusion from the press conferences. She made a few notes on her clipboard and then decided to head up towards the ward. The dinner hour was too busy a time for staff to take too much notice of her presence.

Katy Barlow was running late. She wanted to get home in time to see 'Crossroads' but extreme nervousness had delayed her final task for the afternoon, making that unlikely. She was a qualified and very experienced blood technician but the task she was about to perform was one she would rather have avoided. Collecting blood from hepatitis patients was bad enough but she was about to face her first collection from a patient confirmed to be suffering from AIDS. She took a deep breath before opening the door and pushing her trolley into the private room occupied by William Chalmers.

'I need some blood from you, Mr. Chalmers,' she said cheerfully. 'It won't take long.' Katy's smile rapidly faded when she realised she was being ignored. She unwrapped a parcel on her trolley and donned the long-sleeved, disposable apron and the gloves it contained. She put on a mask and then a pair of clear plastic goggles recommended for eye protection. She felt rather ridiculous and embarrassed by the precautions but was certainly not going to take any risks. Bill stopped staring at the ceiling and took note of the alien form standing beside him.

'Would you like me to stop breathing?' he asked, with no hint of amusement in his voice.

Katy's smile flickered again behind her mask but she didn't know how to respond so she busied herself preparing the disposable units for blood collection. Bill thrust an arm towards her with a sigh and she applied the tourniquet and swabbed the vein at his elbow.

'Could you clench your fist a few times for me please, Mr. Chalmers?'

Bill silently complied. Katy quickly checked her list for the minimum essential quantity of blood required for the test. Holding her breath, she poked the needle at the vein more timidly than usual. Bill winced and the needle slid past the side of the vein.

'Oh, I'm sorry.' Katy's hand was shaking as she withdrew

145

the needle. It might have been an excusable error in some circumstances but Bill's veins stood out like hosepipes and should have been a dream to slip a needle into.

'It's ok,' he said heavily. 'I'd be pretty nervous if I were you, too.'

Katy forced her fingers to remain steady and reinserted the needle successfully. She slowly withdrew the 2 millilitres of blood she required and placed a swab over the needle ready to apply pressure. She withdrew the needle swiftly, in a straight line, and then jumped as a drop dislodged itself from the needle tip to splash on to her apron. She hoped Mr. Chalmers hadn't noticed.

'Can you press on this and bend your elbow, please,' she asked him hurriedly.

Katy started the next stage of the rigmarole which she had read up on carefully before she came. She removed the locking needle from the syringe and placed it in the brightly coloured Cin bin on the bench which bore a hazard warning label and was destined for incinceration. The specimen of blood went into a tube that was securely capped and then placed into a special screw-capped, leak-proof container also emblazoned with the bright warning labels. The request form to accompany the blood was sealed into a plastic bag. Katy disposed of the empty syringe with relief, checked Bill's arm and then peeled off the plastic protective gear and placed it into the appropriate rubbish bag in his room, the contents of which were also destined for incineration. After washing her hands thoroughly, Katy smiled at Bill and pushed her trolley out into the corridor.

She paused when she reached the foyer outside the ward. Her feeling of relief at having accomplished the dreaded task without incident made her want to giggle suddenly. She even smiled in a ridiculously friendly manner at the skinny woman with stringy hair who was approaching her purposefully.

'Hi,' the woman said, indicating the container with its warning label as she spoke. 'You must have a pretty important job. What's the hazard?'

Tony and Bridget were quiet as the car left the outskirts of Newcastle. It was an instant transportation from city to countryside and the night seemed to swallow them as they left the street lighting behind. The roads were white with frost and Tony negotiated the narrow bends with care. He pulled up beside the isolated little cottage and switched off the ignition before turning to Bridget. She tucked a fold of shining hair behind her ear and smiled mischievously.

'Would you like to come in and meet Jody?'

Tony opened his mouth and then shut it again. Her records had said nothing of any children and he was suddenly aware of an aversion towards meeting some male companion of hers. He cast a puzzled glance at the cottage, the darkened windows of which suggested it was unoccupied.

'Come on,' Bridget was laughing as she climbed out of the car. 'You'll like him.'

He followed her up the path and waited while she unlocked the recessed front door, framed by naked rose vines.

'This must be very pretty in the . . .' His words were cut off as the door opened and something large and mobile seemed to be everywhere at once. Joyous barks and the flash of a pink tongue revealed the creature's species and as Bridget switched on the hall light, Tony grinned widely.

'This is Jody,' said Bridget, a little unnecessarily.

Friendly dark eyes regarded him for an instant, then the dog leaped on Tony in a frenzy of welcome. He laughed delightedly and patted parts that came within reach, then Jody suddenly squirmed through his legs, nearly throwing him off balance, and pounded up the small hallway of the cottage.

'What is he?' asked Tony as he closed the front door behind them.

'Mostly Otterhound – more like an overgrown puppy than anything else, though.'

Bridget led the way into her living room. Tony gazed around in admiration when she turned on the small lamps positioned around the room. The focal point of the small room was a beautiful open fireplace of dark polished wood with intricate carving of leaves and vines down each side. The hearth was a patchwork of antique tiles, all different from each other but with backgrounds of complementary earthy tones of brown, terracotta and green. A large flokati rug lay in

147

front of the fire flanked by an old, rolled-arm couch covered in brown velvet with bright patchwork cushions in shades to match the tiles. An ancient hutch dresser displaying pottery, a rocking chair and a small round dining table in the alcove formed by the bay window filled the remaining space. The wall containing the door to the hallway had shelving from floor to ceiling. Most were filled with books but some held fascinating collections of objects, like a group of pottery owls and several painted wooden elephants of varying sizes. Ferns hung from the ceiling inside the bay window and the wide windowsill was covered with pot plants. A rainbow hued toy parrot also hung from the ceiling, peeping out from behind ferns.

Bridget disappeared through the arched doorway by the hutch dresser to deposit her bags in the kitchen. Tony's appraisal of the room was interrupted by a heavy paw batting at his legs. He looked down. Jody sat in front of him with an admirably upright stance. His plumed tail swept the polished wood of the floor in large arcs. A tennis ball was carefully positioned by Tony's right foot. Jody looked as if he was laughing with delight. He looked from Tony's face to the ball, and back again, and Tony grinned.

'Are you allowed to play ball inside?'

Jody barked impatiently so Tony picked up the ball and threw it gently towards the dog. Jody leaped up, caught the ball as it sailed towards him and shot under the table with his prize. Bridget came back into the room, smiling as she handed Tony a box of matches.

'You'll get sick of it before he does. Could I ask you to light the fire, please? I'll see what I can offer you to drink.'

The fire was already set with crumpled newspaper, a layer of pinecones and needles, and small kindling on the surface. A few touches of the match and there was a satisfying crackle as it ignited. Tony sat back on his haunches, waiting until the heat built up enough to add a couple of small logs from the wicker basket on the hearth. It was years since he'd had the pleasure of making a fire. Catherine had replaced their open fireplaces with gas fires before they'd even moved into the flat. He shook his head slightly as though to dispel any thought of his wife.

148

'Do sit down,' Bridget called. 'I'll just feed Jody. I hope you're not in a hurry.'

'Not a bit.' He sat back on the couch and allowed his gaze to travel the fascinating room again. Being here, especially with the frosty blackness outside, bathed in the warmth of the crackling fire, felt rather like waking up on a cold Monday morning and then realising it was still Sunday and there was no need to leave the comfort afforded by the warm nest of bedding. He had no desire to go anywhere. He shut his eyes for a moment and drank in the heat and the fresh smell of the burning pine. He opened them smartly when he felt something cold on his knees travelling swiftly towards his groin.

He encountered first the level gaze of Jody, sitting directly in front of him, and then glanced down at his lap to see the tennis ball nestled in his crotch. It was distinctly soggy, as Jody had been happily sucking it under the table while Tony had been occupied with the fire. He picked it up gingerly between forefinger and thumb. Jody's eyes sparkled appreciatively.

'Jody,' called Bridget from the kitchen. 'Dinner!'

He was torn. Tony could almost see the wheels turning but was surprised by the decision. Jody's head snaked forward, plucked the ball delicately from his fingers, and then he took it into the kitchen with him. Bridget came and warmed her hands before the fire.

'Could I interest you in something to eat?' she inquired. 'I have some leftover stroganoff which only needs reheating. It won't take long.'

'I'm not in any hurry,' Tony assured her. 'I'm thoroughly enjoying myself, and yes, stroganoff would be terrific.'

'Great. Would you like a glass of wine? I've only got white, I'm afraid.'

'It's the only sort I drink,' replied Tony happily.

Bridget excused herself and a brown shadow insinuated itself around the end of the couch. Tony found his lap now contained a decidedly soggy tennis ball, peppered with shreds of jellied dog food.

'Yuk,' he told Jody firmly, and rolled the offending article under the couch. 'Sorry, fella.'

Bridget came and stood by Tony, ignoring Jody who was sniffing resolutely around the base of the couch.

'Look what I've found hiding in the 'fridge.' She held out a bottle of Moet et Chandon for his inspection. 'I've been saving it for a special occasion. Would you like to open it?'

Tony met the solemn gaze from her dark eyes directly.

'Do you think the occasion is of sufficient merit?'

Bridget smiled gently and handed Tony the bottle in answer. He twisted off the wire and held the bottle at a forty-five degree angle as he carefully eased out the cork. There was a satisfying, if muted, pop and a spray of mist. Bubbles rose from the neck of the bottle, subsiding before any of the champagne was lost.

'Oh, well done,' congratulated Bridget, holding out two tall glasses. 'I do hate to see any wasted.'

Tony half filled the flutes, waiting for the bubbles to subside before topping them up. Bridget chattered on.

'I grit my teeth when I see ships being launched or, even worse, sportsmen shaking it up and spraying it everywhere.' She touched her glass to Tony's. 'Cheers,' she said and curled herself up on the mat close to the fire.

The conversation was general as they sipped their first glasses of champagne and soaked in the warmth and light. They laughed at Jody, stretched full-length on the floor, poking a paw under the couch where his ball was firmly stuck.

'Are you really thinking of emigrating?' Bridget asked as she refilled their glasses.

'Mmm.' Tony watched the streams of tiny bubbles rushing to the surface of his glass. 'My mother moved out to Canada a few years ago when my father died, to live with my sister who's married to a dentist. We're not particularly close though, unfortunately, and Canada is a bit big to appeal to me. New Zealand seems friendlier and far away – a perfect place to start a new life.'

Bridget frowned in concern but she remained silent. Suddenly Tony found himself talking to her, about his hopes for the future and about Catherine.

It was the first time Tony had really spoken to anyone of his marriage and once started, he couldn't stop. It was an exorcism of the guilt and unhappiness accumulated over years

150

and Bridget was a perfect listener. Her movement to add logs to the fire and at one point to refill their glasses did nothing to interrupt the flow. When Tony hesitated and his voice caught, she gently touched his hand in encouragement. They both stared into the fire, hypnotised by the flames as the buildup of charcoal on the back of the chimney glowed. When Tony finally stopped talking they were silent for several minutes. Then, still watching the flames, Bridget began to speak.

She made Tony chuckle by telling him of her meeting with Peter in the overcrowded Underground. She spoke about the hopes they had had for the future and a family, the frustrations and setbacks they had experienced. Tony shook his head and then nodded in sympathy as she told him about Peter's problems with the practice. Bridget's voice was a whisper as she talked of the unendurable grief of Peter's death. Tears rolled down her cheeks as she spoke of it and Tony eased himself slowly off the couch to kneel beside her. He stroked her hair back from the sides of her face, and as she turned towards him he wiped away her tears and softly kissed the tip of her nose. She laughed shakily and touched his cheek.

She moved within the circle of Tony's arms and for a long time they held each other, sharing their grief and drawing comfort from the special contact of mutual empathy. The emotions they experienced within the embrace changed from the need for simple comfort and both recognised the altered climate. When, eventually, Tony's lips touched Bridget's her response was avid. They made love urgently, desperate for the closest contact possible and to confirm the beginning of a relationship that both felt could be vital.

Afterwards, they lay together on the soft white fluff of the rug, bathed in the glow of the dying fire. Tony raised himself on one elbow and brushed his lips over Bridget's closed eyelids. She opened them when she heard his chuckle and followed his gaze to where Jody, sitting on the couch, was eyeing him resentfully.

'He's not used to this sort of entertainment,' Bridget laughed.

'I should hope not.' Tony traced the outlines of her face with a gentle touch. 'Though I think he might just have to get

151

used to it from now on.' He drew Bridget's face closer and kissed her nose softly before seeking her lips. He released her when she shivered suddenly.

'Put your clothes on, lady. I don't want another case of pneumonia on my hands. I'll get this fire going again.'

'And I'll get that stroganoff, which is probably a dried up lump by now,' she finished apologetically.

'Who needs food?' grinned Tony. His smile faded as Jody's stare made itself felt.

'I'm sorry,' he said contritely to the dog. 'Will you forgive me if I get your ball back?'

Chapter Seventeen

Alister Cunningham had been employed as a technician in the respiratory department of the Northern for five weeks now. He was totally unaware of how much he was disliked and had every confidence that the new career he had embarked on was perfectly suited to his abilities. He was keen to learn everything he could and sit any examination which would lead to promotion and more responsibility. Alister could see himself in a few years time as totally indispensable – being called in at night to supervise the mechanics of ventilator machines for critically ill patients, being able to run bronchoscopy sessions practically single-handed, and in charge of some research project that would produce an amazing breakthrough. He was a little frustrated at present because all he was allowed to do was run blood through the gas analyser or administer spirometry tests.

Using the analyser was an exceedingly boring task which involved injecting a minute quantity of blood through the inlet valve of the machine, watching to see that it filled the tiny piping along the length of the screen without forming bubbles, waiting for the computer to do its thing, and then recording the figures on the readout and ringing through to the ward with the results. He had done hundreds of samples by now and the process was as dull as it was automatic.

He had also perfected his other task of running the spirometry tests, admittedly a little hectic on outpatient clinic days but still dead easy and well below his capabilities. He would have a row of patients sitting in the room and for each one he would fit a new cardboard tube, like the inside of a toilet roll, to the mouthpiece of the spirometer and encourage the patient to take as deep a breath as possible and then expel it as quickly as they could manage.

'Push harder, Mrs. McConnell, harder . . . harder . . . HARDER!' his voice rising to a squeak as he coaxed the last bit of air out of their imperfect lungs. They would get three goes and then have a huff on one of the supply of bronchodilators kept in the laboratory. The patients would return to the back of the queue at that point to wait five minutes before repeating the process to see what, if any, improvement had been achieved. Alister felt he treated his patients in a very professional manner. In fact, he knew it was, as he had modelled it from his first day on the behaviour of the physician he had observed – Arthur Stewart. It was faintly patronising, with a somewhat insincere tone of concern, but Alister didn't recognise it as such. Just as he didn't recognise the fact that none of the staff he worked with could stand him.

It was partly his looks. There were no two ways about it: Alister was as ugly as sin, as Sue had commented to the other girls in a horrified undertone in the locker room after they were first introduced. He had very small eyes, set rather far apart, which made them appear even smaller. 'Like a rat's,' Barbara decided. His nose was large. 'What a conk!' Jackie had said with disdain, thankfully admiring her own snub variety in the locker room mirror. Alister's mouth was also oversized with rubbery, moist-looking lips, and he had tried – unsuccessfully – to obtain the latest fashion in haircuts, almost a crew cut on top but shoulder length at the back. It did not suit his gingery and wiry locks. Even Amanda was disturbed by Alister's skin problems. He had the skin problems experienced by a large proportion of Tyneside youth, brought up on a grease-laden diet, almost total lack of exposure to sunshine and with an overabundance of bakeries and sweetshops available. His acne was so bad that it was difficult to discern any normal patches of skin. Most of the inflamed areas never erupted although two or three were usually active at any given time – helped by his almost unconcious habit of fingering his face whenever his hands were idle.

Overall, Alister's body above the shoulders was a disaster. The rest was not much better. At only five foot two, most of the female technicians topped him by several inches. He was also rather overweight which he managed to accentuate by wearing tight jeans. After seeing a housesurgeon that the girls all raved over, Alister had emulated his style with the white lab coat he was so proud to wear and pushed the sleeves up to his elbows in the manner recently adopted by pop heroes. As he had to get a fairly large size of coat to accommodate his shoulder width, it descended almost to mid calf, giving him the appearance of a child playing at dressing-up.

His colleagues might have become used to Alister's looks and accepted him, if only he had displayed the humble lack of security that such an appearance would have engendered in any normal human subjected to adolescence and the standards of beauty expected by society. But Alister simply oozed confidence. He seemed to know everything already when being given instruction, nodding sagely and often interrupting to ask rhetorical questions. He greeted the girls as if he had known them all his life, and there was no way they could avoid his presence at their lunch table. They had certainly tried their hardest. He would join in any conversation with the air of a trusted confidante, undeterred when his suggestions were ignored. When they became silent, as they often did these days, he had a wealth of experiences with which to entertain them. It seemed that Alister had gone skydiving, scubadiving, surfing, swimming in shark-infested waters, attended brothels in Cairo and Amsterdam, seen a murder and numerous horrific car accidents, run a marathon and kissed Princess Di's hand. The girls had been somewhat amused initially by these accounts of Alister's action-packed nineteen years but now they actively hated his company and plotted ways to avoid it. They hid in the locker room to have their lunch on one occasion but Alister found them, produced a packet of sandwiches from the pocket of his white coat, pushed his sleeves up a bit further and happily settled himself, cross-legged, in their midst.

Alister's confidence that everybody loved him was the fault of his upbringing. His father, Malcolm Cunningham, had been a steel worker, and his mother, Marysia, a shopgirl at Marks and Spencers. Malcolm had considered boys to be the only acceptable form of offspring and Marysia had been proud to produce one nine months after their marriage. They had doted on Alister, more so when his birth was followed, in rapid succession, by the arrival of five daughters, the youngest twins.

When not working overtime to try and keep his family in food, Malcolm escaped the dreary and cramped tenement they lived in by taking his son out. He would sit him proudly on the bar of his local while he had a few pints with the boys, or on his shoulders at football games, encouraging him to yell support for their team, Newcastle United. Alister adored his father. He was bewildered at Malcolm's absence after he was killed in an industrial accident at the steel works when Alister was six, but his mother and sisters gradually made up for it. Right from the moment of her husband's death, Marysia had turned to Alister as the male head of the family, the only sort she recognised, seriously discussing with him any decisions to be made about ways of supporting the family. The girls followed her example and Alister became the centre that the Cunninghams' universe revolved around.

As he grew up, he shouldered his responsibility for the family with increasing confidence. He worked as a paper boy then a milk boy and a shop assistant to supplement their meagre income from benefits and Marysia's job at a local laundrette. By the time he was sixteen, he was up at 4 a.m., often not getting to bed until midnight. He always had time to provide protection for his sisters, however, to talk about their problems and produce surprises like a new lipstick for them to share. When younger, they had begged for tales of his adventures, real or imagined, and the repetition of these stories over the years to the adoring and believing audience they commanded at home had firmly established them as real events in Alister's mind.

The family were thrilled at his new job. Every evening they waited for him to come home and tell them of his day. He had impressed them immeasurably by bringing home his white lab coat and modelling it for them. He had a good short-term memory and was able to give his family a daily resumé of the information he had absorbed.

'The main function of the lungs is to transfer oxygen from the air to the blood,' he told them through mouthfuls of mince and mashed potatoes. 'Oxygen travels to every part of the body and combines with glucose which is broken down by chemicals to release energy. This, in turn, produces carbon dioxide which the blood takes back to the lungs which get rid of it.'

Over the icecream came snippets of anatomy. 'The trachea divides into two branches, the bronchi, one into each lung. The bronchi divide up lots of times like tree branches.' Alister produced a pen and scrap of paper from his pocket to illustrate. 'And each one has a little air sac at the end called an alveolus. The air sacs have very thin walls which lets oxygen in and carbon dioxide out.'

The Cunninghams tolerated their favourite television programmes being interspersed with fragments of medical lore, though they did encourage their star to confine his gems to when the advertisements came on.

'The term asthma comes from the Greek word meaning "to pant". It makes the bronchi get narrow because the muscles around it squeeze up. Bronchodilators make the muscles relax so it's easier to get air in and out.'

As far as his family was concerned, Alister was as good as a doctor. Wanting to impress his fellow workers to a similar degree, he decided that the best course of action was to become an expert in the field of respiratory medicine. He was no stranger to hard work and long hours and he had arranged permission to use the departmental library after hours. He stocked up on notebooks and biros. He was going to become indispensable before they knew what had hit them.

The plan was put into action by the end of that week. Alister ate an early, solitary dinner in the hospital cafeteria at half-past five, after finishing work for the day. He had stayed on until the other technicians left as he wanted to surprise them with the results of the work he planned to do. He chose an unexciting meal of sausages and chips, the fat already congealing in puddles around the edges of his plate and ate quickly, feeling rather alone in the vast room. The only other tables occupied were near the kitchen door where staff were having a cup of coffee before the dinner rush began. Their sudden bursts of laughter made Alister feel a little left out of things. He slotted his empty tray into the trolley standing in the centre of the cafeteria and unwrapped and ate a Mars bar as he walked back in the direction of the respiratory department.

The outpatient area was completely deserted now but the doors would remain unlocked for another hour or so, or until one of the porters remembered the task. Alister walked up the silent corridor, lit only dimly by outside lights shining through uncurtained windows. He switched on the light by the locker room and retrieved the key from its hiding place in the cold store room before collecting his bag with its booty of notebooks and pens. The library was also locked but due to his careful planning of this operation, Alister knew where to find that key as well. The sliding glass windows of a secretary's office in the same corridor could be opened from the outside and the key hung on a nail within easy reach.

Once inside the library, he turned on as few lights as necessary. He walked around the small but well-stocked room and chose several textbooks, carefully marking the spaces they had come from with small slips of paper. He didn't want any complaints from the librarian curtailing his self-improvement programme.

Alister worked steadily with determined concentration and didn't notice the time slipping by. It was a long process, meticulously copying out information, and he spent a moment wondering the best way to learn shorthand. There was a lot he didn't understand but he was sure that a bit of application and prolonged exposure would bring comprehension – like learning any foreign language. He made a long list of symptoms of respiratory disease, putting headings in capitals and neatly underlining them before making further notes.

ORTHNOPNEA – breathlessness lying down.
                    – a symptom of heart failure.
                    – may also be caused by pressure of the abdominal contents on the diaphragm in patients with lung disease.
PAROXYSMAL NOCTURNAL DYSPNOEA

It made Alister feel knowledgeable just to pronounce the words. He chanted them softly to himself several times, like a

magic incantation, after first carefully enunciating each sylla-
ble of the unfamiliar terms. He delighted in noting that an
electrocardiogram, spirometry and a search for eosinophilia
might be indicated. He had no clue as to what these eosinophilia might be but he could just imagine Nicola's admiring
glance if he suggested it in a conversation about an appropriate patient.

He filled four pages of his notebook with information about
sputum. He felt no revulsion as he noted details about the
purulent yellow or green varieties, frothy, black, grey, foul-
smelling or bloodstained secretions. This was all fascinating
medical stuff and it was obvious that a diagnosis could just
about be made by having a look at what the patient spat out.
He made lists of the possible diagnoses with each heading.
Bronchiectasis, pulmonary infarction, tuberculosis, lung
abscess, acute pneumonia, trauma, Goodpasture's
syndrome. At least he'd heard of tuberculosis and pneumonia. Eosinophils cropped up a few times more so Alister made
a note of them on a separate sheet of paper. They would need
investigation.

He was getting a little tired as he finished wading through a
chapter on physical signs in chest disease but carried on when
he found a section on clinical lung function tests. Here was a
picture of someone using a spirometer and a diagram of what
was being measured. It might make the test much more
interesting if he accurately understood what was going on,
and it would give him something to tell the patients about at
the same time.

Alister made a heading of 'Vital Capacity', as he did know
that was what he measured. He noted that the maximum
volume of air which can be expelled from the lungs after full
inspiration can be reduced by restrictive defects, deformity of
the chest and airways obstruction. The fraction of forced vital
capacity (FVC) expelled in the first second (FEV_1) is reduced
by increased airways resistance. Abbreviations began to
accumulate. PEFR, MEFV, TLC (wasn't that tender loving
care?), TLV, and RV.

By the time Alister had laboriously traced over a diagram
showing measurement of functional residual capacity by gas
dilution methods, and its formula of $HE_1 \times Vs = HE_2 \times$

159

(Vs + V1), his brain went on strike. He simply could not read any more.

Alister rubbed his eyes and looked at his watch. He was horrified to find it was nearly eleven o'clock. His family must be worried sick, and all the doors would certainly be locked by now. He decided to ring home from the phone in Nicola's office before sneaking out through the adjacent fire escape door at the end of the corridor. He would have to hurry as he didn't want to miss the last train home. Alister's salary didn't run to luxuries like taxis. He quickly replaced the textbooks and gathered up his pens and the notebook he had almost filled. His sisters would be so impressed when they saw this – especially those abbreviations which always made anybody sound as though they knew a lot more than they really did. He could see himself arriving home to the pot of tea and toasted sandwiches they would make for him. 'Paroxysmal nocturnal dyspnoea', he would intone, 'very interesting, you know.' He practised saying it aloud as he walked back to the office.

Alister tried the door of Nicola's office, before remembering that it would, of course, be locked. He shrugged and hauled open the heavy door to the cold store to get the frosty bunch of keys out again. His hand ran over the surface of the shelf several times before he realised that the keys were not there. Alister frowned and checked his pockets. He could have sworn he'd replaced the keys after closing the locker room. He would be in big trouble if he'd lost them. Alister bit his lip and then remembered in relief that a spare bunch of keys was kept hidden behind the ECG machine in the exercise lab. He would replace the lost ones with those until he could locate the originals.

As he passed Nicola's office, Alister heard a distinct noise, which sounded like the chink of roughly handled glass. He tried the handle of the door again but it was firmly locked.

'Miss Jarvis?' he called softly, uncertainty in his voice. 'It's Alister . . . Can I use your phone, please?'

There was no answer and complete silence from within. He waited, puzzled. He must have imagined the noise, or perhaps something had simply overbalanced.

Without turning on the lights he made his way through the computer room to the exercise lab. Small bright red and green

160

lights pierced the darkness from the banks of machines, like eyes following his progress. He edged around the treadmill to the ECG machine, resting on a table against the wall. Alister moved mostly by sense of touch as he didn't want to put on a light and alert anybody who might be nearby. He would probably get into trouble for being in the department at this time of night. He felt behind the machine and found the keys, but at his touch they slipped through the gap between table and wall to land with a loud jingle in the dust of the laboratory floor. He squatted down and reached under the table. He could just feel them with the tip of his fingers and he shut his eyes to help his arm stretch just a little bit further.

A sudden awareness that he was no longer alone made Alister shiver and crane his head up from his awkward position. He peered into the dimness and his exclamation was one of surprise.

'I thought you might be security and I'd be in trouble,' he said, relieved. 'You're working late as well.' He peered under the table. 'I'm just getting the keys so I can make a . . '

Alister Cunningham never knew what hit him. It was, in fact, a small cylinder of compressed oxygen of the type that hangs on a wall with an attached mask, ready for dealing with emergencies. In this instance, it created one.

Sam Donnelly was thankful he wasn't on night shift as he changed from his dark blue orderly's uniform into his street clothes. He was nearing retirement after thirty years' employment at the Northern and lately his back had been playing merry hell: too many years of lifting obese patients, heavy stretchers in and out of ambulances and manoeuvring the awkward large beds with their tall, solid railings at either end. His view of patients as he pushed them, framed by high-railed bedheads and wearing their hospital-issue striped pyjamas, always made him think of them as prisoners. His own dark, plain uniform added to the impression so Sam had always gone out of his way to be cheerful. Many patients remembered with kindness the patter of the grey, stooped porter, delivered with a warm smile, that eased the nervousness of the ride to theatre or a boring wait for an ambulance or x-ray.

Sam straightened slowly and rubbed the small of his back

where the familiar throbbing sensation was gaining intensity. He walked slowly to the side door he always exited from as he lived only a few blocks away and leaving by the main entrance added almost ten minutes to the time the journey took. The frosty air nipped at his ears and his normally rosy veined cheeks and nose swiftly turned a deep purple. He turned up the collar of his jacket and debated whether to light a smoke to warm the air before it reached his lungs. He decided against it as the thought of his cosy living room, with his slippers warming up against the pot belly stove, occurred to him. He would wait and enjoy a pipe in the warmth with the welcome companionship of his wife, Mavis. The picture of her nodding over her knitting, with their old labrador, Ned, asleep with his head on her foot made him quicken his pace.

As Sam turned a corner, his foot slipped sideways slightly on a patch of ice, jarring his back. He stopped, leaning forward with an arm on a lamp post, rubbing his back with his other hand and cursing softly as he waited for the pain to subside. Eventually, with a sigh, he straightened.

He found himself looking at the back of the respiratory wing of the hospital and his eye was caught by a partially opened fire escape door. He stared at it, pondering the possibilities. Someone could have broken in but it was more likely that a staff member had let themselves out that way after hours. They'd had trouble with that happening recently, but nobody would ever admit to it and increased security had failed to catch anybody. Sam knew he should report it but the pain in his back and the lure of the aspirin and hot cocoa he was heading towards were too much. He turned his gaze resolutely away from the gently swaying door and walked painfully on, his hand still resting on his back. He would telephone the head porter's office and report it as soon as he reached home.

A hundred yards on, Sam stopped again.

'Damn it,' he said aloud angrily, turning to retrace his path.

Minutes later, the respiratory department ground floor was lit up like a Christmas tree. The security men were careful not to touch surfaces which would be dusted as soon as the police arrived but the arrest button in the exercise laboratory was depressed instantly to summon assistance for the lad lying

162

beside the treadmill, his face grotesquely squashed against one of the forest of tall gas tanks.

Mike Jennings, on night shift in casualty again, arrived with the rest of the team in response to the strident alarm. They gently moved Alister as there was no room even to examine him wedged between the tanks and the treadmill. Mike quickly checked for vital signs. Alister's pulse and breathing were detectable but dangerously faint. Mike shone his pen light torch into Alister's eyes as one of his colleagues held an oxygen mask in place. The pupils were reacting but sluggish and one looked larger than the other. Gently palpating the skull, Mike's fingers quickly found the damaged area.

'Put an IV line in,' he directed his companion. 'I'm going to call neurosurgery.'

Several frantic phonecalls were made as Alister's limp body was gently prepared for transfer. A neurosurgeon was not available, thanks to ongoing emergency surgery. No one could see him until morning and there was no hope of an immediate brain scan. Intensive care had no ventilator space available due to the Legionnaires' cases but if the equipment was available in the respiratory ward they could fit him in somewhere. Mike rang for the respiratory registrar on call, delighted to find it was Bob Matthews.

Bob's arrival in the exercise lab, in record time, coincided with that of the police. They moved in efficiently and rapidly arranged themselves around the department. The number of personnel made the scene one of confusion with orders being shouted more than once to gain compliance. A large German Shepherd strained at a heavy choke chain that looked capable of towing ships. The dog and his handler were directed towards the fire escape door.

'My God,' said Bob, as he recognised Alister. 'What the hell's going on?'

'Do you know this gentleman, sir?' One of the police officers was flashing a badge in his direction.

'Yes, of course. He's Alister Cunningham, one of the technicians in this department.'

'Do you know why he would be here at this time of night?'

'I have no idea.' Bob shook his head, still dazed by the shock. He moved towards Mike. 'What happened?'

163

Mike edged back over the treadmill to allow room for the gurney to enter.

'He's had rather a nasty blow on the back of the head.'

'Have you moved him from the position he was found in?' a heavily built, plain-clothes detective asked Mike.

'Yes, of course we did,' he snapped. 'We couldn't have examined him squashed amongst those tanks.'

Bob was still cornered by the first officer. 'Would you have a home address for Mr. Cunningham?'

'Could you demonstrate the position he was found in please, Doctor.' The detective raised his voice to be heard over the confusion.

'Not right now.' Mike was incredulous. 'We've got a critically ill patient here.' To emphasise his point he began to follow the gurney being eased through the door of the lab. Bob made to follow.

'Excuse me, Doctor.' The detective switched his attention to Bob, laying a restraining hand on his arm. 'Are there any drugs kept in this vicinity?'

'Yes,' said Bob tersely, pointing towards the computer room. 'In the first office on the right in that direction. It's a pretty well-stocked supply.'

'Any narcotics?'

'No.' Bob shook his head. 'Look, I'm sorry but I'll have to go.' He shook the detective's hand off his arm.

'Please don't leave the hospital, Doctor Matthews. We may need to talk to you again.'

Bob was already at the door. 'Not much chance of that, Inspector, don't worry.'

Chapter Eighteen

The bedclothes were thrown back instantly as the electronic alarm clock began its insistent beeping. Nicola Jarvis barely noticed the chill of the morning as she made her way into the bathroom and turned on the shower. She soaped her body slowly and luxuriously with masses of shower gel, enjoying the feel of her warm slippery skin. Her face was turned into the hot needles of water and her hands chased foam and then lingered between her legs. Abruptly she withdrew them and reached for the shampoo. Masturbation had lost any appeal now that the real thing was on her agenda. After blow drying her hair, Nicola broke with a long standing tradition and failed to scrape the locks back from her face and secure them in her usual prim knot. She let her hair wave softly to her shoulders, tucking it behind her ears while she attended to her make-up.

Studying her face critically for a moment, Nicola felt pleased with what she saw. Her skin was clear and required only the faintest touch of foundation to conceal the minor flaws and barely discernible lines. The electrolysis treatment had effectively removed the hint of moustache she had been developing. She had suffered for hours having her underarms and legs treated at the same time but it was worth it for the wonderfully smooth, unshadowed skin that shaving could never achieve.

She needed mascara only to colour the tips of her dark lashes and add some body. Nicola used a magnifying mirror to aid application as there was no way she could do it with her glasses on. She brushed on a touch of green eyeshadow, though the sparkle which had appeared in her eyes in the last few days needed nothing to accentuate it. She put on her glasses to survey the finished effect and smiled at her reflection. She had an appointment with an optician this evening and was going to have another go at wearing contact lenses. She had tried them some years ago and had been unable to tolerate the irritation they caused her eyes, but there were the new soft ones available now and Nicola was sure they were going to be perfect. A slight green tinting would add depth to the colour of her eyes.

She dressed in the new outfit she had purchased the day before; a forest green wool skirt that hung in flattering folds, a soft white viyella blouse with lace trimming on the collar, and a white angora cardigan with a decoration of tiny green fir trees above the waist band and cuffs. It was very frivolous for Nicola Jarvis but she loved the sudden transformation into femininity it produces. She zipped up long black boots and decided the two hundred pounds the outfit had cost was well worth it.

She made her toast and coffee and then took another new purchase from the cupboard, Marmite. She knew they ate a lot of in New Zealand and she was sure she would love it. A surge of warm emotion went through her as she spread the mysterious mixture thickly on her buttered toast, remembering her conversation with Tony Lawrence the day before.

They had been alone in her office, too briefly, but Nicola had taken the opportunity to express her sympathy over the break-up of his marriage. He had looked surprised, even angry for a moment or two but then he had thanked her. She knew it was too soon to offer anything more than sympathy but had ventured a remark that perhaps the near future might hold unexpected happiness. Tony's smile had been definitely friendly then, and he had confided – 'Just between you and me' he had said – that he intended emigrating to New Zealand. A job had been advertised in the *New Zealand Medical Journal*. He was holding a copy of the journal and had shown her the advertisement. A job for a specialist physician with an interest in respiratory medicine was available in a place called Gisbourne. The salary was $52,600 to $66,400 per annum, in accordance with the specialist automatic scale. That sounded pretty good.

Nicola had skimmed through the details of hospital size, staffing, supporting services and expected duties of the appointee to read that Gisbourne offered a superior town and country life style. There were miles of beaches nearby and prolific opportunities for outdoor pursuits including hunting, fishing and tramping. The city also had some four hundred and fifty clubs and organisations available. Nicola had been about to express her approval to Tony when they had been interrupted by Sue, who wanted to organise the next week's drugs for a trial patient who was due. Tony had folded the journal and stuck it into his coat pocket, winking at Nicola as he excused himself.

'Just between you and me,' Nicola whispered to herself with delight as she carried her breakfast to a coffee table and seated herself beside the fan heater which was puffing out a welcome circle of hot air. She jumped up again almost immediately and hurried into the bedroom to retrieve the book she had been reading until 2am – the final purchase she had made on her shopping spree of the previous evening. She studied the glossy large format book again. It had cost £25 but she would have happily paid twice as much. It was entitled, *New Zealand – A Celebration*, with a beautiful cover photograph of a still lake reflecting the craggy mountains surrounding it.

Her coffee grew cold as she flicked through the masses of colour photographs once more. It seemed like a fairyland of greens and blues. Rolling pastureland, exotic forests and water in so many forms. The sea was always close but there were also so many lakes, rivers, waterfalls and even geysers. The snow on the mountains seemed another shade of blue, reflecting shades of water or sky. Nicola shut the book with reluctance. She would reread the history again tonight and then make her plans for the invitation Tony would not refuse. She wouldn't wait to share the book with him but it would have to be nonchalantly handled.

'You were talking about New Zealand?' she would say, casually. 'I've got a book about it – it's been tucked away on a shelf for years but perhaps you'd like to come for a cup of coffee sometimes and have a look?' The cup of coffee could easily be extended to a dinner and Nicola would reshuffle her cards after that.

Thinking of the invitation made her remember her own breakfast. She took a large bite of her toast and then her face puckered with distaste and she washed her mouthful away with the cold coffee. What horrible stuff Marmite was! It looked dark and smelled deliciously like gravy in the jar but was pale and anaemic-looking on the toast. And so salty! Nicola emptied the toast into the bin and the coffee down the sink. It was well past her usual time to leave for work, anyway.

She wasn't surprised to see a huddle of outpatient staff behind the reception desk as she passed. She had never been included in the popular gossip sessions and indeed suspected that she herself was a common topic. Well, she'd really give them something to talk about soon! She was surprised to find the administrative head of the hospital, Mr. Jackson, in the company of two men outside her office, especially as one was in police uniform.

Mr. Jackson met her cool look of enquiry. 'Ah, Miss Jarvis.' He indicated the man in street clothes beside him. 'This is Detective Inspector Willis. He'd like a word with you.'

'Certainly.' Nicola was unruffled, as though speaking to the police was a normal start to her working day. 'Just let me hang up my coat. I'll be with you in a moment.'

The girls in the locker room fell silent as Nicola entered. She looked at each of them with an expression of faint irritation. Her gaze fell lastly on Amanda, whose face was swollen and blotchy.

'What on earth is going on?'

Amanda's tears flowed anew and Sue patted her on the shoulder and glared at Nicola.

'There was some sort of a break-in here last night,' she said reluctantly.

'It's happened before.' Nicola hung up her coat and new cardigan in her locker. 'People are always after drugs,' she continued. 'What's so upsetting about it?'

Barbara's voice was cool. 'For some reason Alister Cunningham was here after hours. He was attacked and is now on a life support system with suspected brain death.'

Nicola clicked shut her locker and donned her white lab

168

coat. 'That's very unfortunate. He certainly shouldn't have been here after hours. No doubt that's why the police want to speak to me. I suggest you all get on with your work. It's not going to do anybody any good if you let it interfere with what needs to be done.'

'Bitch!' Barbara quietly but vehemently voiced their collective reaction when she mistakenly thought Nicola was out of earshot.

She marched decisively into her office and sat with her back to her desk.

'How can I help you, Inspector?'

'Well, firstly, Miss Jarvis, we'd like you to have a good look around your office and see whether anything has been touched. At this point in time we don't believe the intruder actually got in. The keys were untouched and there are gouge marks around the lock but no evidence of it having been forced.'

Nicola rose and looked at the door. It was largely covered with black fingerprint dust but the scratches in the metal fitting around the keyhole could be seen. Judging by the mess of powder with no clear impressions, the search for prints had been unsuccessful.

She stood then in the doorway and surveyed her office carefully. Her large desk was as tidy as always with the numerous items sorted according to size and priority. The container beside the telephone housed ECG rulers, pens and pencils. Neatly rolled tourniquets, peak flow meters and a sphygmomanometer filled the space between the container and the pile of patient notes needing attention. In front of them lay patient files, protocols, spirometry results and computer printouts of various types. A Hewlett Packard programmable calculator lay in the centre of the desk with its adaptor. Nicola frowned.

'That should have been locked away. It was careless of me.'

She surveyed the remainder of the office briefly and then walked towards the wall of cupboards. Finding the doors locked as normal she returned to her desk and pulled open the top right hand drawer. Reaching in behind an assortment of stationery items she removed a small bunch of keys from amongst the paper clips and showed it to her visitors.

'That's in its usual place. I'm quite sure it hasn't been disturbed.'

The detective nodded. 'Can you just check on the drugs as well for us, please?'

'Certainly.' Nicola's heels clicked against the lino as she moved back to the cupboards. She dismissed the first one, tapping on its glass door.

'The only drugs there are associated with trials we have running currently. Unmarked bottles which are boxed as you can see – no incentive for a thief even to open it, I wouldn't think.'

She opened the next cupboard door and gazed at the stack of lidless boxes containing syringes, needles and IV equipment.

'Impossible to tell if anything's been removed, but it doesn't look any different than it did yesterday to me.'

The detective nodded a little wearily.

Nicola unlocked the last door. A wealth of tiny boxes filled the shelves. Alphabetically sorted into irregular heaps, the drugs covered a wide range. Every type of available inhaler was represented: Fenoterol, ipratropium, isoprenaline, salbutamol, terbutaline, budesonide, sodium cromoglycate – Nicola's gaze flicked over at least a dozen of them. Many of these drugs were also there in other forms – tablets, capsules, syrup, dissolvable tablets and sprinkling powders. The cupboard was well stocked with various corticosteroid drugs, emergency items such as antiarrhythmics, atropine, adrenaline and calcium in case of an arrest in the department as well as numerous other pharmacological supplies of dubious value.

'It looks fine to me.' Nicola stood back to allow the inspector a better look. 'There's really not much here that would be of any benefit to someone looking for street drugs,' she told him. 'Narcotics are kept in a safe in the outpatient nurse's station.'

'Yes, thanks.' Inspector Willis motioned for her to sit down again. 'Tell me, Miss Jarvis, is it common practice for any of your technicians to be in these rooms after hours?'

'What time are we talking about?'

'We got called shortly after 11 pm. We believe the attack on

170

Mr Cunningham had occurred about thirty minutes or so before that.'

'No.' Nicola's lips pursed. 'Alister should not have been here at that time. Nobody should have. The department would have been locked by the porters hours before that.'

'We found this in Mr. Cunningham's bag.' He held out the notebook to Nicola. 'And his mother said he had planned to work in the library. We understand he had his dinner in the hospital cafeteria earlier.'

'That's quite possible, I suppose.' Nicola leafed through the notebook. 'He's certainly been doing some reading and if this was all written last night he could well have been here until a late hour. I knew nothing about it, however.'

'Right.' Inspector Willis nodded at Nicola and the uniformed officer pocketed the notebook. 'Thanks for your assistance, Miss Jarvis. We'll be in touch if anything else crops up. We've been unable to contact Dr. Anthony Lawrence, by the way. Would you have any idea where we might find him?'

Nicola glanced at the wall clock in surprise. 'He's usually in the hospital very early. You could contact the ward if you can't reach him by page.'

Nicola noticed Bob Matthews talking quietly to Sue in the corridor as the police left. Sue looked deliberately away when she approached them and her face betrayed her revulsion at the tone of Nicola's query to Bob about Alister's condition. The only interest she seemed to have in his condition was the inconvenience it was going to cause her.

Bob was looking very subdued. 'The neurosurgery boys have got him at the moment. They're going to operate for a subdural this morning but I don't think there's much hope, personally. He's alive, but the electroencephalogram was pretty damning.' Bob rubbed his chin, uncharacteristically shadowed by a heavy stubble. 'I must go and find a shave. I haven't even been in my room since I came on duty.'

The news of the break-in and critically ill victim sparked off a new wave of enthusiasm from journalists now familiar with the layout and personnel of the Northern. Jemima Pride was slow to find out about the new incident which annoyed her considerably. She had spent most of her day researching the

171

previous information published on AIDS and working on her item which she was confident would provide front page material. 'AIDS Strikes Newcastle' or perhaps 'Two Killers in the Northern'. She spent an hour wondering what paper to submit the scoop to, finally deciding it was time to move to a classier publication like *The Journal*. She was furious when, having contacted an editor, she was thanked for the story but told they would put their own reporters on to it and didn't want her work. Well, there were plenty of other papers who would be grateful to pay her!

Disgruntled, she arrived back at the Northern in the late afternoon and her mood worsened when she read about the new development at the hospital in the evening edition of the newspaper she had picked up. The break-in was attributed to someone on the hunt for drugs and the police had no leads at present. What was more interesting to Jemima was that it had occurred in the respiratory department and was therefore linked to Dr. Anthony Lawrence – the son of a bitch! Jemima felt a surge of malice towards him and a certain glee, knowing what his reaction might be when he read her morning's efforts – if she could get them published, of course. He wouldn't be able to brush journalists off so easily after that.

Outpatients were packing up for the day when Jemima entered. She didn't approach the reception desk but pretended to be absorbed in material on her clipboard, walking purposefully in the direction she wished to go. No one questioned her. There were any number of employees roaming the hospital on various tasks and if someone held a clipboard or wore a white coat and looked as though they knew what they were doing, they could go almost anywhere unchecked.

She walked past the empty examination rooms with a quick glance into each one. When she heard voices coming from one room she ducked into the examination room next door to it, holding the door almost closed and listening carefully. Somebody was upset, by the sound of it, and Jemima found eavesdropping one of her most successful techniques.

The room beside Jemima was the outpatient kitchen. Muriel was making Amanda a cup of tea, having found her sobbing a few minutes previously in the female staff toilet.

'I'm sure he'll be all right, lovey,' Muriel was saying. 'They say the operation went very well this morning. They got all the blood clots out and fixed up the fracture. He'll wake up and want his breakfast tomorrow, you just wait and see.'

'No.' Amanda shook her head tearfully. 'I know he'll die. It's the third, don't you see?'

'Third what?' Muriel was a curious as Jemima.

'Death. It comes in threes.' Amanda sniffed and then blew her nose noisily on the paper towel Muriel handed her. She didn't need any further prompting.

'There was Sharon Andrews – she was only twenty-eight and I'd talked to her only the day before, and then there was Bruce Matheson and he was young too. He was married and had two little children. There wasn't anything really wrong with them – they were in the trial because their asthma wasn't too bad.'

Muriel clicked her tongue sympathetically. 'What happened to them, lovey?'

Amanda wasn't listening. She stared into her teacup. 'Now there's Alister, and nobody liked him. It makes it even worse.'

'Drink your tea, pet.' Muriel advised. 'Things coming in threes is only an old wive's tale, you know.'

'No.' Amanda shook her head firmly. 'It's happened to me before. My younger sister was run over and killed just before my mother got sick, and then my grandfather died, and my grandmother only six months later. It really is true.'

Amanda's unusual eloquence was beginning to fade and she sipped at her cup a few times before she spoke again.

'At least it means that the rest of the people in the trial will be OK, I suppose. I really didn't want to do it any more, you know, waiting for the third? Dr. Lawrence was very nice about it really.'

'Ach, that poor man.' Muriel's tone was disgusted. 'With that trollop of a wife running off like that. Would you like another cuppa, dearie? You still look a bit peaky.'

The department was almost empty as Jemima quietly made her way into the exercise lab. She paused and added some notes to the pages she had just filled with a rapid scrawl. The germ of an idea had planted itself and its growth was reflected in the increasing speed with which her pen ran across the paper.

She moved through the computer room and looked around her with ferret-like darting glances. She knocked softly at the open office door and smiled warmly at the woman who looked up. Nicola's face reflected the disappointment she felt at not yet having seen Tony. She did not want to waste the inaugural appearance of the new outfit but she also had no intention of missing her appointment with the optician.

'Sorry to disturb you,' Jemima said. 'Do you by any chance know Dr. Lawrence?'

'Yes, of course.' Nicola was tidying up her desk and picked up a stapler before looking at Jemima again. 'Why?'

'My name's Jemima Pride, from *The Journal*.' She waved her clipboard by way of a pass. 'I've been assigned to cover the way he's coping with the problems here at present. He's a wonderful man, isn't he?'

'Yes.' Nicola smiled possessively. 'We're proud of him.' She lightly stroked the stapler she now held in her lap.

'Are you his head technician, Miss Jarvis?' Jemima took note of the details afforded by the lapel badge. 'Our photographer will be arriving shortly. Perhaps we could get a photograph of you both together?'

Nicola smoothed back her hair. 'I'm not sure about that. He's a busy man.'

'I understand he has personal difficulties at the moment as well.'

'I beg your pardon?' Nicolas was wary.

'I believe it was not his wife that I saw him leaving the hospital with last night.'

'What on earth are you talking about?'

'A very attractive young woman with long black hair.' Jemima licked her lips.

'I think you'd better leave.' Nicola's voice was cold.

'Their relationship didn't look very professional to me.' Jemima edged back towards the door. The atmosphere was definitely not friendly.

'Get out.' Nicola stood up and advanced towards Jemima, still holding the stapler.

'OK. I'm going. Don't get your knickers in a twist, love. But I'll be back.'

Nicola slammed the door on the retreating journalist and

locked it. Her face twisted into a mask of fury, she crashed the stapler on to her desk top hard enough to mark the woodwork and jam the appliance irreparably. She took several deep breaths then yanked open the desk drawer, sticking her fingers with drawing pins as she scrabbled for the keys. With the door to the cupboard unlocked, files and patient notes were thrown heedlessly behind her as she sorted through the pile.

Bridget Gardiner. Patient ten. She withdrew the file and dropped it on to her desk. It wasn't true, of course, that malicious slut of a reporter had invented it. But then, how would she have known about Mrs. Gardiner? A page in the folder ripped as Nicola looked again at the final completed entry, knowing already that the patient had been in the department for an exercise test the day before. And Tony had been unusually late in arriving this morning. . . . Everybody had noticed. She tapped her pen against the desk in a furious staccato, then ripped a corner from her desk blotter and scribbled on it an item from Mrs. Gardiner's personal details in the front of her file. The scrap of paper was shoved into the pocket of the green skirt. Nicola heaped the files roughly back into the cupboard. Finding the door couldn't close properly on them, she gave it a vicious shove then left it ajar, locking her office and storming past Amanda, finally on her own way home. The optician was in for an uncomfortable appointment with the last client on his books for that day.

Jemima had remained outside the locked door of the office for several moments, listening with interest to the sounds of fury within. She jumped with fright when she found she was not alone in her eavesdropping.

'I think you may have upset somebody.' The stranger's smile was relaxed, revealing very white and even teeth. Jemima clutched her clipboard protectively and eyed the immaculate pin-stripe suit the man was wearing.

'You don't really think that Dr. Lawrence is having an affair with one of his patients, do you?'

Jemima moved away from the office door. Her eyes narrowed shrewdly, she demanded: 'Are you a friend of his?'

'Not exactly. I do work with him quite a lot though, which is why I'm here now. I heard about the attack on young Alister

175

and I wanted to find out how he is.' He looked at the closed door behind them and smiled at Jemima. 'But I don't think now would be a very good time to make enquiries, do you?'

She sniffed. 'You don't need to, anyway. I heard that his brain surgery this morning went very well and he's probably going to recover.' She moved away, wanting to end the conversation. Being present when Miss Jarvis emerged from her office was something Jemima could do without. And besides, in spite of, or perhaps because of, the good looks of the man beside her, she suddenly felt distinctly ill at ease in his company.

Tony Lawrence received none of the previous welcome from Jody and tried to coax him from his position tucked firmly behind his mistress's legs, postponing his apologetic glance at Bridget.

'I hope you don't mind. My car just sort of automatically came in this direction when I left the hospital.'

Her smile began in her eyes. 'You're in luck. It's not a lump of dried up stroganoff tonight.'

The telephone rang as he followed her into the already familiar and welcoming room. The fire was blazing and Tony picked up the tennis ball from the couch to woo Jody.

'Want a game?' he offered, but the dog padded past him without a glance and flopped down with a grunt in front of the fire.

'You've gone right off me, haven't you?' Tony asked, amused. 'Well, I still think you're the nicest almost Otterhound I've ever met.'

Bridget had answered the phone and given her number, smiling at Jody's blatant disapproval of her visitor. She replaced the receiver with a frown a few seconds later and Tony looked at her, puzzled.

'I've been getting weird calls all evening,' she explained. 'No one answers.'

'Has it happened before?'

'Well, some kids at school got my number once, but they usually give themselves away by giggling. These calls are totally silent – like the line's dead.'

Bridget answered the phone again twenty minutes later and she spoke curtly. 'Cut this out, whoever you are. There are much more interesting things to play with than the telephone.' She smiled at Tony as she cut off the call. 'I can't be as rude as I'd like to be, just in case it is one of my pupils.'

They were laughing about Jody's jealously of Tony when the telephone rang again only ten minutes later. He rose quickly. 'I'll get it.'

He picked it up on its second ring and waited. No one spoke. He counted to ten and then said, slowly and clearly, 'If you call this number again, it will be reported to the police. Why don't you grow up and stop making a bloody nuisance of yourself.' Tony thought he heard a gasp at the other end of the line and the call was disconnected.

'That's fixed the little buggers,' he grinned at Bridget. 'Probably scared the pants off them.'

After that, the telephone remained silent.

Chapter Nineteen

Patient number 11 in the Northern's respiratory department's current drug trial, Dougal Dewar, awoke with a pleasurable feeling of anticipation. He was due for exercise and lung function tests at 9.15 a.m. and today he was going to take the plunge and ask Amanda to go out with him. She was the reason he had agreed to take part in the trial in the first place. He had noticed her some time ago when he had gone to a routine outpatient's appointment and she had done his spirometry test. Her smallness and slightly pathetic aura roused Dougal's protective instincts. He longed to put an arm around her and feel that petite body snuggled against him. He had been surprised at his initial reaction to Amanda as she was so unlike the type of girl he had been attracted to in the last few years. It must be a mark of maturity on his part, he decided. At twenty-three, with a secure job and £300 in the bank, he felt ready to settle down. He had sown enough wild oats to last him the rest of his life.

Dougal dressed in his jeans, a clean shirt and a heavy pullover, lacing up his boots before making his way quietly towards the bathroom. His flatmate, Frank, was still asleep, probably with company, and Dougal didn't want to be held up this morning. He scraped a razor over his face with care but the heaviness of growth made him permanently look as though he hadn't shaved for a day or two. Not that this had ever hampered his success with the ladies, though. Dougal was immensely popular. He had a delightfully good nature, with a wide grin and a ready sense of humour. He was also very attractive in a rough diamond fashion. His mop of black curls and twinkling dark blue eyes topped an impressive body. At six foot two, Amanda would have to stand on tiptoe to see over his shoulder but that only increased her attractiveness for Dougal. He was tired of the more voluptuous and often brassy females he had conquered in the past. The ease with which they all leaped into bed with him, usually on the first date, had been an ego boost initially but Dougal's gentle nature had made it very difficult for him to bring an end to these empty relationships when the novelty wore off – usually on the second date. There had been a very embarrassing incident not so long ago when two of his female acquaintances decided to battle for supremacy in his affections with a fist fight in his local. They had both moved on now, but he was still ragged about it by his mates, getting ribald requests for ringside seats when he entered the pub.

In spite of being aware of his physical attractiveness, Dougal was, for the first time, nervous of making an approach. Amanda was in such a totally different category of womankind and he was worried that she might not even consider him as a potential date. If she was unattached, that is, which seemed unlikely to him. He scrubbed hard at his hands, unsuccessfully trying to remove the traces of engrained grease that outlined his fingerprints and the base of his nails. He thoroughly enjoyed his job as a mechanic, loved to work with a reluctant engine and make it run sweetly again. Permanently dirty hands had up until now seemed a small price to pay. He was also lucky enough to have landed a job in a thriving business with a great boss. He even had permission to be late on these mornings of his trial participation. His boss was impressed by anything medical and felt he was making his own contribution to the furtherance of medical science by allowing an employee time off to be studied. Dougal always made the time up anyway. He hated to leave a job unfinished and often worked on for an hour or more after knock-off time to complete a task. He was good, too. Promotion to head mechanic was on the cards in the next few years.

He didn't have enough time for any breakfast and instead drained the bottle in the 'fridge of almost a pint of milk, no doubt earning Frank's wrath by condemning him to water on his Weetabix. He let himself out of the basement flat and

179

started up the steps to street level before abruptly turning and re-entering the flat as he remembered that he needed his capsules and diary to take into the hospital. He retrieved the diary from under the battered paperback copy of the Harold Robbins novel he was reading at present, and after a search found the bottle of capsules hidden under a discarded dirty sock. He had even forgotten to take the morning's capsule in his haste to leave so swallowed it without water as he made his way outside again.

It was nearly 8.40 a.m. and he ran the two blocks just in time to leap on to a packed bus. Panting from the exertion he pressed himself into the only space remaining at the base of the staircase and was still trying to catch his breath as the bus halted again and a new knot of people struggled on. The bus moved away jerkily and an obese woman settled heavily against Dougal for support. He almost fell on to the stairs and gave up the unequal struggle to stay near the exit. He clambered up the spiral staircase with difficulty and found that the many upper deck occupants were all taking advantage of the permission to smoke. Dougal hung on to a pole near the stairs, still trying to catch his breath but recognising with dismay that it was going to be difficult. The cold, running for the bus, and now the heavily smoke-laden atmosphere seemed to be triggering an asthmatic attack. He wasn't too worried. He had never had a really bad attack and he concentrated now on breathing slowly and calmly. He would come right once he was out of the smoke, and he had an inhaler in his pocket if it should become necessary. He was going to the right place anyway, he thought, hoping it would not interfere with his tests. He was fervently hoping that Amanda would be looking after him today and planned to ask her out when she was sticking ECG electrodes to his chest.

Being out of the bus didn't seem to help much and then he had to hurry the block from the bus stop to the hospital as it was ten-past nine and his appointment was for nine-fifteen.

He grinned with delight in spite of his heavy wheezing when he found Amanda waiting for him.

'Are you all right?' she queried, her face concerned.

'Yeah, fine,' Dougal puffed. 'Running for the bus . . . had to go upstairs . . . too much smoke.'

He handed the diary and bottle to her and sat down unbidden. He was fighting hard to control his breathing and his embarrassment at the situation wasn't helping. He had always felt that asthma was a vaguely sissy complaint to have, and to be having an attack in front of the woman he hoped to date was seriously undermining his resolve.

Amanda was marking the time of the attack in the diary – the only episode in the last three weeks. She looked worriedly at him.

'I think you'd better have a puff of your bronchodilator. Have you got it with you?'

He nodded and produced the plastic case from his pocket. He expelled as much air as he could from his lungs and fitted his lips firmly around the mouthpiece of the aerosol. He began breathing in deeply and then depressed the canister, continuing his inspiration as far as possible. He tried to count to ten before expelling the air again but didn't have that much control. Amanda was watching him carefully.

'OK. We'll wait a few minutes and you can have another puff if you need to. I'll give Dr. McGinty a call while we're waiting. I'm not sure that we should do any tests on you today.'

Dougal felt slightly easier by the time Amanda returned. He had already given himself a second dose of the bronchodilator and she recorded it meticulously in the diary.

'I'm ready for anything now,' he told her.

He watched as she sorted out the forms for the day's visit. She depressed the button on the intercom to ask Gwen to come and do a pre-exercise venous blood gas. Dougal took off his pullover and rolled up the sleeve of his shirt, waiting until Amanda was tying the tourniquet to his upper arm to speak.

'I was wondering if maybe you'd like . . .' he began, but broke off abruptly as Sue dashed into the lab.

'Mandy, have you got the drug cupboard key?'

'Oh, yes. Sorry.' Amanda fished in the pocket of her white coat. 'I forgot to put them back.'

'Where on earth is Nicola?'

'Is she still not here?' Amanda was astonished. 'It's not like her.'

'Well, she can stay away forever as far as I'm concerned,' Sue took the keys from Amanda, 'but she's got a patient waiting right now and that guy from the drug company's coming at 9.30. I know who's going to have to take over. As if I hadn't enough of my own to do this morning.' Sue hurried off with an exasperated expression.

Amanda frowned. 'She was supposed to be looking after you this morning, too. It's not like her to be late.'

Dougal was delighted with his luck. 'I'm glad it's you,' he said. 'Do you like being called Mandy, rather than Amanda?'

'I don't mind.' She smiled shyly.

He tried to ignore his still wheezy breathing as he searched for the right phrasing for his invitation. He was thwarted before he even opened his mouth by the arrival of Gwen, who bustled in with a stainless steel kidney dish full of ice and a small syringe balancing on the top.

'Hullo, there. Mr. Dewar, isn't it?' Gwen checked the tourniquet and tightened it, swabbing his elbow and deftly removing the 1 millilitre of blood required almost before he noticed. She spoke to Amanda as she inspected the sample for unwanted air bubbles.

'When's the exercise test schedule, love? I've got a list of gases to collect on the wards a mile long.'

'I'm not sure that we'll do one. We're waiting for Dr. McGinty to come down.'

'Mmm.' Gwen looked thoughtfully at Dougal. 'You don't sound so good, young man.'

Dougal's breathing was worsening again and was clearly audible. He was trying to lean forward unobtrusively and was breathing through his mouth.

'I'm fine,' he said, with some difficulty.

Gwen turned back to Amanda. 'I'll run this through the machine now, before I go upstairs, and let you know. If I'm not down again in time, you can do the next one.'

Amanda giggled. 'You must be kidding.'

Dougal smiled at her. 'I don't mind.' As far as he was concerned she could stick as many needles in him as she fancied.

'It's OK,' she assured him. 'Dr. McGinty can do it.'

The intercom crackled into life a few minutes later when

Gwen called through the blood gas results. Amanda scribbled them down and handed them to Hugh who had just entered the lab.

He scanned the results with a frown and turned to Dougal, asking him to remove his shirt. The door of the lab opened while he was following the instruction and Tony Lawrence looked in.

'Has anybody seen Nicola this morning?' The query faded as he noticed Dougal. He had the earpieces of his stethoscope in place by the time he crossed the room and he placed the bell directly on Dougal's back.

The silence in the room for the next minute or so was broken only by Dougal's increasingly laboured breathing. Tony removed the stethoscope and felt for his pulse. He shook his head in puzzlement as he glanced from his watch to Amanda.

'That's odd,' he muttered, without clarification. 'Can you please get the wheelchair from reception, Mandy? I want to take Dougal here around to A & E.'

Hugh's eyebrows were raised but Tony ignored the unspoken question.

'Don't worry, Dougal. I just want to get this attack of yours under control as soon as possible. We've got more facilities in casualty than here.'

Dougal nodded.

'Any idea of what might have triggered it?' Tony asked.

'Ran for the bus . . . smoky . . .' His words were punctuated by his lengthy and noisy attempts to expel air.

'Have you eaten anything this morning?'

He shook his head. '. . . just milk . . .'

Amanda was waiting with the wheelchair, her expression frightened but determined. For once there was no hint of approaching tears. They supported Dougal on either side and transferred him into the wheelchair.

'Lean forward a bit more and hang onto your knees,' suggested Amanda, giving his hand a squeeze.

'Dougal, have you taken any medication this morning?' Tony began to propel the chair briskly through the corridors with Amanda trotting alongside. She turned her head towards Tony.

'He had two doses of bronchodilator about twenty minutes ago.'

'What was that?' Amanda bent her head to his level and nearly tripped. She placed a hand on the arm of the chair to steady herself.

'Capsule . . . Eight o'clock . . . No, half-past.'

Tony checked his watch. About an hour ago. He lapsed into silence and his face was uncharacteristically grim as he negotiated a turn and began a rapid journey along the corridor leading to A & E. People scattered and stared curiously after them, their own missions temporarily forgotten. Something pretty serious must be wrong with that patient, judging from the faces of the staff with him.

Mike was standing outside a curtained cubicle speaking into a dictaphone, starting his first day shift in casualty. He put the dictaphone down when he saw Tony approaching and stood back to allow them room after indicating that the resuscitation room was free. The nursing staff followed quickly and helped Dougal on to the gurney, one of them automatically slipping a mask onto his face while another collected the items necessary to start an IV.

'Not another trial patient?' Mike directed an incredulous look at Tony.

'Yes, it is. I'm beginning to think there's something a little odd going on. I want him to have some bloods off before he's given any medication for a toxicology screen, and I want the results as soon as possible.' He looked at Amanda as Mike issued directions to the staff. She was standing, pressed against the wall, her eyes fixed on Dougal.

'Mandy, go back to the department, get the code broken on Dougal and bring it back here as fast as you can .'

She nodded silently.

'Don't worry, love,' he added. 'He's going to be fine. We'll make sure of it.'

Tony nodded at the senior registrar who pulled back the curtain.

'I can give Mike a hand with this, if you're busy.'

'That's great, thanks. There's a car accident on the way in. We may need this room but I'll let you know. They're ten minutes or so away at the moment.'

A nurse took a rack of blood samples with the request forms Tony had scribbled out to the laboratory for urgent analysis but it might be some hours before any results would come through. Dougal looked shocking by the time he received his injection of aminophylline. Mike turned up the flow of oxygen coming through the nebuliser and then adjusted the IV Tony had placed.

Tony injected 200 mg hydrocortisone and felt for Dougal's pulse again. He was almost pleased to find the rate had increased from the last time he had checked. It was more normal for the condition the patient was in. An aminophylline infusion was started and the atmosphere was tense for the next couple of minutes, all eyes fixed on Dougal. The staff were all thinking of the recent disaster with Sharon Andrews – a scene that was remembered by all present with dreadful clarity and which seemed to be replaying itself again now. It was Mike who broke the silence, removing his stethoscope from Dougal's chest.

'He's coming right.'

Tony let out a long breath, until then unaware he had been holding it. Dougal's faint grin under the mask was mirrored on the faces surrounding him. They all watched with pleasure the dramatic recovery he was making. His colour became healthier and his breathing quieter and easier. With a smile, Tony read out the improved blood gas results that came through.

Amanda slid through the curtain, clutching a scrap of paper. Dougal gave her a thumbs up sign and her frightened expression lightened into relief and pleasure.

'OK to shift him?' Mike asked Tony as the confusion of ambulances unloading was heard.

'Yes.' Tony nodded and smiled at Dougal. 'We'll have you in for a while, though, and keep an eye on you.' He looked at the sister. 'Can you watch him here for thirty minutes or so and then have him transferred to the respiratory ward?'

She nodded.

'I'm on my way up for a ward round,' continued Tony, 'so I'll be there to admit him. Mandy, would you like to stay and keep Dougal company for a while?'

She looked gratefully at Tony and spoke more firmly than usual. 'Yes, please, Dr. Lawrence.'

'Good. I'll let Nicola know where you are. Dougal might like his boss contacted as well.'

Dougal mumbled something inaudible under the mask. He made a satisfied signal with forefinger and thumb circled at Tony before returning his gaze to Amanda.

Chapter Twenty

Colin Ingram sat on the swivel chair alongside Nicola Jarvis's desk, watching the door. He tapped his fingers impatiently on the desk top and glanced at his watch for the twentieth time. Reaching for the telephone he asked the operator for an outside line. He dialled Nicola's home number, taken from the staff list pinned to the wall by the phone, but again there was no reply.

Colin gave the door a shove with his foot to close it and took the keys from the top right hand drawer. Opening the cupboard, he removed the stack of files he was interested in and extracted from them a thin manilla folder which contained only a single sheet. It listed the patients entered in the salbutamol versus placebo trial, giving patient numbers, home addresses and telephone numbers, date entered into the trial and date completed where appropriate. He made a copy of the information, making some quick calculations concerning the later entrants with the help of a Scottish pictorial calendar hanging in a prominent position by the desk. It was about time this trial was wrapped up and Colin was looking forward to seeing the results.

He looked up from his notes when Barbara entered the office.

'Can I get you a cup of coffee or something while you're waiting?'

'No thanks. I'll have to go, I'm afraid. I've got an appointment over at the General.'

'I'll tell Nicola you were here. I can't think what's happened to her. She must have had some problem on the way to work.'

'I'll call in again after I've been to the General.' Colin closed the folder and patted it. 'Do you know what the state of play is regarding entrants for this trial?'

Barbara turned a page on the desk diary beside him. 'Well, there's two being started later today but I don't know what number that will take us up to.'

'That's fine. I've got that.' Colin shut his briefcase and smiled at Barbara. 'It seems to be going very well. By the way, how's poor old Alister?'

'Showing some improvement after surgery, thank goodness,' Barbara replied. 'Looks like he might even regain consciousness before too long.'

'That's great. I'll see you later, then.'

Barbara chewed her lip thoughtfully as she watched the drug rep leave. His comment about how well the trial was going made her wonder how much he knew about his job. None of the department's staff considered it to be going very well. In fact, Dr. Lawrence had called a staff meeting for early that afternoon to discuss it. She wondered if she should have mentioned the meeting to Colin Ingram. He would find out about it when he returned later, though, and Barbara didn't really have much idea of what it was all about.

Amanda came in late to the meeting and squeezed in behind chairs to perch on the solid pile of boxes containing computer paper which filled a corner of the office. Tony noticed her entrance and broke off his quiet discussion with Hugh McGinty and Bob Matthews.

'How's Dougal?'

'He's fine now. Says he wants to go home.' Amanda smiled. She had agreed to go out with him the following evening and was delighted with the prospect.

Tony shook his head. 'We'll keep him in overnight, just to make sure. He can go home in the morning.'

'I'm sure Mandy will be available to carry his bag.' Jackie's comment made Amanda blush furiously. Tony looked across at Sue and Barbara who were busy at the desk, sorting through sheaves of paper and making piles of patient notes and trial folders.

'OK, Sue?'

She nodded and checked the list in her hand.

'First patient in the salbutamol placebo trial was Ian Dalgliesh, completed 31st October. Slight side effects of shakiness noted on active phase. Second was Maureen Scott who completed November 12th.' She glanced at Barbara who was pulling the trial folder from the pile. She scanned it quickly before adding: 'No side effects noted. Some improvement on active phase.'

'Third patient was Alan Henderson,' continued Sue. 'Completed November 15th. Fourth was . . .'

'Hang on a minute,' Hugh interrupted. 'Didn't Henderson have some problems?'

Barbara handed the folder to Hugh who licked his forefinger and turned pages rapidly.

'Yes, I thought so.' He frowned. 'I remember writing this up. He had quite a severe attack of asthma and had an exercise test postponed. Came right at home with bronchodilator treatment but it lasted several hours.'

'Unusual attack?' The query came from Tony.

'Well, he had several mild attacks over the trial period but they were of gradual onset and usually at night. This one came on fairly suddenly in the morning. It was during placebo phase though we didn't crack the code at the time.'

Tony made a note and the file was passed back to Barbara. Sue cleared her throat.

'Patient 04 was Sharon Andrews.' She paused. 'Died due to an asthma attack, week 5, while on placebo.'

There was silence for a moment then Hugh spoke again.

'I've been through her notes pretty carefully. She had had severe attacks previously, hospitalised twice in the last four years.'

Tony shook his head. 'Perhaps she shouldn't have been enrolled in the first place.'

Hugh grunted. 'She was well within inclusion criteria. No hospital admissions in the last twelve months, not using bronchodilators more than five times a week beyond regular t.i.d. dosage. She was using a corticosteroid aerosol as well which was stopped for trial purposes.'

Bob's glance switched from Sue to Tony. 'That could have affected the severity of the attack.'

'Yes.' Tony sighed. 'I don't want to get into a death review

189

right now, though. It's an overall picture of the trial that I'm interested in.' He nodded at Sue again.

'Patient 05 is William Pearson. He's due to complete this week and hasn't had any major problems. A few more attacks than usual in the last couple of weeks. We assume he's on placebo at the moment.'

'Mmm. Put his folder to one side, will you, Barbara? I'll have a look at it later.'

'Patient 06 was Irene McTavish who withdrew herself from the trial in week 7.'

'And died the following week,' put in Hugh.

'What?' Barbara was shocked.

'Didn't you read it in the paper? She died in a house fire.'

'Good grief. I didn't know. That's awful!' Barbara looked about at the other girls who all shook their heads. It was news to them as well. Amanda had paled slightly.

'Sue?' Tony stopped her imminent comment and she searched for her place on the list.

'Patient 07 was Bruce Matheson. Died week 8 while on active phase.'

'That was the possible aspirin reaction, wasn't it?' Bob said to Hugh.

The registrar nodded briefly, watching Tony making his rapid notes.

'Go on, please, Sue.' Tony's tone delayed any further discussion.

'Patient 08 is Jim Moore, on washout at the moment. No problems with the first phase. 09 is Hamish Wright who's . . .' Sue waited for Barbara to reach the latest entry in his folder.

'He's week 4,' she said. 'Due for an exercise test tomorrow.'

'10 is Bridget Gardiner. Week 2, no problems and . . .' Sue turned the page. '11 is Dougal Dewar who's also week 2.' She looked at Tony. 'Shall I put him in as withdrawn?'

'Yes,' said Tony slowly. 'I don't want him to continue. What do you think, Hugh?'

He nodded briefly in agreement and said in an undertone, 'I see what you mean. It's pretty odd.'

Sue was speaking again. 'Patients 12, Melanie Crawford, and 13, Joan Foster, are both on week 1. Mrs. Foster is having problems with persistent wheeziness and has been using her bronchodilator several times a day but it doesn't seem too serious. And that's it.'

Barbara waved another piece of paper. 'There are two further patients who checked out and are due to start week zero this afternoon and three more potentials who haven't been seen yet concerning participation.'

They all waited for Tony's comment. He pondered the notes he'd made.

'Who's seeing the week zeros today?'

'Nicola was supposed to but I expect I will.' Sue sounded resigned.

'Has anybody found out what's happened to her?' Tony queried.

Barbara shook her head. 'That guy from Atlas rang her at home this morning a few times but she wasn't in.'

'Perhaps she had an accident on the way to work.' Jackie sounded interested rather than concerned.

'Maybe she eloped with the milkman,' suggested Barbara which provoked a giggle from Sue. Amanda gave her a stony look.

'It's not very funny, you know. Something must have happened. She's never away.'

'Worse luck.' Barbara's motionless lips belied the fact she had spoken.

'I'll try ringing her again after the meeting,' Sue said tolerantly to Amanda. 'I'm sure it's nothing to get upset about.'

'Let me know when you get hold of her.' Tony folded his piece of paper. 'I won't keep you much longer. Two other things, though. Sue, I want you to postpone starting the new patients this afternoon.'

'It's too late to cancel their appointments. What do I tell them?'

'Just that we're not sure they're suitable or something. Say we'll contact them again if need be.'

Sue looked unconvinced and rolled her eyes at Barbara in a 'What's going on?' expression. Bob's face sported an identical expression but Tony ignored them.

'The other thing I want to check on is the drugs for the trial. What form are they coming in?'

Barbara edged behind Tony's chair and removed a small

191

brown box from the cupboard with some difficulty.

'All the bottles for each patient are in a box like this,' she explained. 'They come from the drug company and all the bottles and boxes are sealed until we start the patient with that number.'

'Who breaks the seals on the bottles. Patients?'

She shook her head. 'We count the capsules in each bottle before the patient takes them for the next week, so we can check if they've missed any on their next visit. Sometimes it's done a day or two before they come, depending on how busy we are.'

'Have you noticed any seals broken before you count them?'

Barbara shook her head slowly. 'But then, we've all sort of pitched in a bit on this trial. Nicola usually does it but other times any of us might look after a visit and then seals might already be broken because somebody's already counted the capsules.'

The other technicians nodded agreement. Hugh was preoccupied reading a patient file and Bob was preoccupied watching Sue. Jackie looked at the clock.

'I've got a patient waiting now.'

'Off you go then.' Tony dismissed the meeting. 'We've all got plenty of work waiting for us. Thanks for your help.'

The girls drifted away apart from Sue who remained to tidy the files. Bob started to follow Tony and Hugh but changed his mind when he saw his opportunity to be alone with Sue.

'I think I'll have another look at the Andrews notes,' he told the others.

Hugh flashed him a wink but Tony nodded gravely.

'Let me know if you find anything that strikes you as odd. We'll be in ICU for a while.'

Sue's face was expressionless. She gave the office door a nudge shut as Bob re-entered.

Tony gave the lift button another impatient jab and then headed for the stairs. Hugh quickened his pace to keep up with the older man.

'What do you think is going on with the trial?' His question was directed at Tony's back, ahead of him by two stairs.

Tony slowed his pace and paused on a landing.

'I'm beginning to wonder if there's some kind of contaminant in the trial medication.'

'You're not serious.' Hugh was frankly incredulous.

'Yes, I am.' Tony moved into the corner as the landing door opened and several nurses came chattering through, their capes held shut in preparation for the chilly walk to the cafeteria for afternoon tea.

'The trial is a disaster,' Tony continued quietly. 'And it's unprecedented. I've never had an asthmatic dying on any previous trial and we've had two deaths, possibly three and a near miss this morning.'

'What do you mean, possibly three?'

'It seems an odd coincidence that Irene McTavish died when she should have still been in the trial.'

'But she withdrew.'

'She didn't return her capsules.'

'It was a house fire.'

'If you were having an acute asthmatic attack, it would make escaping a fire pretty difficult. It was an odd time of day for someone to be trapped like that, don't you think? That sort of accident usually only happens if people are asleep when the fire breaks out.'

Hugh shook his head. 'That's pure speculation.'

'True, but look at the others. There's an increase in number and severity of attacks with almost every patient coming through.'

'We take them off prophylactic treatment. Maybe this brand of oral salbutamol is useless.'

'OK. Even granted that it's useless, we've still had two deaths in young people, both of whom arrived in hospital in plenty of time for emergency treatment that should have been successful.'

'It happens, Tony. Asthma is a killer – you know how dangerous a severe attack can be.'

'Damn it, Hugh.' Tony's voice rose. 'It shouldn't have happened. Acute asthmatic attacks are the most treatable emergencies there are. It especially shouldn't have happened with the kind of monitoring these people had.' He ran a hand angrily through his hair. 'The chances of a young, otherwise healthy person dying in even an acute attack are minimal.

We've had two, nearly three, in the space of as many weeks.'
His voice lowered suddenly as the landing door below them
banged shut and a housesurgeon bounded up the stairs, his
expression harrassed. Hugh waited until he was well past
them.

'So, what are you saying?'

'What if there's something wrong with the medication
we're dishing out? Something in them that's causing bronchoconstriction through allergic response.'

'Such as?'

'I don't know. Aspirin, maybe.'

'You'd have to be allergic to it.'

'Sure. But some of these trial patients are getting through
with no problems.'

'How could the drugs have been contaminated?'

Tony shook his head. 'I can't imagine and it's bugging me.
Could be in the factory, I suppose, but I doubt it. I'm sure
there's something funny though. I ordered bloods for analysis
on Dougal this morning. I asked the lab to check for aspirin
and so on but if it's something out of the ordinary then it's a
needle in a haystack proposition.'

'Maybe somebody's infiltrated the drug company's supply
depot,' suggested Hugh with a smile. 'Someone with a grudge
against drug trials. Weirdoes like those animal liberation
groups.'

Tony snorted. 'I know the idea's preposterous.'

'What made you think of it?' asked Hugh curiously.

'The problems with this trial have been nagging me but with
the hassle of the Legionnaire's outbreak amongst other things
I hadn't given it enough time to come up with any answers. It
was that chap this morning that really triggered the idea. He
had such an uncharacteristically severe attack, coming on
about an hour after he'd taken a trial capsule.'

'That's a pretty slow allergic response.'

'Ah, but he drank about a pint of milk before he took it.'

Another group of nurses edged past them. The sight of
doctors earnestly conversing in awkward places was hardly
unusual and didn't merit a second glance but it prompted
Tony to move on up the stairs. He paused again briefly as
Hugh caught up with him.

'I know it's a crazy thought, but it occurred to me that someone might be deliberately tampering with the trial drugs after they've arrived in the department.'

'So that's what those questions to the girls were about! That's impossible.'

'Is it?' Tony pushed open the door leading to the ICU floor. 'Why was Alister Cunningham cracked over the head, and what was he doing in the department at that time of night, anyway?'

'Maybe he'll be able to tell us.' Hugh reached for overshoes, gown and mask in the ICU ante room. 'There was some pretty encouraging signs of returning consciousness this morning. Reactions to mild pain stimulus, and he even opened his eyes for a second.'

The ICU sister was in Alister's room when they entered.

'How is he?' asked Tony.

'We've had a problem,' she said reluctantly. 'We're waiting on another EEG.'

'Why?'

The sister avoided Tony's eyes. 'We tried to call you earlier. The operator thinks your beep is malfunctioning again.'

'Come on, Clare,' Tony was impatient. 'Out with it – this isn't like you.'

'You're not going to like it.' She drew in a deep breath. 'Shortly after your new registrar visited this morning, some-one checked on Alister because of an arrhythmia alarm. The oxygen setting on the ventilator had been changed. We corrected it, of course, and the arrhythmia –V. Tachy, settled but we don't know how long it was like that and . . .' She bit her lip and her glance trailed from Alister's face to her own hands, nervously twisting a corner of the sheet.

'What was the oxygen setting on?' Hugh spoke for both of them.

Her voice was a whisper. 'Zero.'

'Jesus Christ.' Tony snatched at the wall phone and punched a button. 'Get me Bob Matthews.'

The operator flinched at his tone of fury. Tony leaned with one hand on the wall, his head turned, staring at the frozen scene before him. Hugh looked stunned. Clare agonised. The only discernible movement was Alister's chest, and the only

195

sound the hiss of the ventilator.

Bob's reply was cut short by Tony.

'What were you doing in Alister Cunningham's room this morning?'

'Sorry?'

'Alister Cunninghan. ICU.' Tony spoke deliberately. 'Why did you visit him earlier today.'

'I'm sorry, Tony.' Bob sounded puzzled. 'I don't know what you're talking about. I haven't been near ICU today.'

Chapter Twenty-One

The low pressure area moved in a westerly direction from Siberia and lessened only a little in intensity before pausing over Northern Britain. The dense cloud cover over Newcastle was a deep grey, with a luminous yellow-pink tinge towards the horizons. Small flakes of snow, scudding about in a light breeze, heralded the start of one of the city's few annual falls, melting as they touched tarmac and vehicles.

By the time Bridget Gardiner had parked her Citroën and collected the grocery bags to take inside, the flakes had grown feathery and now drifted straight down to settle into a soft powdery blanket. Bridget halted her path towards the cottage to turn her face skywards. She screwed her eyes shut and held out her tongue, making a wish as she tasted the first flakes. It was a ritual preserved since childhood and faithfully performed with every snowfall but she did feel slightly ridiculous doing it now. She glanced quickly about her for reassurance that there were no passers-by in the lane. It was a silent and deserted world, with the special quietness that a shroud of snow provides. Daylight was fading fast and Bridget shivered. Jody's joyous greeting could already be heard from within the cottage and she would need to hurry to give him a run before it became completely dark.

Having deposited the shopping and given Jody his expected cuddle, Bridget removed her leather boots and donned a pair of thick woolly socks that had once been Peter's. She wrapped a scarf around her neck and tucked the ends into the neck of her anorak. Winding her hair into a ball with one hand she shoved it inside the woollen hat which she pulled firmly down over her ears. Jody sat watching her, quivering with suppressed excitement, a tennis ball clutched firmly in his jaws.

'I don't suppose you'd prefer to stay in front of a fire?' Bridget inquired hopefully.

Jody wagged his tail and a muffled bark came from behind the ball.

'No. I didn't think so.' Bridget shoved her feet into the Wellington boots by the back door and put Jody's lead into her pocket. 'Come on, then.'

They went out through the back garden gate which led into a field belonging to the McMurray's neighbouring farm. It was free of its bovine inhabitants at present and Jody bounded in widening circles, returning periodically to his mistress to deposit the tennis ball and demand a response. His eyesight was excellent. Bridget could barely make out the arc of the ball in the gathering gloom.

Snow was collecting over Jody like icing sugar on a chocolate pudding. Bridget trudged to the far end of the field, noting with some anxiety the depth to which the snow was rapidly accumulating. She hoped desperately that it wouldn't interfere with Tony's planned visit that evening. She whistled for Jody and quickened her pace, leaving the field through another gate which led to the cottage of her nearest neighbour, Miss Bell.

An elderly spinster, Miss Bell lived alone and Bridget made a point of checking on her frequently in cold weather. There had been increased publicity on the dangers of hypothermia in the elderly this year, due to alarming statistics on the number of deaths amongst pensioners during last winter's cold snap. The old lady's cottage was dark and there was no response to Bridget's hammering on the door. The door was locked and she could see nothing by peering through the windows. She made her way past the cottage into the lane, clipping on Jody's lead at the sound of a vehicle approaching. The tractor chugged easily through the snow and the driver shouted a greeting.

Bridget moved to one side of the lane and walked beside the tractor as it slowed, raising her voice over the engine noise.

'Miss Bell isn't at home, Mr. McMurray. I'm a bit worried about her.'

'She's right enough, lass,' Mr. McMurray bellowed back. 'She was feeling a bit poorly when the wife went to see her this morning, so we've got her up at the farm for a day or two.'

Bridget smiled in relief. 'Let me know if I can help.'

'Come up to supper with us, Lass. There's always plenty.'

'Thanks, Mr. McMurray, but I've got a friend coming to visit – if the snow doesn't prevent it, that is.'

'Right enough. Keep yourself warm.' The farmer raised a bare hand in a wave as the tractor speed increased and Bridget fell behind. His weathered skin was testimony to years of work in bitter cold and gloves an unnecessary encumbrance.

The engine noise faded and Bridget and Jody walked the last hundred yards home in companionable silence. It was only four o'clock but the only light outside was the soft white glow of the snow, making the lamplit cottage a welcoming haven. Bridget towelled off Jody and shut him inside while she transferred a supply of dry fuel from the woodshed to the house. With the fire established, she moved into the kitchen and lit the gas oven, giving it time to warm up before placing the roasting tray containing the chicken and vegetables inside. Jody was stretched happily asleep in front of the fire and Bridget shoved his hindquarters to one side to make room for herself.

She extracted her workplan from her school bag. The concern over a reading group that was not making satisfactory progress had developed to a point where a new campaign needed planning. She removed the running records she had done on the group that day in the hope of finding clues to common problems that needed attention.

Bridget gave up on the reading group twenty minutes later, finding it impossible to concentrate. Thoughts of Tony Lawrence which had been uppermost in her mind in the last few days claimed precedence and she stared into the flames, the warmth licking at her body only in part a product of the crackling logs. Her anticipation of the evening ahead made her restless and she fussed with the chicken for a while, basting it with fat from the roasting pan. Jody sleepily padded after her into the kitchen and watched the process approvingly. Bridget tapped the dog gently on the nose.

'You be nice to Tony tonight. You're just going to have to get used to sharing me again.'

She lit another lamp in the living room and straightened the folds of the velvet curtains. A photo of Peter on the bookshelf caught her roving glance and she smiled reflectively. It was with a sense of profound relief that she noted the absence of a feeling of guilt when contemplating his picture, in contrast to her feelings during any of her previous tentative forays into new relationships. An irresistible urge compelled Bridget to pick up the telephone. She wanted to hear Tony's voice and confirm that this wave of happiness was no illusion.

The dial tone was absent but returned after she depressed the cut off button a few times. She dialled the number of the Northern and counted the rings as she waited for an answer. At the fifth ring she thought she might be disturbing Tony at a busy time. By number ten she was convincing herself it was not a good idea but at the fifteenth she decided he needed warning about the potential condition of the roads. The call was answered on number eighteen and the operator's voice was faint. Bridget shouted her request twice but a loud crackle interrupted the operator's reply. She came back on the line after a wait and Bridget caught the word 'paging'. The crackles then reached an intensity too painful to listen to. She held the receiver at arm's length and shook it, to no avail.

Bridget cut the call off. There was no point in keeping the line open in that condition. Prepared to try again she waited for a dial tone. Weather conditions like today's often caused some interference. She had to admit defeat ten minutes later. The phone was dead.

Bridget and Jody's footprints and the tracks left by the tractor in the lane disappeared as the thickly falling snow erased the blemishes. The carpet of snow was soon marred, however, by a crisp, new set of prints that marked a trail directly towards Bridget Gardiner's cottage.

Chapter Twenty-Two

Tony Lawrence noted Jemima Pride leaving the Northern through the automatic doors of the main entrance as he snatched a few minutes for another trip to ICU. A wave of irritation tightened his facial muscles into a frown but he quickly dispelled it with the thought that she was, at least, travelling in an acceptable direction.

The irritation was replaced by a sense of disquiet which had no immediate grounds. Her presence was understandable as a few reporters wanted daily progress reports on the Legionnaires' patients being treated and were waiting for news of any further cases, now unlikely. Some also hovered, vulture-like anticipating the more likely demise of the unfortunate Alister Cunningham. There would be a fresh story if the assailant could be charged with murder rather than mere assault. Tony's disquiet turned into apprehension as he considered the effect it would have if the media learned of the incident in ICU earlier that day.

As he put on protective clothing and tied on a mask, he glanced at his reflection in the changing room mirror. It was clear that Bob Matthews had not been in the unit that day and also horribly clear that garbed like this, a total and unauthorised stranger could easily be mistaken for a new and unfamiliar staff member. Who the hell had visited Alister Cunningham, and should the episode be reported to the police? The possibility that the adjustment of the oxygen setting had been deliberate had occurred to Tony because of his suspicions concerning the salbutamol trial. His personal assumption was that perhaps the assailant had returned to ensure his victim was not going to recover. Tony had so far kept this thought to himself, as it seemed too far-fetched to be believable. It was the sort of event that belonged in Hollywood, not part of the daily routine of a Tyneside respiratory physician. Tony was in ICU now to observe Alister's electroencephalograph print out. If it showed deterioration in the patient's condition he would have to report the incident with the ventilator, however far-fetched his interpretation might seem.

Tony sighed heavily and made his way into a room now even more cluttered with equipment. A nervous young technician was fixing electrodes to Alister's skull. Clare was standing at the base of the bed, gripping the bedrail and staring intently at Alister's still face. She jumped slightly as Tony moved to stand alongside her.

'Any more arrhythmias?' he queried quietly, his eyes on the cardiac monitor which traced a steady and normal sinus rhythm.

'No, he's stable.' Clare's gaze didn't waver as the technician hooked up the electrodes and set the needle positions and speed for the trace. They both fell silent, watching the screen of the EEG as the dots of light sprang into action with an erratic leap. The paper began to spill out, recording the trace, as the beams collected the information on the electrical activity present in Alister's brain. The atmosphere in the room lightened and the technician looked towards the figures at the end of the bed.

'Thank God,' breathed Clare.

'You must have corrected the oxygen setting in time to prevent any further damage.' Tony squeezed her shoulder. 'Well done.'

They watched in silence again for a few moments and then Tony nodded to the technician who switched off the paper feed, ripped away the trace and handed it to him. It slid rapidly through Tony's hands as he scanned it again.

'It's showing more activity than the last one, don't you think?'

Clare nodded excitedly. 'I'll get the last trace so we can compare them.'

Tony's beep sounded, drowning out the quieter ema-

202

nations from the room's equipment. He moved to the phone as Clare left and the technician finished removing the electrodes and wheeled the machinery from the room.

'Dr. Lawrence? Ross Wilson here.'

'Have you found anything?' Tony was surprised to hear from the biochemist so promptly. Although Dougal's blood had been delivered to the laboratory that morning, assays were generally time-consuming and he hadn't expected a result before the next day at the earliest.

'I had an assay set up when your samples arrived this morning. It wasn't a requested check but since you wanted some information urgently I spun down a sample and added it in. I can't give you the exact reading yet, but I thought you might like to know that the blood contains a very high level of beta blocker.'

The silence was palpable.

'Are you there, Dr. Lawrence?' Dr. Wilson's voice was puzzled.

Tony replied with a slight gargling noise and cleared his throat twice.

'Could you repeat that, please?'

'As I said, the blood went in with an assay I'm doing to measure levels of beta blocker in a trial for cardiology that's testing the efficacy of various doses. Your sample has a higher level than any of the others and some of the trial patients are on a daily dose of 150 milligrams.'

'Are you quite sure?'

'Quite sure, Dr. Lawrence.' The biochemist sounded offended. 'Would you prefer to come to the lab and check for yourself?'

'No, I'm sorry.' Tony rubbed his eyes. 'It's just a bit much to believe. Thanks for your help. You may well have saved somebody's life.'

'I don't understand.'

'I can't explain at the moment. Thanks again.' He disconnected the call and strode towards the exit of the unit, removing his mask and gown as he walked. Clare was talking animatedly to other staff members at the nurse's station, gesturing towards the rolls of paper unfurled in front of her. She smiled delightedly as Tony approached them but her expression changed to one of bewilderment as he strode past without a glance, not even pausing as he threw his rolled up gown into the linen bag by the door, which swung gently shut after him. A nurse broke the amazed silence.

'He's forgotten his overshoes.'

The large clock in the outpatient waiting room was indicating four-thirty as Tony Lawrence passed, unheeding, beneath it. The department was emptying and the door to Nicola's office was locked, the surrounding areas deserted.

'Shit.' He fought his rising agitation and rattled the door handle angrily. The staff must have packed up and left with remarkable speed. He knew the keys were kept in the cold room but it took several minutes of feverish searching to locate them. He left them swaying in the lock as he stepped into the office. Sue had done an efficient job of tidying up after the afternoon meeting and the files were not in sight. Tony moved to the cupboard and spotted them through the glass door on a lower shelf. He tugged at the cupboard door but it too was locked. Placing a foot against the adjoining frame he tried to force the lock, to no avail. Tony had no idea where these keys were kept and threw open desk drawers and overturned containers in a hasty search which failed to locate them. He thumped his fist on the desk top in frustration and looked about him for inspiration.

Moving decisively, he took the towel that covered the couch pillow. Wrapping it into a bulky glove around his hand, he considered the cupboard door. He paused in his task long enough to shut the office door, then with a surprisingly small amount of noise broke away the glass in front of the lower shelves. Tony lifted out the folders carefully, avoiding the shards of glass left around the edges of the frame. He found the single sheet folder that listed all the trial patients, and pulled the telephone close as he seated himself at the desk.

Scanning the list rapidly, he felt his heart rate increase as Bridget Gardiner's name caught his eye. He dialled her number first, cursing quietly when he heard an engaged signal. He went back to the head of the list. The first three had completed the trial so were in no danger. Sharon Andrews and Irene McTavish could not be helped, but 05, William

Pearson, was in his final week now. Tony got another outside line and punched the telephone buttons swiftly. A long wait was rewarded by a childish voice.

'Hullo? Elizabeth Pearson speaking.'

'Hullo,' said Tony. 'Could I speak to Mr. Pearson, please?'

'Daddy's not home yet,' replied the child.

'Is Mummy there, please?'

'Yes.'

Tony waited, listening to the child's breathing. His brow creased. 'Could I speak to her, please?'

'Yes.' The phone was laid down with loud bangings and he could hear Mummy being shouted for at increasing distances. Eventually the phone was picked up again.

'Jan Pearson speaking.'

'Hullo, Mrs. Pearson. It's Tony Lawrence, Northern Infirmary here.'

'Yes?'

'Your husband is involved with an asthmatic drug trial we're currently running.'

'That's right.'

'Could you please tell him not to take any more of his trial medications,' Tony said slowly and clearly. 'It's very important.'

'Yes, I'll tell him. But . . .' Mrs. Pearson sounded curious.

'I'd like him to return them to the hospital tomorrow if possible,' Tony interrupted. 'If he should have an asthmatic attack tonight, please bring him into the hospital immediately but don't use any of the trial drugs. Is that all clear?'

'Yes, but . . .' Mrs. Pearson paused, trying to phrase her query.

'Thanks very much.' Tony finished the call as quickly as he could. He had to avoid lengthy explanations as he felt under increasing pressure to contact the rest of the trial members. Besides, at the moment he didn't have an explanation he cared to give.

Bruce Matheson. Tony groaned aloud as he read the name. If only he'd looked into this a bit sooner! The signals had been there all along. Too many uncharacteristic attacks, lack of response to treatment and the unusually slow pulse rate in a situation where a tachycardia was normal. Beta blockers

205

slowed heart rate as well as being capable of causing severe bronchoconstriction. But how could he have suspected something so bizarre?

'*Christ!*' Tony clenched his fist and tried to suppress the anger he felt at himself.

08, Jim Moore, was on washout but Tony rang as he didn't know when he might be due to start a new bottle of capsules. His wife was unquestioning and promised to deliver the message. Hamish Wright, patient 09, was at home by the time Tony rang his number and wanted to know why he was to stop the capsules.

'They're doing me a lot of good, Doctor. Haven't been able to do this much for years.'

Tony cleared his throat and thought quickly. 'It's possible that some of the capsules have been made with the wrong strength of drug and we want to avoid any side effects it could produce.'

'Well, I've nearly finished this bottle and haven't noticed anything so they must be OK.'

'Please, Mr. Wright,' Tony spoke curtly. 'Do not take any more of them. It's very important.'

'All right, then, Dr. Lawrence. Whatever you say.' Hamish Wright was miffed. 'But I don't think there's anything wrong with them myself.'

'Probably not, but we need to check. Could you bring them into the hospital tomorrow, please?'

'No problem, Doctor. I'm coming in for the check up, anyway.'

Tony tried Bridget's number again with no success. It was still engaged. Dougal Dewar was safe now, though the narrowness of his escape made Tony shudder. Patients 12 and 13, Melanie Crawford and Joan Foster, were contacted with some difficulty but Tony felt immense relief at hearing that they felt fine and would discontinue the trial capsules. The last patients on the list were the week zeros who had been due to start that afternoon and had been postponed. Tony then tried the Grangewick number for a third time, slamming the receiver down after listening briefly. He reached for the telephone directory and consulted the troubleshooter's page before gaining another outside line. It was a long wait before a gruff voice barked, 'Faults.'

'I'm trying to reach a Grangewick number that has been giving a persistent engaged signal. I got a 'no such number' the last time I tried and it's very urgent that I contact the party.'

'Number.' The voice sounded supremely disinterested.

'It's in the Stamfordham district – 986 239.'

'Number you're calling from.'

'It's a hospital extention – Northern Infirmary, extension 693.'

'We'll look into it.' The click dismissed Tony and he replaced the receiver wondering whether they would even bother to contact him again. He sat with his head in his hands, his posture reflecting his bewilderment as he pondered the day's events. He answered the unexpected phone call on its first ring.

'Tony Lawrence,' he said automatically. 'Extention 693.'

'Faults here.' There was an almost satisfied-sounding sniff from the speaker. 'Lines are out in Grangewick due to problems with snow. Can't say when service will be restored.'

Tony's reply was cut off and he bit his lip, staring out of the office window at the blizzard he had been unaware of. No wonder the department's staff had headed home early. He was glad of the fact that he kept his car keys in the pocket of his white coat. There was only one way to contact Bridget and he wanted no delay in setting out. Draping his coat over the back of Nicola's chair, he opened the office door to leave.

The beeping from the coat pocket made his pause indecisively, then move out of the office. It was probably nothing but perhaps it might be Bridget trying to contact him. He turned abruptly and picked up the phone. It was one of the laboratories. He groaned in frustration and resisted the impulse to disconnect the call.

'We have the results on the HTLV-111 antibodies test on Caroline Chalmers, Dr. Lawrence.'

'Yes?' Tony's staccato response made the technician hold the phone away from her ear.

'They're completely negative. She hasn't been infected.'

'That's great news. Thanks.' The surge of relief vanished as Tony replaced the receiver. He couldn't take the time to visit the ward himself but equally he couldn't prolong Bill's torment now that he had the means to dispel at least part of it. He punched the buttons on the telephone again and asked the ward sister to pass on the results. Tony put the receiver down so hurriedly it bounced out of its slot and lay buzzing faintly on the desk top as he turned to leave the office for the second time.

Detective Inspector John Willis, accompanied by Gordon Davies and a uniformed officer, barred his passage.

'Ah, Dr. Lawrence.' The detective's gaze swept the room and his eyebrows rose expressively as he noted the disruption of the desk top, the scattered files on the floor and the broken glass of the cupboard door.

'I can't stop, I'm sorry, Inspector.' Tony tried to edge past the trio. 'I have some urgent business.'

'I'm sure you do, Doctor,' replied Willis levelly. 'But I'm afraid I must insist.'

He gestured Tony back into the office along with the officer and Davies before firmly closing the office door.

Chapter Twenty-Three

Bridget grinned at Jody when she heard the knock on the door.

'He's made it,' she said delightedly, quickly uncurling herself and moving towards the door in the dog's wake. 'You behave yourself, now, Jody.'

She could feel the breeze created by his wagging tail. Opening the door, however, Bridget was confronted by a man's back encased in a black woollen greatcoat, a layer of snow on the shoulders. Even before he turned, she had recognised that this was not the visitor she had been expecting. Jody's behaviour seemed to register disappointment as well. Instead of his usual indiscriminate friendliness he was sniffing carefully at the man's calves.

Bridget felt a wave of uneasiness at the awareness of the isolation of her situation. She was normally more careful about opening her door. The feeling was dispelled by the friendly smile on the vaguely familiar face before her.

'Hullo, Mrs. Gardiner. I am sorry to be calling on you in such inclement weather.'

Bridget smiled uncertainly, trying to place where she had seen him before.

'I'm Colin Ingram. I represent the Atlas drug company which commissioned the trial you're involved in. I met you one afternoon when you were doing an exercise test.' His smile was warm. 'Doing it exceptionally well, I might add.'

'Oh, yes. I remember.' Bridget's relief was tempered with puzzlement. She brushed away the snow that Jody deposited on her skirt as he edged past, moving back into the warmth of the house.

Colin glanced over her shoulder. 'Might I come in for a few minutes, Mrs. Gardiner? Then I could explain my presence on your doorstep before you catch pneumonia.'

'Well, I . . .' Bridget couldn't have explained her reluctance to invite him inside. She bit her lip as she watched him stamp the snow off his shoes, moving back instinctively when he took a step towards her. He smiled warmly again and waited in the hallway while she shut the door. Silently, she indicated the living room door though the warmth and delicious smell of roasting chicken made her direction unnecessary. He eased his coat off while still in the hall and hung it on a wall hook, uninvited.

'It's going to drip, I'm afraid,' he said apologetically.

'Don't worry about it.' Bridget didn't smile, waiting for him to enter the room ahead of her. He made straight for the fire and held out his hands to the warmth.

'Ah, that's better.'

'I didn't see your car outside, Mr. Ingram.' Bridget eyed his back again, now outlined by a well cut pin-stripe suit.

He turned towards her but put his bands behind him, palms outward to the fire.

'Please, call me Colin.' He met her solemn stare directly, his practised smile flashingly briefly. 'No, I had to leave the car in the main road. I wasn't sure of the depth of the snow in the lane and didn't want to get stuck. I do have a few more calls I was hoping to make this evening.'

'Oh?' Bridget remained standing on the other side of the couch.

'Firstly, please let me apologise for not phoning you about my visit but the lines appear to be out of order here at the moment.'

'Yes.' She waited for him to continue.

'We're contacting the people involved in this trial for a survey the drug company wants done. We want to ensure that people are not being inconvenienced by, or having any problems with, the way the trial is set up. We intend to use the survey to help with the planning of future trials.' Colin's face registered concern as he continued. 'As it is, you see, we find that we have quite a dropout rate in some trials, of patients who simply don't want to continue. I'm sure you can understand the cost it represents to us in terms of time and money invested in these people. If we can identify common reasons for unwillingness to complete trials then perhaps we can eliminate some of them in the future.'

'I see.' Bridget nodded. 'But I'm not sure how I can help, Mr. Ingram. I have no intention of withdrawing my participation in the trial.'

'Colin,' he said firmly.

'All right, then. Colin.'

'The way you can help, Mrs. Gardiner . . .' He paused, smiling confidently and waiting for a return invitation towards less formality. When it didn't come he quickly covered the awkward pause by coughing lightly. '. . . is by giving me your comments about various aspects of the trial management that we have identified as potential problem areas.' He indicated the briefcase that he had deposited at one end of the couch. 'I have a list that shouldn't take too long to complete if you can spare a few minutes.'

'I'll be happy to help.' Bridget smiled finally, feeling slightly guilty at her desire to be rid of her visitor as quickly as possible. Tony probably wouldn't get here for another hour at the earliest and she had no pressing tasks.

'Would you like a cup of tea or coffee?' she made herself ask.

'Thanks very much. Coffee. Milk, no sugar.'

As she moved into the kitchen Colin looked at the dog sitting beside him. Jody wagged his tail and moved closer. The drug rep's hand rested on Jody's head.

'He's a lovely dog,' he said loudly. 'What's his name?'

'Jody.'

Colin's fingers found the base of a floppy brown ear. They tightened and then gave a sudden and vicious tug. Jody squeaked with pain and indignation.

'Oh, I am sorry, fella.' Colin's loud comment was contrite. He shrugged bemusedly at Bridget who came quickly into the room. 'I think I must have trodden on the poor chap's paw.'

'He does tend to get in the way a bit.' Bridget made a fuss of Jody who had rushed up to her, cringeing slightly. He followed her back into the kitchen and sat on her feet while she poured coffee, his head pressed against her leg. She stooped to give him a quick cuddle.

'Nasty big feet, eh?' she whispered sympathetically, planting a kiss on the moist brown nose.

Colin had settled himself on the couch but had not made any move to open his briefcase. He sipped at the coffee Bridget handed him.

'Perfect.' He eased himself further back on the couch and eyed Jody who was still staying as close as possible to his mistress. Jody eyed him back suspiciously.

'Wonderful things, pets.' Colin said conversationally. 'My mother had eight cats.'

'Eight! That's rather a lot.'

'She would have had more if she could. She doted on them. They all had their own baskets and brushes with their names on. She even had a special saucepan that she cooked their meals in.'

'She must have been very fond of them.' Bridget gave Jody a scratch on his nose, just between his eyes, which half shut in ecstasy.

'Well, they were all she had – apart from me, of course. She was widowed shortly after I was born. I guess the cats began to take over as I grew up and needed less of her attention.' His voice mellowed to a softly sympathetic tone. 'I understand you too are a widow, Mrs. Gardiner.'

'Yes,' answered Bridget shortly. It was not a subject she wished to discuss with him. 'What sort of things did you want to ask me about the trial, Mr. Ingram?'

Colin was staring into the fire, his fingers gently stroking his coffee mug. Bridget finally broke what seemed an unusually lengthy silence.

'Mr. Ingram?'

His gaze was slowly transferred to her face. He was no longer smiling.

'I believe you know Dr. Anthony Lawrence rather well, Mrs. Gardiner.' The tone was almost a sneer on the word 'rather' and it was matched by the singularly unpleasant expression on his face.

Chapter Twenty-Four

Tony Lawrence looked at the faces of the three men he was confronted by in Nicola's closed office. The uniformed officer was standing with his back to the door, gazing impassively towards the window and the hypnotic pattern of swirling snow. Gordon Davies was also standing, his back to the wall, arms folded. He met Tony's gaze squarely, his expression puzzling. There was the habitual hostility but mixed with it almost a hint of smugness. He looked like a lawyer about to give a final summing up in an open and shut case against a client he thoroughly disliked.

Tony broke eye contact and turned towards John Willis. The inspector thoughtfully nudged the broken glass on the floor with his foot, and then cleared the files from a corner of the desk and perched on it. The silence continued, a deliberate, heavy silence that made Tony increasingly nervous.

He made his frustration at being trapped evident but his angry query was cut off by the dismissively raised hand of the detective.

'I understand, Dr. Lawrence, that your marriage has recently broken up.' The man's voice was matter-of-fact. He sounded only slightly interested.

Tony barely controlled his anger. 'What the hell has that got to do with you?'

'It appears to have quite a lot to do with us, Doctor. Might I ask the reason for the separation?'

'I think that's my business.' Tony strode towards the door. 'And I'm not going to stay here listening to you pry into my personal affairs.'

The uniformed officer stood as before, barring the door, his gaze still fixed on the window opposite.

'Excuse me,' Tony said curtly. The officer ignored him.

Willis shifted his position on the desk slightly so he could see Tony's face.

'I'd like you to tell me what your relationship was with Miss Nicola Jarvis, please, Dr. Lawrence.'

'What?' Tony's expression was of angry incredulity. 'Jesus, what is this? She's a technician in this department, as you well know.'

'Did you have a relationship with her outside of working hours?'

Tony laughed – a short sound, devoid of amusement.

'No, Inspector, I most certainly did not. She's worked here for five years and has never even called me by my given name.' The memory that she had, in fact, done just that only recently, made Tony shake his head, puzzled.

'Would you like to sit down for a moment, Dr. Lawrence? I'm sure you'll understand the reason for this interview when I inform you of my day's activities.'

'I'll stand, thanks. As I said, I'm in a hurry.'

'Yes, we'll come to that. Very well, Doctor.' Willis stood up and walked a few steps towards the window before turning unexpectedly.

'At 1 p.m. this afternoon a call was received by the police concerning a rather unpleasant incident. An elderly woman, a Mrs. Goddard, had noticed a small stain on her bathroom ceiling earlier this morning. She did not investigate at the time, but went out to do her shopping. When she returned some time later, she found a couple of the neighbourhood dogs taking an inordinate interest in an outside drain. She did not investigate this either, but on getting inside was horrified to find the stain in her bathroom had spread and that there was, in fact, water collecting in her bath. She knew that her bathroom was directly below the same room in the flat above and assumed that a tap had been inadvertently left on. She went up to the flat above and knocked on the door, not surprised to receive no answer as the occupant was normally at work all day. At work, in fact, in this department, Dr. Lawrence. In this very office . . .' He paused, and his gaze swept the room again.

214

'I don't see what . . .' Tony's objection was again dismissed as the inspector continued.

'Mrs. Goddart returned to her flat, and tried to clean up the fluid dripping into her bath. It was at this point that she came to the conclusion that it was not simply water. It had a reddish tinge and a faint smell that made her think it contained blood. She tried to ring the caretaker of the apartment block and when she found he was unavailable, she very sensibly called the police. I was called in, Dr. Lawrence, because, as you know, I deal in homicide.'

The colour was rapidly draining from Tony's face. Willis turned his back on him and spoke to the window.

'However, this was not homicide. It was a rather nasty example of suicide. One of the nastiest I've come across, in fact, and I've seen quite a few. She had used a surgical scalpel, you see, Doctor – to cut her own throat. I don't know how she managed it, but she had almost severed her head from her body.' Willis traced a pattern on the window in the steamy area he had been breathing on before he continued. 'She did it in the bath, a hot bath. Supposed to be less painful that way, you know.' He peered out of the window with interest at the thickly falling snow. 'Neater, too. Except that she left the hot tap dribbling. When the overflow became clogged with clotted blood, water began to seep over the edges of the tub. It flooded the floor, of course, and eventually began to make its presence obvious in the flat beneath.' Willis paused, fixing Tony with his gaze again.

'You wonder what all this has to do with you, Dr. Lawrence? Well, scattered around Miss Jarvis's bedroom were a number of items. A rather nice book – a photographic study of New Zealand – had been mutilated, with most of the pages torn out. It had obviously been of some significance to Miss Jarvis, but what interested me more was a photograph, nicely framed in silver. It had also been partially destroyed, the glass broken and the picture badly slashed – probably with the scalpel. It was still easily recognisable, however . . .' His voice tone changed slightly, becoming more thoughtful. 'Miss Jarvis was naked and appeared to have recently used a variety of . . . ah, shall we say, auto-erotic devices?' The detective paused yet again and watched Tony's face closely as he continued. 'It was a photograph of you, Dr. Lawrence.'

Tony blanched. 'Oh, my god,' he said softly. He shut his eyes for a long moment.

Willis was relentless. 'I came to the hospital a short time ago and, of course, went to the head of this department to explain my presence. A second unpleasant incident concerning this department in such a short period of time seemed rather too much of a coincidence. Dr. Davies had a visitor in his office when I arrived and I found him in a somewhat concerned state.' He transferred his gaze to Gordon Davies, inviting him to speak for the first time. Tony listened numbly as the living nightmare increased.

'I was visited by a reporter, Lawrence,' he said forcefully. He had evidently been waiting for the opportunity to speak for some time. 'A Jemima Pride. She asked me, or rather informed me, of the picture created by the trial you are presently running. Recent deaths, I might add, that I was unaware of.'

Tony stared at Davies in disbelief. The accusatory voice of his superior was raised still further, his anger obvious.

'Not only this, she informed me of her belief that you are having an affair with one of the patients enrolled in this trial.' Davies spluttered indignantly, giving Willis the opportunity to interrupt the tirade.

'Another item we found in the possession of Miss Jarvis, Dr. Lawrence, was a piece of paper with a telephone number on it. A Grangewick number that might have some significance to you, we believe.'

'Oh, Jesus.' Tony sat down heavily. 'It all makes sense,' he groaned. 'Horrible sense.'

'What do you mean?' The inspector strode towards him, glass crunching underfoot. He leaned down, gripping the edge of the desk.

'This . . .' Tony's hand wearily indicated the chaos of the desk and office. He glanced up to meet Willis's intense stare and spoke quietly.

'I have only just found out, this afternoon, that the medications involved in this trial have been tampered with. Some of the capsules seem to contain a high dose of beta blocker.'

216

Gordon Davies advanced towards Tony, barely in control of himself.

'I knew it,' he shouted. 'You're trying to destroy this department. You think you can make trouble for Atlas by fucking up their trial, and that way you can get at me!' His face was turning a mottled shade of purple. 'But your accusations won't work, Lawrence. You're crazy –'

At a nod from Willis, the uniformed officer laid a restraining hand on Davies' arm. He shook it off angrily but lapsed into silence, folding his arms and glaring balefully at the three men around him. Willis ignored him.

'Go on, Dr. Lawrence.'

'Not to put too fine a point on it, Inspector, a beta blocker can have a devastating effect on an asthmatic, causing bronchoconstriction that can lead to a fatal attack in some cases. I now believe that the fatal attacks during this trial have been caused by beta blockers within the trial drugs.' He waved towards the desk again. 'That's what all this is about. As soon as I discovered this fact I contacted all the patients involved to warn them off taking any more of the trial medications.'

Willis nodded. 'How did you find out?'

'We had another patient who had a severe attack this morning. The picture of the trial had already been causing me a lot of concern –' He broke of, glancing at Davies. 'In fact, I approached Dr. Davies a week ago and said I thought the trial should be discontinued.'

'What was his response?' Willis spoke to Tony as though Gordon Davies was not present in the room.

'That the trial would be completed. If not by me, then he would do it himself if necessary.'

All three men looked at Davies. His lip curled. 'You're mad, Lawrence,' he said derisively.

'When this morning's attack occurred,' continued Tony, shifting his gaze away from Davies, 'I ordered blood sample analysis to look for some kind of toxin.'

'You're going to pay for this, Lawrence,' Gordon Davies said through clenched teeth. He was frantically trying to consider the repercussions this news might have, both on the Atlas drug company and, more importantly, on himself. The prospect was not appealing.

217

'I am already,' Tony said softly, without raising his eyes from the telephone receiver, still lying on its side amongst the clutter on the desk, the buzzing noise long since discontinued. 'I doubt if there's anything you could do, or say, Dr. Davies, that would make me feel any worse about this.'

'Why didn't you look sooner?' Willis spoke with none of the veiled hostility his tone had carried initially.

'Because there seemed to be reasonable explanation for the attacks in earlier cases. Because I've been under a lot of pressure dealing with Legionnaires' outbreak here and haven't been so directly concerned with the running of what should have been a completely routine drug trial. Because Dr. Davies had made it so clear that he intended the trial to be completed, and because when I contacted the drug company they promised to investigate the matter and deal with it. Most of all, I suppose, it was because it was an idea so horrendous that it just didn't seem conceivable. But now, with what you've told me . . .'

'What do you mean?'

'I couldn't understand how it could possibly have happened. I thought that some dreadful mistake had been made by the pharmaceutical company in the packaging of the drugs, but that's almost impossible. To believe that it's been happening means considering the possibility that someone has been deliberately tampering with the medications before they reached the patients.' He looked directly at Willis and shook his head as he spoke. 'Nicola Jarvis had access to these drugs . . .' His voice trailed away.

Willis nodded again. 'And now, possibly, a motive. She was obviously in love with you. Unrequited passion in someone who may be unbalanced can be a very powerful force.'

Gordon Davies didn't like the tone Willis was taking which seemed to be becoming sympathetic towards Tony.

'What about this affair with a patient, Lawrence?' he snapped caustically, 'I'll see to it that you're struck off –'

'Bridget!' Tony stood up, his gaze still on Willis who straightened with him. They both ignored Davies.

'She's the only patient I haven't been able to contact.'

'Grangewick?'

'Yes. The phones are out because of the snow. That's where I was trying to go when you –'

Willis held open the office door. 'We'll take my car.'

Chapter Twenty-Five

Bridget Gardiner was unaware of the lukewarm puddle of coffee seeping through the fabric of her skirt and still dripping over the edge of her sharply tilted mug. In spite of the warmth of the nearby fire she felt a chill spreading through her. Her gaze was fixed on her visitor, Colin Ingram, much as a rabbit is transfixed by the headlights of an oncoming car, but the drug rep's eyes were shut, his head resting on the back of the sofa. When he slowly opened them this line of vision met that of Bridget's and she shivered involuntarily, causing more coffee to slop on to her lap. She looked quickly away and placed her mug on the floor, mopping her skirt ineffectually with her hand.

Colin's lips parted company in a smile that looked as if it were controlled by strings, but when he spoke his voice was as pleasant as ever.

'He's a nice guy, isn't he?'

'Who?' Bridget avoided his gaze, knowing perfectly well whom he meant.

Colin smiled tolerantly.

'Dr. Lawrence. Anthony James. Rising star of the respiratory department of the Royal Northern Infirmary.'

The crackle of sap igniting in a log in the grate filled the silence.

'Isn't he?' The words were almost spat at Bridget.

She swallowed and her gaze flickered briefly towards Colin.

'I . . . Yes, he is . . .'

'I suppose you think he's a pretty good catch.' The tone

became belligerent now. 'Respected in society, well-paid. Not a bloody arse-licker like me.'

Colin stood suddenly and Bridget jumped. She eyed the door behind him but knew instinctively that any movement on her part would be a mistake at that point. Colin's voice had a sarcastic edge to it when he spoke again.

'Oh, but I forget – *Mrs.* Gardiner. You were married to a doctor before, weren't you? Perhaps they're the only ones good enough for you.'

His face crumpled and his tone of voice changed again abruptly. He spoke almost wistfully.

'I was going to be a doctor, you know. Mother wanted me to be one. I even started the university course.'

Bridget shrank back as his hand reached towards her and she held her breath as he picked up a handful of her hair. He began to let it slip through his fingers.

'She never knew I'd failed my course. Crapped out in every shitty subject.' It was a matter-of-fact statement and Colin caught the end of the lock of hair in his palm as he spoke again.

'If I hadn't, perhaps I would have been good enough for you, too.' He rapidly wound the hair around his hand, yanking Bridget's head back so her face was turned up towards him. She gasped and tried to rise to lessen the pain in her stretched scalp. Jody stood, his hackles rising and emitted a low growl. Still trapped by her hair, Bridget was pulled out of her chair as Colin's gleaming black shoe contacted Jody's jaw with sickening force. The dog was thrown off balance but quickly gathered himself to come to the defence of his mistress. Colin roughly disentangled his hand, uprooting a clump of shining black hair that remained caught in the large signet ring he wore. Before Jody could stand and face his attacker, the heavy-soled shoe dealt a swift and vicious blow to the side of his head and the dog crumpled silently.

Bridget gave an agonised scream '*NO!*' and hurled herself towards Jody. Colin's fist lashed out and the knuckles adorned with the chunky signet ring caught her cheekbone, the force of the blow knocking her back towards the chair. As her vision cleared she felt enormous heat on that side of her face, a heat that would soon become a throbbing pain. Her hands found the arm of the chair and she gripped it, dragging herself into a kneeling position.

'That's right.' The calm voice came from directly overhead. 'Sit down, Mrs. Gardiner. I want to have a chat with you.'

Bridget fought back a wave of dizziness and pain as she stood. Her next move was a stumble in the direction of the door but her upper arm was caught in a vicious grip and she was forced on to the soft cushion of the armchair. She uttered a stifled sob as she saw the inert brown body on the floor in front of her. A trickle of blood was matting the hair on the dog's chin into a dark tangle.

'Can't have him bleeding on the carpet, can we?' Colin sounded concerned. 'Come and open the door for me.'

Bridget stood slowly, supporting herself by gripping the arm of the chair. She gazed in horror as the dog was dragged towards the door of the kitchen by his back legs, his head bumping against the floor and a trail of blood marking his passage.

'Come on,' said Colin cheerfully.

Bridget walked numbly towards the door and then into the kitchen, stopping before the back door. She turned the heavy old iron key in the lock and opened it slowly. The frigid snow-laced air cleared her head instantly and she jerked the door wide open, ready to flee. Even before the decision could be translated into action it was defeated. Reading her thoughts, Colin dropped Jody half out of the door and caught Bridget's arm, twisting it behind her back. He drew her body against his as he used his foot to shove the dog on to the snow-covered porch. Bridget's face was hard against his chest and her free arm was trapped as he reached around her in a bizarre embrace to close the door again. She heard the metallic clunk as the key was turned.

Bridget struggled to move her head, crushing her injured cheekbone painfully against Colin's collarbone. She felt the encircling arms increase the intensity of their grip and couldn't breathe. Her mouth and nose were pressed against her attacker, almost in his armpit and she was aware of the warm musty odour and the dampness of his perspiration. She bent her knees in an attempt to free herself by a downward slide but was jerked painfully upright by the arm still held

222

behind her back as Colin withdrew his free arm, still holding the heavy key from the back door. He propelled Bridget ahead of him into the living room, pausing by the couch to press her into a sitting position. He eyed the key in his hand and then walked towards the fireplace, with its nest of glowing coals. There was a soft crackle as the key was dropped into their midst. Colin turned and stood quietly, watching Bridget.

She sat hunched on the edge of the sofa, rubbing her upper arm which felt badly bruised. She couldn't shake off the sensation she had felt while trapped in that terrifying embrace and her breath came in short gasps. A picture of Colin's foot shoving Jody's body out into the snow replayed itself before her eyes over and over and despair made her wait passively for what was to come. When nothing immediate happened, she looked up just far enough to see the gleaming black shoes, the toe of one dulled by a smear of blood. Terror made her catch her breath and she inhaled with rasping difficulty.

The shoes moved towards her and then knees came into view as Colin squatted before her. He tilted her chin upwards gently and the gesture reminded her instantly of Tony. With the thought of him came a determination to survive. She only had to hold out until he arrived, and surely he was on his way by now.

'Do you know how easy it is to kill a cat?' the drug rep asked softly, not expecting a response. 'You pick them up with one hand around the neck and let them struggle for a bit.'

Bridget straightened her back, moving her chin from Colin's touch. His hands kneaded air as he continued. 'Then you twist the body, further and further and . . .' He made a gargling sound deep in his throat. Then he giggled. 'Of course, it's a good idea to wear some gloves.' His tone faded wistfully. 'Yes, it's easy to kill a cat. It's easy to kill eight of them.'

Colin touched Bridget's bruised cheek lightly. Her head jerked and she met his gaze. He smiled at her.

'Do you normally get asthmatic attacks under stress?' he queried.

Her hand went to her throat as she became aware that her difficulty in breathing was increasing. She could feel her pulse

223

beating rapidly. A deliberate effort to calm herself seemed a little inappropriate given the circumstances and she looked quickly around the room. Colin had followed her gaze and noted where it ended.

'Is your inhaler in your handbag?' He sounded as he had when he had first arrived at the cottage – apologetic for disturbing her but friendly and eager to please.

Bridget frowned slightly, making no reply. Colin's knee joints cracked loudly as he straightened.

'I'm sure it is.' He picked the bag up and unzipped the main compartment, then upended it so that the contents spilled into a heap on the floor.

Bridget stared at the jumble of possessions and felt tears prick the corners of her eyes. There was the small container of doggy Choc-Drops she had bought this afternoon for Tony to try and win back Jody's affections with. The bright plastic case housing her chequebook also caught her eye. It had the words 'Big Spender' emblazoned on it. Her clear memory of Peter laughingly presenting her with the case years ago when they had just accumulated a large overdraft was interrupted by the sound of Colin's voice.

'I think a capsule might be a better idea, don't you?' She looked up to observe him holding her salbutamol inhaler in one hand, the other containing the bottle of trial medication capsules. She shook her head slowly but Colin had placed the inhaler on the arm of the chair as he seated himself. He unscrewed the cap of the bottle and leaned forward as he shook the contents on to the floor.

'The thing is, you know, to pick just the right one to take.'

Bridget watched in puzzlement as he picked up each capsule in turn, holding it to the light, shaking it and then twisting the halves as though to separate them. His face was thoughtful as he sorted through the drugs, then his eyes narrowed sharply as he paused to glance at Bridget.

She tried to breathe quietly, to no avail. The sensation of bands gripping her chest increased and she knew her face was flushed from the effort of expelling air. Her injured cheek felt like a traffic light.

'It's dangerous to enter drug trials,' Colin said seriously.

224

'Did you know that several people have already died in this very trial that you're doing?'

Bridget's eyes widened but quickly clouded with disbelief. She looked desperately at her inhaler, balanced on the floral cover of the chair arm.

'Don't you believe me? There have been at least four deaths so far – all from severe attacks.' His white teeth glinted as he gave a quick grin. 'Rather like the one you're having at the moment, I imagine.'

He turned his attention to examining the last of the capsules, the join of which was still too firm to have been tampered with, as all the others had also been.

'Shit.' The expletive was angry and he swept the capsules up with one hand and threw them towards the fire. Some bounced on the grate and the few that landed on the coals ignited with soft popping sounds. Colin picked up the inhaler and flicked the plastic casing open as he stared at Bridget again.

'I'll tell you why, shall I?'

She returned his stare miserably, knowing a reply was not expected.

'It's your precious Dr. Lawrence, that's why they're all dying like flies. He's poisoning them.'

Bridget's face reflected her disgust and disbelief and Colin sniggered.

'Bit of a shock, hmmm? Lover boy a murderer.' Colin's voice rose in pitch and volume. 'He's killing off his asthmatic patients by giving them beta blockers.' The tone became snide. 'My theory is that he's being paid by a rival drug company to discredit our product.'

Colin's hand clenched, opening the inhaler case beyond its capacity, the snap of the breaking plastic making Bridget jump and the back of her neck to prickle. The sharp edge of the broken casing pierced Colin's thumb and with a sudden movement he hurled the canister into the fireplace. Bridget watched in horror as the plastic rapidly melted and bubbled, giving off a pungent smoke. As the acrid smell reached her she shuddered, her head touching her knees in her fight to expel the air trapped in her lungs.

A pulse in Colin Ingram's temple throbbed visibly. 'It's not

225

the first time,' he shouted. 'He killed my mother.'

Bridget's head rose and her face was contorted with the effort of shouting the words. 'It's not true.'

'How the fuck would you know?' Colin sneered. 'You probably hadn't even gotten around to screwing doctors when it happened.'

His mouth twisted and his voice became harsh. 'So long ago, Dr. Anthony Wonderful Lawrence doesn't even remember me – but I'll never forget him.' His fists clenched. 'The bastard,' he added, the soft words infected with loathing. His head jerked sharply towards Bridget.

'They had their explanations, of course. They said nobody knew she was asthmatic. She got a bit wheezy at times, sure, but then she had smoked for years.' He smiled tolerantly at his memories. 'She swore she had given up but I used to smell it sometimes when I got home and once I caught her hiding behind the shed at the back of the garden. She got a bit of chest pain sometimes too, you see, and had been told to stop smoking but she was fine most of the time.' Colin's lip curled. 'Until she was persuaded to enter that fucking trial. Angina, they said she had, and would she like to try out a new drug.'

Colin seemed oblivious to Bridget's harsh breathing sounds and continued without pausing, becoming increasingly agitated as he spoke.

'The first week of the bloody trial, she made my breakfast and took the pills. She always got up early and cooked me breakfast before I went to university. I didn't say much to her that morning because I knew I was getting the last of my marks for the year's course that day and didn't want her to know that I'd failed.' His voice quietened to become barely audible as he continued brokenly. 'She never knew I'd failed – she thought I was doing so well. "My son the doctor," she said when she kissed me goodbye. She was so proud. All those years of making do worthwhile.'

Tears rolled down Colin's cheeks and he sniffed. 'I never even saw her again. She had an attack, the neighbour said, and got taken to hospital. I got to the hospital and nobody would tell me anything. I had to wait for hours before her doctor came to see me – along with the bloody junior house-surgeon who had been responsible for my mother when she

226

was brought in. The doctor said it had been an asthma attack brought on by the beta blocker – taken in that fucking trial for angina that didn't even bother her. "I'm sorry," he said to me, "but your mother is dead. Dr. Lawrence did all he could." All he could! It wasn't bloody enough, was it?' Colin drew in a shuddering breath and let it out again in a series of jerky sobs. Then he laughed bitterly. 'And now it's beta blockers that are going to destroy him – ruin his marvellous bloody career and finish off his precious lover.'

At that instant, the salbutamol canister, resting on the hot coals in the grate, exploded. Shards of metal flew out and several splinters hit Colin Ingram on the side of his face nearest the fireplace. One splinter pierced his cheek, another sliced open the top of his lip and a third splinter embedded itself in his left eye.

He screamed, his hands groping at his injuries. He found the piece of metal projecting from his cheek and tried to remove it but his blood-smeared fingers were unable to find purchase.

'Oh, Jesus,' Colin moaned. His tongue licked tentatively at his lip and he winced.

'My eye. Oh, Sweet Jesus – I can't see,' he shrieked in rising panic.

The pain from the fragment of metal embedded in his eye was incredible and made worse each time his eyelid dragged across it in uncontrollable spasm. The eye looked like a science fiction creation, a livid red pulp with glutinous tears of blood oozing from the corner.

Bridget stayed unmoving, lying on her side on the floor where she had dropped when the explosion occurred. She didn't look at Colin and kept as still as possible, hoping he might think her unconscious, or dead. Her breath sounds were becoming quieter now, through no effort on her part, and the sounds of Colin's moans and movements were taking on an unreal quality – as though a television set had been left on in the next room. She shut her eyes and let herself drift, only vaguely aware that the stumbling sounds of footsteps and moans had receded, the end point punctuated by the slamming of her front door.

Chapter Twenty-Six

The dark blue Volvo idled quietly by the main entrance of the Northern. Tony had rushed back into the department while Willis collected his car to gather drugs which might be needed if they were too late to prevent Bridget taking a contaminated capsule.

An evening porter, fresh at the start of his duty shift, scowled suspiciously at the man behind the wheel and then looked pointedly at the 'No Parking' signs surrounding the vehicle. He was ignored by John Willis who sat drumming his fingers on the dashboard, his eyes glued to the brightly lit foyer behind the porter. He had opened the car door and had started to climb out, one leg outside the car, when he saw the figure hurrying towards the doors.

He quickly eased himself back into the driver's seat, leaning across to swing open the passenger door. Tony Lawrence put his weight on the swing door of the hospital's entrance with his shoulder, his hands full. The small oxygen tank he was carrying threatened to escape from the crook of his elbow and stuck out at an awkward angle, the metal projections of the fitting scraping the arm of the porter as Tony passed.

'Sorry,' he called back. 'Emergency.'

The porter nodded briefly. Emergencies were his line of business and he strode after the doctor to close the car door on him. He tipped his cap as the car glided away, wondering what sort of emergency would call a doctor out from a hospital in a car equipped with short wave radio when an ambulance would surely have been more suitable.

The occupants of the Volvo were silent as the car built up

228

speed on the A1058 travelling towards the centre of New-castle. Tony was sorting through the handfuls of objects in his lap, filling his pockets with the drugs and syringes. He balanced the gas tank on his knees and checked the mask and hosing attachments. He discarded one length of plastic tubing as being superfluous, tucking it on to the ledge below the glovebox. The car wheels sucked at the road surface. The sound was interspersed with the whine of the electronic window washers sending periodic jets of water over the glass surfaces and the click of the wipers clearing the remains of the ice accumulating constantly on the windscreen. Willis glanced across at his passenger and broke their silence.

'Put your seatbelt on, old chap.'

Tony obediently reached over his shoulder with his right hand and groped for the retracted safety belt, his left hand resting protectively on the equipment in his lap.

'Got everything you might need?'

Tony clicked the belt catch into its slot between the seats.

'God, I hope so.'

They were silent again as the detective concentrated on the lane signs that were leading them through the complexities of the ring road and on to the A6127. The traffic had remained reasonably heavy on the main road so far and the slushy area in the lane centres between the ridges of snow posed little hazard. Willis increased his speed, staying in the right-hand lane as they drove past the Town Moor and travelling at nearly 45 m.p.h. Some of the drivers in the line of cars crawling in procession in the left lane shook their heads in disbelief as the Volvo shot past.

They had to wait in a line of traffic giving way at the roundabout by the turnoff to Blakelaw. Willis rubbed his hand nervously across the top of the wheel.

'Nasty business, this, Lawrence.'

'I'm afraid you don't know all of it, Inspector.' Tony stared grimly through the windscreen. The engine revved in complaint as the wheels failed to find purchase instantly when it was the Volvo's turn to move. Willis sighed in annoyance and then moved carefully towards the left lane as the dual carriageway reduced to two-way traffic. They were forced to stay in the slow-moving queue of traffic heading towards Ponteland and Darras Hall.

'You know something more about this Jarvis woman?'

'No.' Tony shook his head. 'That's all been a total surprise – I still can't believe it.'

'Then what the hell are you talking about?' Willis snapped.

'I was going to report it,' Tony said defensively. 'It only happened this afternoon and I couldn't see how it might be connected to this business – still can't, as a matter of fact.'

'Would you mind letting me in on it?' The detective's tone was heavily patient.

'You remember Alister Cunningham?'

'Of course. The unfortunate lad who nearly had his skull crushed through being in your department after hours. How is he?'

'That's just it. He was doing pretty well. He suffered a setback today but it looks as though he'll still pull through.'

'Good.' Willis steered the car into the slight skid as they cornered and then straightened up again.

'The attack on him must have been by who ever was tampering with these trial drugs, wouldn't you say?' Tony asked.

'Seems more than likely,' responded Willis.

'And it looks as though that person was Nicola Jarvis?' continued Tony.

'Well, the odds on a woman overcoming even a healthy young male like that aren't all that long – especially if she took him by complete surprise, which I imagine she would have at that time of night.'

'Alister Cunningham was visited in Intensive Care today by someone dressed in the theatre gear they use for sterility – someone not recognised by any of the staff.'

'And?'

'Shortly afterwards an alarm went off in his room and it was found that the oxygen setting on his ventilator had been reduced to zero.'

'Jesus.' Willis turned to look at Tony and the Volvo edged towards the mounds of snow banking the road. The wheel crunched through the top layer of new ice and the car skidded. 'Christ,' he muttered, while expertly regaining con-

230

trol of his car. The roads were becoming more of a problem as they turned off onto the minor roads leading towards Callerton and Grangewick. The narrow, twisting road stretched ahead like an unmarked white sheet, a flat area between lines of shrouded trees and hedges, no demarcation visible at the road sides. Willis changed into a lower gear and slowed the car. The sucking sounds of the tyres were replaced by soft crunching as fresh icy snow compacted beneath them. Willis didn't risk another glance at his passenger as he continued their conversation.

'Could it have been an accident?'

'No,' Tony said with conviction.

'Holy shit! What time did this happen?'

'About mid-day.'

'But Nicola Jarvis had been dead for hours by then.'

'I know,' Tony said grimly. 'Even if she hadn't been, it couldn't have been her.'

'What?'

'The visitor was male. The staff thought he was a new registrar of mine and therefore didn't question his presence. When I contacted the registrar he denied ever having been near the Unit.'

'Do you believe him?'

'Oh, yes. No question about that. I found out about the incident almost immediately after it happened and, as I said, I considered reporting it then, but while I was in the room I got the call from the biochemist giving me the information about the contamination of the trial drugs with the beta blockers and my prime concern from then on was to contact the other patients and prevent them taking the pills.'

'What exactly does this beta whatever do?'

'It's a drug widely used in the treatment of several disorders, predominantly hypertension. It's avoided with anyone who may have asthmatic tendencies because it can trigger bronchoconstriction and a possibly fatal attack of asthma.'

'Is the reaction common knowledge?'

'Yes. Though incredible as it may sound, there are still cases of patients actually being prescribed a beta blocker for the treatment of asthma.'

231

'Is it fatal in every case?'

'No, which is perhaps why a lot of trial patients have been OK and why I didn't suspect something earlier on.' Tony rubbed at his eyes. 'God,' he groaned, half to himself. 'I did have my suspicions about this damn trial – I just let other things get in the way of doing anything about it. The Legionnaires' outbreak, my marital hassles . . .' His voice trailed off and he stared sightlessly through the side window to his left, unaware of the signpost indicating the turn off to Throckley Marsh.

Willis filled the awkward pause. 'Don't blame yourself too much, Lawrence. None of us is clairvoyant.' He laughed shortly. 'Hell, I wish I was – my job would be a bloody breeze.' He took one hand off the steering wheel and reached carefully into his pocket, extracting a packet of cigarettes and depressing the lighter in the dashboard.

'Do you have any objection to my smoking?'

Tony grinned fleetingly. 'I will have if you don't offer me one.'

Willis smiled with genuine pleasure. 'Ah, a doctor who's human. Be my guest.'

Tony took two cigarettes from the packet and lit them both, handing one to Willis. They both drew on them deeply and Tony unrolled his window an inch to clear some of the grey cloud they expelled.

'What's Davies got to do with this mess?'

Tony was taken aback by the question. He was silent as he drew on his cigarette again.

'I don't know,' he said at last. 'His relationship with the drug company responsible for this trial is close, to say the least. He . . .' Tony hesitated.

'Yes?' prompted Willis.

'He receives quite a lot of financial considerations from the company. No one really knows what form they take. It's possible he could be receiving a personal retainer for making the department's facilities available.'

'Sounds pretty corrupt,' Willis commented.

'There's a fairly large grey area concerning the ethics of relationships between the medical profession and phar-maceutical companies,' Tony admitted. 'But I really don't

232

think Davies would be involved in anything he knew was unsafe. He would have too much to lose. Certainly he was adamant about continuing this trial, but there could be a lot of reasons for that.'

'We'll be looking into it,' promised the detective. 'I'm finding this case more fascinating by the minute.' He fell silent as he slowly negotiated the single lane bridge and a ninety degree corner after passing the Plough Inn.

Tony was also silent. He didn't want to talk anymore and decided not to tell Willis of the compensation paid to Shane Andrews. No doubt he would find out soon enough. Tony's concern for Bridget's welfare was becoming overwhelming. He stubbed out his cigarette in the dashboard ashtray and rolled up his window. The silence continued until Willis cleared his throat lightly.

'Don't worry about Bridget,' he said gruffly. 'We're not going to let this snow stop us.'

Chapter Twenty-Seven

Grangewick snuggled at the base of the hill, resting quietly beneath the bright blanket of snow, the smoking chimney-pots and glowing windows indicating the havens of warmth that protected its inhabitants.

Jemima Pride dropped her half smoked Camel cigarette out of the partially opened car window and reached for her hat and gloves, cursing the impulse which had led her here.

She had arrived well over an hour ago, before the snow had been much of a problem on the roads, and now she recognised the difficulty she was faced with in returning home. She had sat in her car for some time on her arrival, waiting for a likely-looking local to pass. The elderly woman she had finally approached hadn't minded standing in the cold to talk. Oh, yes, the lady knew Mrs. Gardiner well. Jemima had received the directions to the cottage she wanted and a lot more besides. Dr. Gardiner had been the woman's doctor for some time before he was so tragically killed. Lovely man he had been. So sad for his young widow.

Jemima had returned to her car and spent half an hour writing out the entire conversation, making other notes as she pondered what line to take in her interview with this Mrs. Gardiner. Eventually, she elected to say she was writing an article about Grangewick and would like some impressions of what it had been like for someone in general practice here. With a bit of subtlety and any luck she would be able to confirm at some point that Dr. Lawrence was indeed having an affair with one of his patients. That should make good copy.

Jemima elected to leave the car where it was. She rather liked walking through fresh snow, listening to it squeak under her feet. She fastened the studs of her oilskin parka and pulled the hood up over her woollen cap. As she was about to open the car door, her attention was arrested by the sight of a figure coming towards her from the lane she intended entering. 'Drunk,' she decided, her pale green eyes following its stumbling path. The high-pitched giggle she heard through the gap of the window she had neglected to close confirmed her opinion and she stayed put, waiting for the figure to pass. She stared as the person came closer, noting that the hand clutching one side of his face was covered with blood. He was talking aloud to himself, babbling sentences that were broken and only partially comprehensible, but the sound of his voice made Jemima take a closer look at his face.

'. . . didn't do so bad in chemistry, Ma . . . Cats . . . I'll feed the cats . . .'

With a shock, she recognised him as the good-looking stranger she had spoken to outside Nicola Jarvis' office. The man who worked closely with Dr. Lawrence. What on earth was he doing here? She opened the door and called after him but he appeared not to have heard, slipping and stumbling in the snow and aparently making for the only other car to be seen – parked half on the footpath on the same side as Jemima's but facing in the opposite direction, back towards Newcastle.

With a premonition of disaster, Jemima leaped out of her car, leaving the door ajar as she followed the line of footprints Colin had left up the lane. She was panting with exertion and a kind of excitement by the time she reached the cottage. Whatever was going on, it was bound to provide a better story than she'd ever had access to before.

Jemima rapped smartly on the front door of Phoenix Cottage and stamped the snow from her feet. She peered through the glass panel at the side of the door but could see nothing except the beam of soft light from an open doorway at the end of the hallway. She picked her way around the side of the house, stooping as she passed beneath the low branches of the Weeping Elm and went up the steps to the porch by the back door.

Jemima reached over a snow-dusted mound to pound at the door with a gloved fist. As she waited her toe prodded the mound and she uttered a stifled half scream when she felt it move. Quickly she crouched down and brushed the snow away. Soft brown eyes were half closed but seemed aware of her face only a few inches away. A tail gave a feeble wag which displaced its covering of snow.

'What's happened to you, fella?' The sickened feeling in the pit of her stomach turned to anger as she cleared away the blood-stained snow from the dog's jaw.

'Which bastard did this?'

Softly she stroked the cool nose and head and ran her hands down the length of the damp, shaggy body.

'Don't worry, fella,' she said firmly. 'You're going to be all right.'

Jemima stood up and stripped off her oilskin, then she saw the attempt at another tail wag and without hesitation removed the heavy sweater she was wearing. She folded her woollen cap and very gently eased it under the dog's head, then tucked the sweater around him. She covered the whole body with the oilskin parka for good measure and then knelt to touch his nose delicately with her fingertips. Jemima Pride cared little for people in general and suffered not at all from investigating and exposing aspects of their lives they preferred to keep private. Animals were another matter entirely, especially dogs. Even dog owners whose animals were subjected to unwarranted cruelty entered another category in Jemima's affections.

'Don't move,' she told the dog. 'I'm going to find out what's going on around here.'

By standing on tiptoe, she could see into the small kitchen. Through the open door leading to an inner room she could make out the shape of a body lying on the floor. She rattled the handle of the back door and cursed quietly. Her notebook sank, discarded and no longer of any importance, into the snow under her foot as she ran back to the front of the cottage. Clad now solely in tee-shirt and jeans she failed to register the freezing temperature in her consternation. She balanced on one foot by the door, removing her shoe and using the heel to smash out the pane of glass in the side panel. She reached through and turned the snib lock.

Bridget's eyes flickered as Jemima crouched beside her and felt for her pulse. She was breathing in agonisingly slow and painful cycles and either couldn't hear or respond to Jemima's queries. The reporter wasn't sure that she could feel any pulse but the woman was obviously still alive. She looked wildly about her and then leaned closer to Bridget.

'I'm going to get help,' she shouted.

She stepped over Bridget's still body to reach the telephone, jiggling the button furiously to try and obtain a dial tone.

'Useless fucking thing,' she shouted angrily after long seconds of frustration. She dropped the receiver and started for the door before turning abruptly. Grabbing a patchwork knitted blanket off the back of a chair she draped it over Bridget with care, then turned again and ran out of the house, leaving the front door wide open. After the warmth of the room, the outside chill struck her like something solid. Her flesh contracted painfully and she rubbed at her bare arms as she ran into the lane. It wasn't until a large stone protruded through the snow to stab her foot that she realised she had forgotten to replace her shoe. She headed for deeper snow and tried to ignore the burning of her toes. The nearest cottage was in darkness but Jemima paused to pound frantically on the door.

'Please, please be home,' she shouted pleadingly. Sobbing with frustration she had to admit defeat and was then at a loss as to what to do next. She stood in the lane, advancing a few steps in one direction and then changing her mind to go the opposite way. Should she go back to the cottage and try to help Mrs. Gardiner, or look for aid elsewhere? She ran to the end of the lane and looked up the main road, past her parked car to where an uncurtained window shone promisingly.

'Thank God,' she sniffed, indecision at an end.

Jemima was partly aware, as she ran towards the distant house, that the empty car she had thought Colin Ingram had been heading for had not moved. Yet he was nowhere to be seen.

The pain of the injured eye was unbelievable, causing blinding flashes that paralysed Colin Ingram's normal thought proceses. His consciousness had retreated from the present to a large degree, the part aware of the pain only periodically overriding the delirious conversations he conducted with himself.

One such occasion was when he arrived at his car and tried to find his keys. He held his head with both hands, rocking his body and moaning softly as he tried to think what to do. He knew where the keys were but couldn't quite pinpoint the thought, like chasing the memory of a fading dream. He got as far as remembering his overcoat, but before he could picture where it was, the hand holding his mutilated eye open slipped and he closed it involuntarily, screaming at the crushing agony the friction caused. He felt that his head was about to explode and the vision in his uninjured eye clouded. He clutched at the bonnet of the car for support but mercifully the pain began to ebb.

'She's a nice girl, Ma – going to be a nurse. . .'

Colin pulled himself up and his legs pumped automatically as he weaved an erratic path along the centre of the road. His words were becoming slurred.

'Of course I'll still respect you, Doreen . . . I won't hurt you . . . There's a good lass. . .'

The approach into Grangewick can be treacherous at any time, with its sharp S-bend on the downward slope of the hill. The dark blue Volvo was only on the brink of control as it negotiated the road, its occupants nervously silent.

'My God. Whats that?' Tony's alarmed shout was not necessary to alert John Willis to the fact that a figure stood on the road before them, but the sound caused his instinctive reaction as he slammed his foot to the brake pedal. The heavy car began a graceful slide, turning one hundred and eighty degrees and collecting the figure across its boot before continuing to slide, at increasing speed, down the slope of the hill. Its path was stopped when it came to rest against the truck of a large Beech tree. The movement ceased with a muted thump of enough force to jar the two men inside and activate the safety locking mechanism of the seatbelts. It had been Colin Ingram's lower chest and abdomen that had provided the cushioning between car and tree, muting the sound of the impact. As the car ceased its movement completely, the force of compression was sufficient to crush out any spark of life. Colin Ingram died, instantaneously and silently.

The occupants of the dark blue vehicle unclipped their safety belts and sprang from the car. Tony went straight to the body wedged between the boot of the Volvo and the tree trunk. As he reached for the neck to feel for a carotid pulse, a gush of blood came from the gaping mouth but the face was unmoving, one eye staring unnervingly at Tony, the other obscured by semi-coagulated blood.

Willis uttered a sickened oath and turned back to shift the car forward.

'Don't bother with that just yet, Inspector . It's not going to help him.'

They both stared at the body, the lower chest crushed and pinning him in a macabre upright position.

'Do you know who this is?' Tony asked quietly.

'How the fuck would I know?' Willis laughed in mild hysteria. 'I only squashed the poor bastard.'

'It's Colin Ingram.'

'Who the hell is Colin Ingram?'

'A drug company representative. One who happens to be involved with our asthmatic trial.'

Willis walked a few paces away from Tony and then turned sharply towards him.

'I don't believe this. What in hell . . .' He snapped his fingers, interrupting himself. 'Intensive Care. Of course. This begins to make sense.'

Tony was ahead of him, stooping to collect the oxygen cylinder from the floor of the car.

'And he's been here in Grangewick for God knows how long, doing God knows what.' Tony straightened to move and almost collided with Jemima Pride whose passage towards the men had been silent and unremarked, her exhaustion and breathlessness combining to prevent her shouting for help. She didn't seem to notice the spectacle at the rear of the car. Her lips were blue and she spoke with difficulty.

'Dr. Lawrence . . . Please help . . . Mrs. Gardiner, she's . . .'

But Tony didn't wait to hear more, running in the direction of Phoenix Cottage as though his own life depended on it.

Tony held Bridget cradled in one arm, the other resting on her cheek to hold in place the mask giving her the mixture of oxygen and salbutamol. A tiny trickle of blood on her arm indicated the site where he had administered the doses of aminophylline and hydrocortisone intravenously.

Tony unconsciously matched his breathing cycles to those of Bridget. A breath in, so slow it was uncomfortable. A pause. His lips parted to let the air seep out again, an agonisingly lengthy process. Surely if he willed it hard enough, he felt he could make their inhalations deeper, the breathing cycles shorter, the tense muscles in their bodies gradually relax. The seconds ticked by and Tony's concentration on Bridget's face was unbroken as a shaggy brown shape limped in through the open doorway to sit beside him.

Bridget's eyelids flickered and slowly opened. The dark brown eyes focused on the intent face so near her own and then slid down to a point below his line of vision. He felt rather than saw the smile beneath the mask, and looked down to see the bloodstained tennis ball carefully positioned beside his knee. A brown paw tapped gently at his leg.

Chapter Twenty-Eight

The fact that it was raining again was nothing unusual in Newcastle.

What was unusual was that Tony Lawrence felt exceptionally happy. His world had been altered dramatically in such a short space of time yet he felt quite at peace with the new direction it was taking.

'Are you sure you feel well enough to be going home?' He looked at the passenger in his car with concern.

Bridget Gardiner glanced back over her shoulder towards the hospital, its rows of brightly lit windows an imposing backdrop to the gathering evening gloom of the carpark. She settled more firmly into her seat.

'Three days in there was more than enough, thank you, Doctor.' She still looked pale and tired but her face brightened as she smiled. 'Besides, Jody will think I've deserted him.' She pointed ahead with an outstretched arm. 'Home, James.'

Tony grinned and started the engine. 'I give in. The vet did say that Jody could go home today.'

Bridget frowned. 'I still haven't thanked that woman for helping . . . what was her name?'

'Jemima Pride. Don't worry, I saw her yesterday.' Tony edged his way into the heavy pre-Christmas traffic heading for the city centre. He laughed and shook his head. 'What a transformation. She wanted to thank me!'

'Why?'

'Well, apparently this story gave her a scoop that got one of the big national papers interested and they were so impressed with her style they've offered her a job. She says it's the start of a whole new career.' He chuckled. 'She's even washed her hair.'

Bridget laughed. 'I'm glad for her. I think it was terrific the way she stayed around the other night when she just about had hypothermia and took Jody to the vet herself.'

'She's very keen on dogs apparently. She was delighted to hear that he was recovering so well. Wanted to know where she might be able to get a puppy like him!'

Bridget laughed again. 'He's a one-off. No dog like him in the entire world.' She sobered and glanced at Tony. 'What's happened to the other people involved?'

Tony pressed his lips together. Glancing in the rear-view mirror he manoeuvred the car into a side lane ready to exit the motorway and began to reduce speed.

'Davies has been suspended, pending a full investigation of all his financial dealings. Administration is absolutely livid about the whole business. I imagine Davies will be forced to resign – might even be prosecuted. The drug company involved, Atlas, is also going to be investigated. I don't think they've done anything illegal exactly but I've heard rumours that they're going to close down at least part of their operation here.' Tony shook his head. 'The whole thing is a real mess. Public outrage at what Ingram was able to achieve will be very damaging to medical research in general.'

'It's terrifying to think how you can be targeted by some insane individual for something you might have done in the past but can't remember.'

Tony nodded. 'The atmosphere at the hospital is unpleasant, to say the least. Everyone seems to be looking over their shoulders or muttering in corners.'

'Is it going to affect your career?' Bridget asked quietly.

'Sure is,' Tony replied grimly. He changed decisively down through the gears and halted at a red traffic light before looking squarely at Bridget.

'Davies is taking the full blame for allowing the trial to continue so I'm not in any danger of being struck off, but it's going to be the start of a whole new career for me as well as Jemima. I'm definitely going to emigrate to New Zealand. I need a complete break – a new life.' His face was serious.

Bridget couldn't see any hint of invitation in his eyes, only determination. 'What do you think?' he asked.

She fought against the wave of dismay that engulfed her. He was telling her that he was leaving and wanted her approval.

'I think it's a wonderful idea,' she said in a small voice. She turned to look out of the window to hide the tears threatening to fill her eyes. She felt weak and shaky suddenly. Perhaps it had been too soon to leave hospital.

A car behind tooted to inform Tony that the light had changed. He accelerated and began to watch the street signs. They had nearly reached the veterinary surgery where Jody was being treated.

'I think I needed some disaster like this to prompt a final decision. Now that I've made it, I can't wait to go,' he said with satisfaction.

Bridget cleared her throat. She tried to sound interested but didn't trust herself to look at him.

'When do you think you'll leave?' Her voice caught on the last word but Tony didn't appear to notice. He parked the car outside the surgery and spoke cheerfully.

'As soon as I've sorted out everything here. I need to wait until the mess at work is cleared up, and I want to sell the flat and make sure there won't be any hassle in getting my divorce through. I don't think Catherine will complain about having matters settled more quickly.' He grinned at his passenger. She turned quickly and fumbled with the door catch.

'I'll get that.' Tony hurried to open the door but Bridget was ahead of him, already opening the surgery door. She was blinking in the strong artificial light of the waiting room as Tony entered and turned to look at a wall chart depicting the evolution of the dog to avoid meeting his gaze, not noticing the entrance of the receptionist.

The girl smiled at Tony brightly. 'Can I help you?'

'You certainly can.' Tony returned the smile. 'We're here to collect Jody.'

'Jody?' The receptionist looked faintly puzzled.

'The almost Otterhound,' said Tony proudly. 'He's been here for a couple of days.'

'Oh, yes.' The girl's smile became broader. 'I'll just see if the vet's free.'

Bridget hunched further into her sheepskin jacket in the far corner of the room. Her joy at her own and Jody's recovery was overshadowed by her increasing misery. Still feeling shaky, it was difficult to try and keep control of herself. Her despair became almost overwhelming when a boisterous Jody dragged the vet into the waiting room and then launched himself into an ecstacy of welcome, not for her but for Tony. The vet gave up the unequal struggle of trying to hold on to the dog's leash. The stitches in Jody's lip did not impede his ability to lick in the slightest and the brown tail was waving furiously in full circles.

'Your dog is fine, sir,' the vet told Tony. 'He's lost a tooth and was pretty bruised and sore for a while but there was no serious damage.' He noticed Bridget standing unhappily in the corner of the room and looked back at Tony who was stroking the by now quieter Jody.

'I take it you are the owner?' he asked doubtfully.

Jody spotted Bridget at the same time and seemed embarrassed not to have gone to her first. She dropped to her knees to hug him.

'Not exactly,' Tony admitted. His eyes crinkled as he grinned delightedly at the vet and Bridget who were now both staring fixedly in his direction. 'That is, unless the dog's mistress wants to make it legal?'

Bridget didn't know whether to laugh or cry. Instead, she cleared her throat and smiled as she spoke to the bemused vet.

'Perhaps you could tell us what the quarantine regulations are for dogs emigrating to New Zealand?'

244